'A high octane adventure. If you like Chris Ryan and Robert Ludlum, you'll love this.' A.J. Dalton (author of the Gollancz 'Chronicles of a Cosmic Warlord' series)

'Lake Fear is a better read than many other action adventures. The characters are real, the motivations are excruciatingly human, and the ending is emotionally powerful.' Nigel Leech

'Wow, this is powerful stuff.' Ann J. Winter

LAKE FEAR

Michael Willetts

Adel Publishing
AP

First published in Great Britain in 2013 by Adel Publishing

Copyright © Michael Willetts 2013

The right of Michael Willetts to be identified as the author of this work has been asserted by him in accordance with the Copyright, Designs and Patents Act 1988.

All characters and events in this publication, other than those clearly in the public domain, are fictitious and any resemblance to real persons, living or dead, is purely coincidental.

The cover photograph is copyright. It was taken by Martti Peramaki.

The chorus of "The Army Goes Rolling Along", The Official Song of The United States Army, is quoted. These words are believed to be out of copyright, and reasonable attempts have been made to check this. If you know these words to still be under copyright please contact Adel Publishing via the web link below as soon as possible.

All rights reserved.

No part of this publication may be reproduced, stored in a retrieval system, or transmitted, in any form or by any means, without the prior permission in writing of the publisher, nor be otherwise circulated in any form of binding or cover other than that in which it is published and without a similar condition including this condition being imposed on the subsequent purchaser.

A CIP catalogue record for this book will be available from the British Library.

Paperback ISBN 978-0-9926992-0-8

eBook ISBN 978-0-9926992-1-5

Set in Times New Roman 11/14

Adel Publishing

www.AdelPublishing.co.uk

Dedicated to my Brothers

To Roland R.I.P.
To Sidney

A heart-felt thanks to the many generous people who have helped me in the writing of this debut novel.

Nigel Leech from Adel Publishing for his invaluable advice, support and editing expertise, Adam Dalton (of AJ Dalton fame) for pointing me in the right direction, Lee Robinson and Lee Kelley for their technical and military advice and finally, my family; my Mum, Dad and Sis and my Wife Joan and Daughter Chloe for their encouragement. *Thank you for believing…*

LAKE FEAR

Hey, watch those clouds boy,
They're black and moving fast.
Feel the wind blast your face boy,
Can't run from your past.
Josh Wild

Prologue

RUMFORD, USA
January, 1994

The boy dreams of his Momma.

He stands at the end of a jetty as the light fades and looks down on her. She floats just below the surface of the water. Her long dark hair fans around her face. A single bubble escapes her mouth and slowly drifts to the surface. It breaks his torpor. He screams, looks around for his brother, but he isn't here. He drops to his knees and reaches for her, frantically grabs her shoulders, but she slips from his grasp and sinks into the darkness.

He goes in after her.

The ice cold water stuns him. He feels for her with outstretched hands. He's submerged now but still screaming, even though he knows that cannot be possible. He kicks deeper. His fingers finally curl around something soft and he pulls it to him, then looks around to find the surface in all this suffocating blackness, to save her, to save himself.

He sees light and swims that way, struggling with the extra weight. He reaches the surface.

He sees that the light is the Moon. Wolf Moon. He's shaking with the cold and the dread as he treads water.

He picks at the mud and leaves caught in her hair and he turns her around. Her face is a grey and bloated ruin. He recoils and lets her go and she sinks back down into the depths.

Gone.

The word detonates in his head.

He cries in his dream and also as he awakes. Because not even in dreams can he save her.

Act 1

We used to wonder where war lived, what it was that made it so vile. And now we realize that we know where it lives, that it is inside ourselves.
Albert Camus

AR RAMADI, IRAQ
November 8, 2010

1

Seth knelt between the two bunks in the confined space of the cell and carefully polished out a scuff from his right boot with a corner of his blanket. He did it silently so that he wouldn't wake his brother.

The late evening sun drenched the building, casting shadows as it slanted in through the single pane of glass, distorting the messages that were written in Arabic, gouged and finger painted in shit and blood on the walls. He had struggled trying to decipher them earlier. One he didn't have any trouble with.

Al mout li Amreeka
Death to America

The room stunk of waste, sweat, piss. It was overpowering, but he was used to the stench of decay. He had moved the slop bucket into the corner earlier and had draped a filthy towel over the shit-smeared seat that was balanced on its rim.

He stood and stepped over his brother to look out the window once more, his frame blocking out most of the remaining light. It would be dark within a couple of hours. He wiped at the greasy, wired glass with the back of his hand and stared out onto a wasteland: an expanse of open land and broken buildings. This cell felt like his coffin, the world outside a graveyard. Two Iraqis in dark suits stood below the window, one on a cell phone, the other smoking and looking up at the window. Seth stared back briefly then looked beyond them, scanning the area. He saw what he was looking for.

To his right, Highway 10 ran past the eastern edge of Camp Ramadi.

The *kill and maim zone*.

In the other direction, at the edge of his vision, he could still make out the blood-soaked sand strewn across the road, the scene of the action that morning.

He relived the moments that would change a thousand lives...

...shouted voices, a blur of automatic gunfire...
and impact sounds echoing off bleached, pock-marked buildings.
Him ducking in reflex scanning for its source, a moped on its side belching fumes, a tangle of bloodied bodies motionless in the dirt, his younger brother Nate on his knees alongside them head raised to the sky, gun raised, calling out to him, him a distance away, Nate closing his eyes and falling silent. Two Iraqi soldiers appearing in view as if by magic, one standing over Nate shouting out in broken English, gun aimed at the back of Nate's head, the other feeling pulses, standing, reaching for the handcuffs hanging from his belt, him slamming the door of the jeep and running to the scene, moving fast for his bulk, dust kicking up with every step, almost blinded by the emerging morning sun creeping around a building, slowing to a skidding halt, front wheel of the moped still turning, a soldier's hand reaching out, almost slipping in the pooling blood, him slapping down hard at the barrel of the gun still aimed at his brother's head sending the soldier to the floor, the other turning his gun on him then, him throwing up his hands in a calming gesture, then leaning over, wrapping his arms around his younger brother, staring down at his

upturned face that was a mask of confusion and wonder.

The whole incident from beginning to bloody end captured quite by chance by a UN aid-worker on her cell phone, including the brothers being led away at gun point.
Sometimes, death is theatre.

Seth had mouthed *rich or dead* to the guard as he and Nate were led into the single cell later that morning, but it had gone ignored. Then the man had slyly spit in Seth's face as he locked the cell bars, the spittle running off Seth's cheek and onto the collar of his combats.

Company management had blocked his calls. Then he'd seen a suit arrive at the jail within an hour with a Ziploc of papers, overheard both their names being mentioned.

Seth didn't like the signs. He'd witnessed enough pandering to local politicos to know that his brother would be hung out to dry. Maybe him too.

Ar Ramadi had been their home for nine long months without a break. They were there, courtesy of Stygian to help protect the local elite. The cure had become part of the disease since Nate, on his way to collect supplies and fuelled by his early morning stims and booze, had panicked and cut down the Iraqi family – father and child shot dead as they appeared, ghostlike, out of the early morning mist on a beat-up moped, his stop warning to the rider ignored or misunderstood.

Nate had calmed down now, thanks to the meds and soothing words from Seth. He lay curled up like a kitten on his bunk in a corner of the cell, covered with a blanket that Seth had placed over him, like he was still a child. Seth leant down and shook his brother awake. He kept his voice low.

'Listen, we're getting out of here before tomorrow's court hearing, because after that we're likely to get U.S. intensive security. We go while the guards are watching the stupid box.'

Nate hardly moved and Seth slapped at his legs and carried on.

'I spotted a motorcycle parked up outside that we can use. Head south, put a call in to Christo. OK Nate? You on it, man?'

Nate slowly threw off the blanket and rubbed at his face. He spoke with a deep raspy voice from behind his calloused hands.

'Use the phone footage Seth?'

'No Nate. That's a once and for all deal, we have to be sure it's gonna count when we play that card. No. I'm gonna call the duty in here. You need to play sick. I just hope to God our stuff is someplace in this building.'

Nate lifted his head. Jesus, he didn't need to act at all, his stale boozy breath hitting Seth full in the face, making him wince.

'On it.'

Seth rapped on the cell bars and called out the first name of the duty guard. He always got a name just in case, a little trick of his that often paid off.

'Hey Malik, you got a minute?'

The young prison guard ignored him at first, carried on playing a game on his cell phone in the dimly lit corridor. Seth called out a second time, more urgently, and the guard pocketed the phone, rose from his wooden stool and shuffled over to the cell bars. He was holding an AK-47 with both hands as he peered through the bars into the gloom of the cell. He looked nervous holding it, like it was a snake. He had taken Nate's own knife when the brothers were brought in and had it now in a makeshift sheath lashed around his waist with a piece of leather strap.

'Hey Malik my friend, my brother here is sick. I think the slop you gave us for lunch was bad or something. You need to take a look.'

Malik tried to appear calm but Seth could see the fear on his face, hear the nervousness in his voice despite the bravado and the fact that he was the one holding the weapons.

'Ha, I tell the cook that the two Americans in our guest wing make a complaint. I am sure he will be most concerned.'

'Hey I'm serious man, he keeps puking and blacking out. I wouldn't want the death of a U.S. citizen on my hands; that would be very bad for you and your family.'

Seth tried to introduce a friendly tone to his voice, but also a warning.

Malik awkwardly pointed his gun at Seth as he fingered the keys one-handed and unlocked the cell. He pushed the door open and waved the gun back and forth between the two brothers.

'Step back please Mr Stone and please keep your hands where I can see them. You see, as instructed, I say *please*, every time, even to murderers.'

The guard took a hesitant step into the mix of harsh sunlight and deep shadows. The heat and stink were intense now, adding to his anxiety.

'Just hold on there Malik. We haven't even been charged with anything yet, let alone found guilty, so I would appreciate some respect for me and my brother here.'

'Oopsidaisy Mr Stone, I forget, we have the *presumption of innocence* now, just like you Americans. But the video, I hear about the video and –'

'Screw the video Malik, they don't always tell the whole story.'

'I see the bodies for myself, see them take them away. For them, the young boy, the father, their story has ended. You saw to that.'

'I'm not saying they weren't killed, Malik, I'm just saying it was an accident is all.'

'The court will answer that in time for you and your brother.'

Nate stirred and groaned as he held his hands to his guts. He still had most of the Jack Daniels pumping through his blood stream from his latest binge and he truly did look like shit.

'I will call a medic for your brother, but only because my job says to do it.'

Malik half turned and started back toward the cell door but he only got a single step before Seth's boot connected with the side of his head dropping him in an instant. The rifle dropped with him and was seized by Seth before it came to rest. He grabbed the guard's legs and quietly dragged him deeper into the shadows of the cell, then stepped over him and took a few steps out into the corridor listening for any movement from the other guards. All he heard was the shouted commentary of a soccer game on a TV and the guards' cheering.

Malik groaned and shifted his position on the floor and Nate instantly came to life. He fell on the guard, his huge hands encircling the man's thin neck, thumbs forcing down onto his windpipe with the strength of a vice, instantly silencing the young guard. Two black scorpions in strike position, tattooed on the back of Nate's hands, distorted now with phosphorus burns, seemed to come alive as his thumbs dug deeper. He repositioned his hands on either side of the guard's head and violently twisted it sideways, making an awful rending noise as muscle and bones were torn and broken.

Seth turned and strode back into the cell, grabbing hold of his brother's shoulders and wrestling him off the lifeless guard.

'No, Nate. Sweet Jesus, why didn't you just knock the guy out? Hell, he can't be more than eighteen.'

Nate looked up without emotion, his heavy-lidded bloodshot eyes intensifying his look of malevolence.

'He pointed a gun at us Seth. That makes him the enemy.'

Seth released him and held a finger to his lips, listening for any movement in the guardroom.

'Come on man, we need to sweep the building, secure the place, get the hell away from here.'

LAKE FEAR

The noise hadn't reached the other guards in the adjoining room over the din of the match. The brothers followed the dingy corridor and headed for the exit door. They knew the building layout well from previous visits inside the wire; they had dropped off suspects here many times. Seth held the gun in front with the safety off, Nate behind, with his knife now retrieved from the dead guard, hanging loose out of sight at his side.

Seth quickly peered through the narrow gap of the partially open door and into the guardroom beyond. Two young Iraqis sat with their backs to the doorway on a filthy sofa watching a football game. Seth turned and put two fingers up and pointed into the room, then stepped across the doorway. He waved for Nate to follow him on, then leaned across him and whispered an instruction in his ear.

'Stay here and keep your eyes on those two. I'll sweep the rest of the building, look for our stuff. Don't engage them unless you have no other option. We'll secure them when I get back.'

Nate made a circle with a finger and thumb and held it in Seth's face.

Seth crept down a narrow stairwell and quietly let himself into an adjoining room. The room was empty save for several rusted lockers leant up against one wall. Seth moved on through the rest of the building. It was clear. Just the remaining two guards to handle. He went back to the locker room still puzzling over their light security detail.

On the floor above, Nate had eased down the corridor and put an ear to the door of the only other room on that floor. He heard nothing. He slowly twisted the handle and looked through the narrow gap. It was unoccupied. He returned to the doorway of the guardroom and stood listening to their banter, all the while fidgeting, his hand flexing absently around the handle of the knife. He eased open the door a little more and stood motionless in the doorway, watching the two guards.

He could make out some of the conversation, mainly about the crappy nature of the game. And then a whistle blew and one of the guards suddenly got to his feet and stretched, turning to face the door as he did, and seeing movement in the shadows.

This guard, younger and smaller than his partner, couldn't make it out at first. He was puzzled; they had no visitors scheduled. The shadows shifted, took on a shape, a form filled the doorway. The guard half-turned, looked for his partner, who was still engrossed in after-runs of the game. He turned back as the form resolved itself. The man entered the room, a huge figure, scarred with the collateral of war, his unblinking eyes froze the guard where he stood. The guard looked down, saw a knife in the man's hand, and looked round again, partner was still absorbed, and back. The man was still staring, the air stagnant. He turned once more, searched for his rifle, but the man caught his action, followed his line of sight, pursed his lips, shook his head, mouthed the word no to him. Nothing, no-one else in the room now, just him and the man with the knife. The guard instantly understood the message: he wouldn't reach the gun in time.

Noise downstairs broke the spell and he stirred, finally found his strength, his voice.

He was far too slow as Nate leapt forward, grabbing him, spinning him around, smashing an open palm dead centre into his face, breaking his nose and sending shards of broken bone upward into his brain. If he ever recovered he wouldn't remember Nate or the events of that day, or much of his life before.

The other guard had raised himself from the sofa, disoriented at first but quickly understanding, and charged for his weapon stood leaning against a far wall, his thin fingers grasping for the trigger guard, all the time frantically shouting out in Arabic, but Nate ran around the sofa and snatched his hair, yanking him back, turning his head around so that he faced him. Nate grabbed the guard's hand that now held the rifle and pulled it upward so that it was at shoulder height. He twisted the man's arm forcing the barrel to aim directly into Nate's own face, covered the guard's trigger finger and slowly squeezed as he looked into the man's confused and fearful eyes. The gun clicked hollowly against the safety catch and Nate whispered to the man, 'You trying to kill me with that thing friend?'

The man shook his head slowly and went to speak but Nate reached for him, put a finger to his lips, made a shushing sound as he brought his knife around in a swift arc, plunging it into the guard's belly and pulling upward when he thought he had reached deep enough inside.

Seth rushed in as the guard was dropping at Nate's feet. The brothers stared at each other momentarily. Seth looked slowly around taking in the scene. He reached forward and slapped heavily at Nate's hand that still held the knife, the blade went skittering into the mess of blood still slowly weeping from the guard onto the greasy floor.

'Holy shit Nate, what the hell is wrong with you man? We could've easily secured them and slipped out of here. They're gonna know for sure we did all this.'

'Yeah? Well they were both about to go walkabouts, what else could I have done? You had the gun Seth. This one tried to shoot me, aimed it right into my face. Him or me. Which was it to be Seth?'

Nate leant down and picked up the knife then wiped the blade on the back of the dead soldier at his feet. Nate's next question came matter-of-factly, his back to Seth.

'You spot our rucks on your travels?'

'That's just exactly what I was looking for you idiot.'

'Don't call me no idiot, I did this for *us.*'

Seth dry-washed his face as he looked at his brother, a mess of bloody bodies at his feet.

'I found some lockers. Nobody else here.' He shook his head at that. 'Come on man; pick up one of the rifles. We need to find our equipment and papers and get the hell away from here.'

They both sprinted down the stairs, footsteps like thunder, into the room below. Seth ran to a window and stood looking out as Nate began prising open the lockers with the blade of his knife.

'The hell is everyone, Nate? You ever seen it so quiet here?'

'Don't care Seth. Hey man, we've lucked out. It's all here.'

A plastic folder with all their papers and two passports lay neatly on top of the two bags. Seth reached around his brother and grabbed the bags, throwing one to Nate. He kept the papers himself.

'All your mummy's still in the bag?'

The brothers quickly searched through the rucksacks as they headed back out of the room. *Mummy's comforts* were the daily battle kit that they kept close to hand.

'What've you got? 'Cause I've got my wallet, map, sat phone, walkie-talkies, my tool kit.'

He reached the bottom of the bag.

'No gun. The cash has gone too.'

Nate spoke as he rummaged through his own bag.

'My kitchen's still here, wallet, bins, flashlight.'

'You got your pad?'

'Yeah, they left my writing pad, but my gun ain't here either.'

Seth closed up his bag and readied to go.

'You take all of the phones off their hooks while I fire up the bike. I don't want unanswered calls making someone suspicious enough to come investigate until we're well away from here.'

Nate held back.

'I'm not going without my weapon, Seth.' He held the guard's rifle out in front of him. 'This piece of shit is just as likely to go off in my face.'

'Listen, someone could easily walk right in here at any time. We're finished if we're caught. I'm going out there and starting up the bike and you'd better be ready or I'm telling you Nate, I'm on my way without you man.'

Seth opened the door and quickly scanned the street but it was quiet, just a few locals closing their businesses for the day. He slung the rucksack and rifle over his shoulder and headed across the street while Nate raced from room to room upending the few handsets that he came across.

Seth casually walked up to the ancient cannibalised motorbike and reached down into the electrics. It took less than a minute to get the engine fired up.

He pulled up to the side of the cell block, all the time on the lookout for trouble. Nate ran out of the building just as an alarm rang out from within the building. The two brothers froze and stared at each other, then Nate swung his leg over the seat and grabbed his brother's jacket.

Seth spoke over the growl of the misfiring engine.

'Survivor?'

Nate shrugged then shouted into Seth's ear from behind.

'Let's get the hell away from here.'

The bike sped east down Highway 10 toward Fallujah. They needed to get away from Ramadi and make a phone call before the bodies were discovered.

They hadn't spotted the man in a dark suit stepping out of the shadows, watching them as they rode away. The man talked for a further minute into his cell phone, closed the call, walked into the prison building.

2

Highway 10 had the world's oddest mix of traffic: military convoys and Iraqi patrols, blacked-out private security SUVs, beat up Japanese and German civilian cars, bullet-ridden trucks and the odd horse and cart, but it was quiet now. Seth and Nate barrelled down the pot-holed road keeping their heads down. They needed additional paperwork to navigate the journey out of the district but they were relying on the usual chaotic communications to avoid being picked up. After around ten kilometres Seth pulled off the road onto a shallow stretch of sand and fired up the satphone.

'I'm gonna try to reach Christo to get us a bird plus some civvies and papers. I figure they may look for us at Baghdad international so we'll have to head for Kuwait.'

'Jeez Seth, that's some drag.'

'I know man, but necessary. There we'll work out how the hell we get stateside before the sky falls down on us.'

Nate nodded absently, whipping his head around from one place to the next, scanning for trouble, agitated and waiting for his next instruction.

'Fuck. The battery is dead. We've got to get some juice.'

Seth fished out the flashlight and map from the rucksacks and searched for the nearest possible source on route. He tapped a finger on the map.

'Here. We go here, Nate.'

Seth shone the narrow beam of light onto a location on the map reading Al Habbaniyah, about twenty five kilometres east of their present position.

'We juice up, get some fresh rations and make the call, OK? OK Nate?'

Nate just nodded.

Seth looked at his brother more closely in the glare of the flashlight. His eyes were bloodshot, the little tic in his left eye working furiously now like he was entering one of his states. A look of bewilderment etched on his face.

Nate's pattern of life was fully formed now.

He was aware of Seth being there, but wouldn't look at him. He was aware of something having cracked again inside him, letting dark memories seep into the present.

And he's 9 years old.

> *…their Dadda comes home sodden and angry…*
> He has lost a day's earnings at gin rummy and is looking for a reason to vent. He goes to the boys' room and slaps Nate for still being awake, that is all, just being awake and reading his comic. The slap turns into a fist when Nate sneers and tries to turn his back on his Dadda. The blows hammer into him as he lies on his side in bed, forcing him against the wall, his Dadda all the time whispering 'Momma's-boy, Momma's-boy' in Nate's ear in time with the blows.
> The commotion has woken Seth who jumps out of bed and grabs at Dadda. Momma runs in and takes a glancing blow, all four ending on the bedroom floor. Their Dadda leaves them that night. He goes, leaving Momma with a gash to her cheek and Nate with a split lip and two cracked ribs. This isn't the first time Dadda has used his fists on them, but it is the last. Seth and Nate vow that much before they finally go to sleep that night.
> It is the following day and the hurt and the anger has bloomed in Nate. He helps to bathe his Momma's

cheek, zoning out the pain from his own bruised body.
He goes out in the yard then and sits alone on a step with his hands clasped under his legs, rocking back and forth, staring at a ladybug that roams between his feet. He finally picks it up and cups it in his hands, then goes looking for more of them, placing them in a discarded Oxo tin before he visits his Dadda's shed to root through his drawers, touching the forbidden tools, taking them from their neat containers and throwing them in the dirt in devilment until he finds what he is looking for.
The ladybugs are plentiful and he plucks them from the tin and arranges them in a row on an old plank. He keeps straightening them as they scurried about until he is ready. Then he takes his Dadda's claw hammer and crashes it down on them one by one until they are just a sticky red pulp, all the time ignoring the burning pain in his side. He clears the mess away, turns the plank over and throws Dadda's hammer into a bank of weeds.
The kitten is the step up. His Momma brings it home from work a few days later in her leather work bag, its tiny head sticking out the top.
'Take her Nate, before she pees in my bag again. She's yours now.'
It is the next day; he asks his Momma if he can bathe kitty because she has gotten all muddy from playing in the yard.
He fills an old tin tub, a leftover piece of rusted shit from the previous tenant, and gently lowers kitty in. He watches her struggle for twenty minutes or more as she makes terrible mewling sounds and paws at the straight sides of the bathtub until exhaustion sets in and she stops moving, just floats there, shrunken and glassy

eyed. He pokes her a couple of times with a stick and she tries to paw at it in reflex action with her remaining strength, but Nate puts the stick against the kitten's neck and pushes her all the way down to the bottom of the tub, holds her there watching the tiny bubbles rise, holding his own breath like it's a competition till his own lungs burn.

He runs then crying to his Momma, dragging her outside and pointing to the tub, saying that he left it only to fetch a rag to dry her off and that was the way he found her. Momma nurses him on her knee that night, promising to get him another.

Other incidents follow: the neighbours barking dog, his artwork to a horse's face with his old bowie knife, more. Seth has no idea what his younger brother gets up to when he's on his own. He meets up with Nate quite by chance after the mutilation of the horse, but Nate had slashed at his own arm and blames all of the blood over his shirt on his own accidental wound.

Memories faded, two decades falling away, and he could feel the brightness in his half-closed eyes of someone shining light in his face from close by.

Seth swung the torch back to the map.

He was getting increasingly worried about Nate. Seth had always been the one, the *only* one ready to catch him when he came down from his high wire act, but he had never seen him this bad, this dangerous. He had to get them both out of the sandbox and back home, back to the place that Nate loved most of all. He could take care of him again, take him hunting and fishing, get him off the recreationals and booze and maybe off the prescription, just the two of them, find a cabin away from everyone until people stopped looking for them. He could work out a plan for them both, new identities, careers.

But first he had to get them away from this hell hole, and he vowed to himself that he would do anything, *anything,* to get his younger brother back home and safe.

3

The house looked unoccupied.

Seth studied it through night-scopes as they lay on a rise looking down into a small valley that lay a mile or so off the main highway. He focussed on the house. No hint of movement. Doors and windows shut. Near the front door were several shallow ruts, indications that vehicles often parked there, but there were none now.

'OK, looks like no one's home, let's get down there and ration up.'

They scrambled to their feet. Seth wiped absently at the dirt and sand that had stuck to where the sweat had seeped through his combats.

The motorcycle spluttered as Seth tried to fire it up. He wondered how much further it would take them if they couldn't get help. If they had to walk later they'd walk, or steal a ride. Finally, the engine caught and he steered them carefully down a narrow rutted path in the semi-darkness.

Close up, he could see the house was a smart white-washed two-storey. Looked after. He rode past a chain link fence that separated it from the desert scrubland and pulled up at the front door.

Nate was off the bike first. For now his training took over. Seth went round back as Nate walked straight ahead, rifle at the low ready, peering through the gaps in the front window shutters. Seth tracked back and joined Nate at the front door.

Nate pointed at something on the wall near the front door. Seth looked more carefully. A handprint in faded blue dye. He nodded and flicked off the safety. This might not be as safe as he'd hoped.

Seth stood back, gun raised, as Nate kicked at the door sending it flying inward. They both went in low, carefully checking each room, looking for trap doors, booby traps.

'Looks like we're in luck Nate.'

Seth pointed into the kitchen as he headed into the living room.

'Check for food. I'll see if the power is still on.'

Seth assembled his sat kit and plugged in the charger. A tiny red light lit up on the handset and he gave a whoop.

'In business Natey.'

Nate appeared at the doorway, flashlight between his teeth, with two plates of dry bread and a chunk of stale cheese. They both dropped down onto the living room floor to eat. Nate looked like a lost boy but he was the first to speak.

'You know I didn't mean to start all this with that family Seth. They … just came at me, I thought they were coming for us both. I shouted for them to stop but they just kept coming.'

He leaned forward and dug straight fingers into his forehead.

'Just wasn't thinking.'

'I know Nate. What's done is done, man. *I* should've gone for the supplies, not you, and none of this would've happened. You should've waited in the jeep or, better still, back at base sleeping things off. I should've gone. I'm to blame.'

'No, that ain't right Seth, I screwed up not you. I'm sorry I messed up bro', really I am. I said the prayer, right there and then, y'know?'

'I know man. I heard you. Don't worry Nate; I'll make it go away.'

He grabbed hold of Nate's arm and held on to it for a few seconds, feeling an almost electric charge of emotion passing between them. Seth stared at his brother and asked him a question to which he already knew the answer.

'Do I need to ask where we head for when we get stateside?'

Nate smiled, rubbing his two-day growth. He seemed to come alive at the thought. He nodded absently as he spoke.

'I guess not. We'll be safe there, Seth, plus we know the area as well as anywhere.'

The brothers were talking about a place that meant a lot to the both of them, going back to their teens. A remote part of Maine, pockmarked with freshwater lakes and woods running along the spine of the Appalachian Trail. They had fished and hunted there as kids many times together while on Cougar trips.

'We could find an empty cabin for the winter and plan our next move.'

Seth had already reached the same conclusion. There was only one destination for them that gave any real chance to disappear for a while and rebuild their lives. Seth elbowed Nate's arm.

'OK Nate, my little troublesome brother, we get out of the sandpit and head for Lake Fear.'

Seth stood and began to clear away the plates but the thought of Lake Fear had left Nate with a distant look on his face, a distance in time and place to what they both referred to as *the Cougar thing*: an event from their teenage years that helped propel Nate on an inexorable path to where he was today. He sat on the floor of a stranger's home in Iraq, leaning against the living room wall and retreated into memory, back twenty years and six thousand miles.

> *…Fifteen year old Nate is sitting on a rock…*
> He is reading the instructions and smiling: 'Make a snare, trap a small wild animal, cook and eat it. Share it with a buddy Cougar.'
> Oh man, they have to be kidding; he can do this in his sleep. His biggest challenge is getting a buddy to work with him. The Cougar leader has split him and Seth up which means he is forced to seek out someone else to share the day's program with him. He eyes the gawky

kid suspiciously when he shows up while Nate is sat on a rock twisting a handful of tall grasses around his fingers to make the snare.

'Yer don't do it like that man, yer 'sposed ter use wire.'

'You want to hurry and find me a piece out here, 'cause I'm getting hungry.'

'Just sayin', is all.'

Nate finishes twisting the grasses and now has a four foot piece of rope that he begins knotting along its length.

'Sposed ter do that together yer know.'

The boy closes the gap on Nate so that he is almost on top of him, blocking out the sun. Nate doesn't look up at him as he says, 'Yep, that's what the instruction says, but I won't tell if you don't.'

The boy seems to hesitate then, thinking about his next words more carefully, perhaps more maliciously.

'You and yer brother, yer don't look much alike do yer?'

Nate wonders where this is going and now he looks up at the kid with eyes half closed against the sun's rays.

'Funny that, 'cause I hear you look just like your sister.'

'Fuck you man, you don't scare me. You and your brother think you own–'

Nate springs forward off the rock, grabbing the boy by the throat.

'Listen you prick, I didn't ask for a buddy so if you are just gonna irritate me all day I just as soon be on my own.'

He lets the boy go, pushing him backward, the boy stumbling into the dirt. He gets up and makes to advance on Nate but thinks better of it when Nate stands square on. The boy rubs at his reddening neck and begins walking away towards the base camp. He half turns and shouts over his shoulder, 'The leader's gonna hear about this, you'll be kicked out this time for sure. D'yer hear me? Your time's up you asshole, your fucking time's up.'

Nate just silently nods at the retreating boy and bends to pick up the grass rope, then turns and heads deeper into the forest towards the lake.

Glenn Ellis Forest forms a small node along the Appalachian Trail. It's truly beautiful here; rows of white Atlantic Cedar and Balsam Fir ring the oval shape of nearby Kennebec Lake. Seen from above, it forms part of a series of lakes whose proximity to each other makes them look like a pearl necklace carefully placed on a cloth of rich green baize, with Lake Fear at the northernmost point.

Nate is completely at home here, beauty, birdsong, sunlight dancing on the lake, trees swaying hypnotically, leaves whispering to him, sweet scent of pine wafting about him in waves on the breeze, warmth on his sunlit face as he lies on the lush grass, all of these things lulling him, pencil and pad in hand, capturing what he sees, then looking up, eyes half closed as he tracks a silver heron sailing across the sky.

He has been thinking of his Momma again, here in this wondrous place, reminding himself of the shittier side of the world he and his brother inhabit and thinking of the complicated medical report the court-appointed suit had read out to him and Seth the previous year, explaining that she had overdosed on a long list of drugs and booze. The suit had seemed to want the boys to get

the list down right because he had slowly mouthed the drug names for them. Seth had stopped him midway and had asked him if he got paid by the word but the suit had ignored him and carried on reading it out loud as if Momma wasn't really dead until he had finished. But she was dead. He was the one that had found her. Found her propped up against –
And then his head is slammed violently from the side, knocking him sideways and dragging him away from his comforting but corrosive thoughts of his Momma. Another blow hits him in his side and he pulls his knees into his body in reflex.
A third blow comes down across his right shoulder. More follow on his head, his body.
He manages to roll away and half stand, his head swimmy, ribs already swelling. He sits on his haunches now to face his attackers. The gawky boy is back and stands looking down at him, a large tree branch in his hands and a stupid smile on his face. The smell of glue reaches Nate's nostrils as he waits, assembling his thoughts. The boy has an accomplice who holds a baseball bat limply at his side. He looks nervous, his reddened eyes darting around as the first boy finally speaks.
'Not so tough now huh? Asshole! Didn't think we could take ya did ya, but now ya know. Now we're boss. Hey, know what? I figured out why you and yer brother don't look much like each other. Wanna know what I think your Mom did –'
Nate springs forward driving his head into the boy's midriff, dropping him onto the soft floor of the forest. The second boy drops the bat and runs, not looking

back once. Nate is on the gawky kid then, hands around his throat, the overwhelming smell of glue making Nate feel nauseous.

'I'll kill you for that, I'll kill you, I'll fucking kill you,' Nate screams, trance-like, into the face of the other boy. He pulls him in a headlock towards the lake.

They reach the water's edge and Nate grabs the boy's long lank hair and pulls his head under the frigid water, holding it there, the boy struggling and fighting and Nate still screaming into the back of the boy's head until he goes limp in his hands. Nate finally lets go and the boy floats there face down, his body swaying gently in rhythm with the ripples of the lake. Nate can't take his eyes off the boy's long thin legs, stiff like wood, doll-like, bobbing and swaying and slowly sinking. He watches the body until it fully submerges and then he runs towards the Cougar base shouting out his brother's name until he is almost hoarse.

Seth appears before him as if magicked up by sheer willpower and Nate just points toward the lake. Seth dives in to the icy waters and drags the body out onto the bank. He starts pumping the chest and breathing air into the lungs in short bursts, almost breathless himself after the run, but knowing he has just moments to save the boy. He works on him as Nate looks on with a growing sense of panic that he has actually killed the kid. He stands, frozen to the spot, his mind turning inward, and then the boy heaves up a great gob of dirty water and bile, catching Seth in the face. Seth keeps pumping as he shouts over his shoulder to his brother.

'Rub his arms and legs ... and put your jacket over him.'
But Nate isn't listening, just staring at the back of Seth

and the body of the boy that he thought already looked like a corpse. He is mouthing the same mantra over and over as Seth works on the boy.
'He shouldn't have ridden me, he shouldn't have called Momma like he did, he –'
Seth slapped at Nate's legs bringing him around.
'I said rub him like this.'
Seth rubbed the boy's legs to aid his circulation.
'And give him your fucking jacket.'

The boy had recovered and the case never made it near court due to Nate's age and self-defence wounds. He was committed to attend anger therapy. Seth had been right there alongside him; he would wait on the ragged canvas chair right outside the office until the shrink was done with Nate and he would question him about their conversations on the bus home. It became part of their lives two evenings a week for six months. On one of the journeys Nate pulled out a notepad and pencil and showed them to Seth. The shrink had given them to him right out of his own desk drawer, told him to write things down, write whatever occurred to him when he got angry, then to step back and see it for what it was, get control again. But the notepad became his tormentor, at first anyway, because nothing came that he could find the words for. So Seth told him to write down any old thing, just to get the juices flowing. And that's what he did. Until the words came. They filled the tightly packed lines, filled up the notepad and Seth bought more.

And at the end of the program? Nate seemed changed for the better. But deep down, he was damaged. He suffered with migraines after, and chewed on painkillers when the pain hit. The other meds for the mood swings came later.

He seemed outwardly calmer and in control of his temper most of the time. But Seth knew different. He figured Nate had simply learned to channel the lava flow a little deeper but it was still there, burning white hot at his centre, and Seth began to develop a fear for his brother and for anyone around him, a fear of the time the full force of this fury surfaced again.

The sound of Seth moving around the house brought Nate back to the present. He looked up at his brother as he spoke, the images of Kennebec Lake dissipating.

'You think Christo will come good for us? We've got major profile now Seth. He could do time if they find out he's helping us.'

'Christo will do anything for money, plus he owes us plenty.'

'He owes *you* plenty Seth.'

'Whatever, bro. We'll find out soon enough won't we.'

Nate was cleaning up after their makeshift meal as Seth pulled out the power cord from the satphone and fired it up. He got a satisfying beep. Twenty seconds later he was on the grid and calling his friend and ally Christopher Maitland Junior' ex Green Beret and now a private babysitter for rich Iraqi families with a lot to protect. The connection was made and the phone answered on the third ring.

'Christo, it's Seth, you good to talk friend?'

'Hell no, Seth, you and your numbnuts brother are all over the wires. You're a circus act, man, and I ain't in to you two no more. I mean what's going on, your brother channelling the wild bunch these days?'

'Listen Chris, one deal and that's it, just one. A chopper, civvies and some paper is what we need and we're out of your life for good, plus, we'll pay retail.'

'Seth, they're saying you lit up a couple civilians, a kid. I also heard you were in custody so how come you're free and calling me. You bust out of jail?'

'Christo, I can't go into that now, we need help and you're the only one we can turn to. We need to get to Kuwait international within twenty four hours. I figure they'll be looking for us at Baghdad.'

'Don't lay that on me Seth, I could do time if I'm caught aiding you. Plus my pension goes down the toilet. I'm not being your fall guy, man.'

'I know friend, but that's it, we have no one else to turn to.'

There was a short silence at the other end and Seth knew Christo was factoring in the times he owed the brothers from their past service together. Seth pressed ahead.

'No one need know, plus I'll bury any evidence when this is over.'

'Jesus. OK Seth, but just you, not your clusterfuck of a brother. I ain't helping him. He's crashing and burning and taking you and the whole security business down with him.'

'No Christo. We stay together, that's the deal, you know that.'

Seth heard rustling as though a map was being unfolded.

'OK OK man, but no chopper; there's a sand storm blowing in. I can get you a fuelled-up town car is all. Give me your current map ref.'

Nate read off the readings from his satphone.

'We're in Al Habbaniyah, holed up in a private residence. We can wait a few hours but that's it, they're bound to look here, plus it's an insurgent safe house so there is no telling who might turn up.'

'OK man, I'm stationed in Fallujah so I'll need five or six hours to assemble and reach you. But that's it friend. It's a one-time deal and after that, you're ghosts.'

4

Agent Byrd was looking out the dirty window of his temporary office inside the wire on Al-Shahid Street in Western Ar Ramadi. It was full dark now and his tired reflection in the glass watched him as he closed a call to his supervisor Mark Slater, Operations Director for CIA Clandestine Services.

Two Stryker combat vehicles tore past heading south kicking up choking plumes of sand and dirt in their wake. He didn't miss that kind of front-line action any more.

He looked round when the comms tech knocked and walked in with a tiny pen drive in his hand.

'Excuse me Sir, would you like me to fire this up for you?'

The man pointed to Byrd's laptop open on the desk. Byrd shook his head, took the drive and waved the man out. He stopped him on the threshold of his airless office.

'This the only copy you have of the call?'

'Yessir, I deleted the original as you instructed.'

'Also, delete the call from your log, soldier.'

The soldier gave a brief puzzled expression but quickly corrected it. He'd heard of Byrd. Not all good.

'Yes Sir.'

The young man saluted and closed the door. Byrd loaded the drive into his laptop and listened to the satphone conversation between the two men. He made a few scribbled notes and then deleted the file. Slater had been very specific on this point: *leave no evidence.* That included enforcing a burn-notice on an idealistic UN worker right here in Ramadi and dealing with an ex grunt going by the name of Christo. He peeled his sweat-soaked shirt from his back and gazed down once more onto the street below. He rubbed his tired eyes and reflected on his plans that were rapidly going bad.

This was becoming one huge laugh a minute, his careful plans for the brothers burning to ashes because they'd decided to escape for themselves. And stick a few expensively trained guards in the process. There's just no helping some people. And what the hell was he doing here anyway, when he should have been back in DC by now after his latest assignment in Baghdad. Instead, two angry brothers make a mess on the carpet and he has to detour to bag it and clean up afterward. He'd pleaded for a couple of hungry young operations officers in the field to handle it, but Slater had been insistent that Byrd attend to matters personally, and alone, on the ground. Abu Ghraib had shook Capitol Hill to its foundations and his orders were to get rid of this latest stink before it escalated. But he had to be careful. The targets had some kind of leverage over the authorities that he didn't quite understand yet and no one was telling.

According to his briefing, the two brothers had been under surveillance long before this recent incident, all the way back before Stygian to their service in Special Forces. The killing of an Iraqi and his son had triggered such a rapid response within the CIA that Byrd couldn't but smell the dead hand of the politicos.

No he didn't have all the Intel on the two brothers yet, but he would. He would find out why he couldn't just leave it to the locals to resolve, why he had to nurse-maid them all the way back to the US.

He stared down at his laptop studying a stationary red dot that blinked like a sclerotic heartbeat on the map. He rolled his head to ease the tension and picked up his cell phone. He had a lot of calls to make if he was to get the brothers stateside, unhindered, within forty eight hours.

Then he would find out what the hell was going on before he completed his mission.

5

It was just past one a.m. when two sets of bright beams lit up the access road. Seth switched off the flashlight and looked out of the angled slats of the window shutters. Two flashes from the lead vehicle confirmed that it was friendly. The other vehicle hung back and switched off its lights.

Christo climbed out of a jeep with two large bags and walked up the path. Seth came out of the shadows from the rear of the property as Nate opened the front door.

'Don't worry Seth, I'm friendly. Just.'

Seth reached a hand to Christo but he just looked at the ground and walked past him and Nate and into the house. He turned on Seth then, full of venom.

'Why didn't you tell me Seth, that you'd taken some Iraqi guards out? Shit, I'm in a world of trouble if they trace any of this back to me.'

Seth didn't answer, just looked at Christo and gave a short shake of his head.

'That's gonna push the price up a lot friend. Listen, I don't have long so we need to go through this quickly man.'

Christo hadn't yet acknowledged Nate who was stood with his hands folded across his body and leaning on the wall in a corner of the living room. He ran through the provisions and arrangements with Seth alone.

'Your ride is fuelled up and I've put two extra cans in the trunk.'

Christo pulled out a heavily creased map of the region and unfolded it on a table. He and Seth leaned over it as Christo pointed to a series of hand drawn red circles.

'I've marked the latest known checkpoints for you as far as Basrah. Most of 'em are rolling, so who the hell knows if they're all still out there?'

'What's this?'

Seth tapped at a hand-annotated point on the map close to a place called Radwaniyah.

'It's an unofficial military field hospital supply depot. We use it in emergencies.'

'Guarded?'

'Light security, just a handful of lab techs live there.'

Seth nodded, calculating its distance.

'There are civvies in the bags and papers for you both to get through the checkpoints and border crossing, plus a street map of Kuwait City. But you're gonna have to ride on your own passports once you reach the airport. I'm assuming you have those?'

Seth nodded although he knew he would have to rely on luck to get through airport security at Kuwait International and US airports now that they were looking for them.

'Beyond this my friend, it's been nice knowing you and I expect ten large in my usual account by the end of the day.'

Seth reached out a hand and this time Christo took it.

'Thank you Christo, from both of us.'

Seth looked over at his brother as he said this but Nate had his gaze fixed on the floor.

'I'm out of here Seth. Find some peace, man, for you, your brother and all our sakes.'

Christo stalled briefly at the front door as if noticing the hand print for the first time.

'And I wouldn't hang around here much longer.'

Christo walked out of the front door and into the darkness to his ride.

Seth and Nate were back down on the living room floor, leaning over the map Christo had left them, discussing the route down to

Kuwait, when a scraping noise at the back door stopped Seth midsentence. He switched off the flashlight and they both crouched silently in the darkness.

Seth pointed to the back door and gestured for Nate to hold his position there. He himself slipped out the front door and followed the path round back, both brothers with their guns at the high ready.

Seth could see a figure at the rear window trying to look in through the shutters. He had a handgun raised and resting across his chest. Seth closed the gap on the man and put the barrel of his rifle against the man's temple.

'Easy friend, nice and easy OK?'

The man nodded slowly.

'Get hold of the barrel of your gun with your left hand and hand it over to me. Any sudden movements will get you killed. Nod again, now.'

The man followed his instructions and Seth tucked the weapon in his belt and patted the man down. Then he knocked hard at the back door.

'Nate, want to open up the door? We have company.'

Seth roughly pushed the man through the doorway and he fell at Nate's feet. Nate pointed his gun at the man's head as Seth closed and locked the door then opened the shutters a little to scan the area. He saw nothing in the complete darkness. He closed them again, switched on his flashlight and aimed the beam at the man's face. The man was Iraqi, dressed in light desert clothes. Seth kicked out at him.

'Any more like you friend?'

The man gave a low moan and squirmed out of reach of Seth's boot, then looked up at him, un-cowed, a sly mocking grin on his face.

'Like me? Many.'

'I mean here, now.'

'Not now, but maybe soon.'

Nate leant down and back-handed the man's face, sending him crashing across the floor and leaving him with an instant red welt.

'How soon, asshole? And don't give *me* that fucking look.'

The man shrugged, pulled his knees up to his chest and looked away, but Nate reached and grabbed his jacket, lifted, and dumped him on a chair. Seth continued to question him.

'What're you doing here?'

'I see the car and the motorbike. I wonder whether I have a visit from any of my brothers.'

'So, you're the caretaker of the place?'

The man nodded.

'Nate, go see if you can find some rope.'

Nate looked at the man and looped an imaginary noose around his neck, then pulled violently upward. Seth saw the movement and narrowed his eyes at Nate.

'For tying him to the fucking chair.'

Seth was flicking through the address book of the man's cell when Nate returned with a length of electrical cord.

He grabbed the man and held him still as Nate bound him to the chair.

'You've got some interesting contacts, lot of activity today. Want to tell me why you would be speaking to the US Embassy?' Seth asked.

'Wrong number.'

Nate cuffed him again, splitting the man's lip.

'Wrong answer.'

'Leave it Nate; we have to get out of here before we have any of his friends turning up.'

'We just leave him?'

'We just leave him.'

They carried the man from the kitchen into a storeroom at the rear of the house. Nate tore off one of the sleeves from the man's top and gagged him with it. Seth tied more cord to the back of the chair and around a timber support.

'OK man, let's collect our gear and go.'

Seth was walking out the front door and heading for the car Christo had delivered when Nate shouted out to him.

'Be a minute Seth, just need to take a leak.'

Nate walked through to the back of the house and collected a candle and Zippo that he had come across while searching for the rope earlier. He lit the candle and opened the door of the storeroom, then knelt and placed the candle on a straw mat, a few metres in front of the bound man. He looked around and spotted a stack of old newspapers and magazines. He grabbed a handful of the paper and began tearing strips and dropping them around the flickering flame of the candle like confetti until a small mound had formed at the base of the candle. He looked across at the man who was already straining against the cord and screaming obscenities into his gag but Nate just smiled and continued tearing.

'Maybe the candle will just burn down to nothing, y'know?'

He closed the door of the storeroom and walked out of the house to join his brother.

6

Seth drove with the window down to counter the stifling heat and sour smell of sweat in the car, but the price was the unnerving sound of the religious wailing reverberating across the desert coming over the countless loudspeakers set high up on metal poles and attached to rooftops.

He'd never got used to the Iraqi night-time. The darkness was punctuated by the flaring lights from burn barrels and fire pits, the sporadic sounds of gunfire and rockets and the hot moaning winds coming from the west over the Mediterranean, kicking up blinding gusts of dirt and sand along the way. Christo had mentioned a full blown sandstorm was on its way and he wished for the first time that it would arrive quickly, give them cover.

They were on Highway 8 now, travelling south. This and the upcoming Highway 80 were known as the *highways of death*: between them over four hundred miles of undulating tarmac laid through desert and surrounded by bleached bones and vehicle carcasses. The two highways provided a main supply route that almost cleaved the country in two running from Kuwait to the Syrian border.

They drove past rows of rundown bullet pock-marked apartment buildings with rugs and clothes hanging off balconies, burst sandbags strewn everywhere like they had been dropped randomly from above, before the buildings ran out leaving just desert.

They had a journey of around three hundred and fifty miles now, and a dozen or so checkpoints to negotiate, with little time to do it. Nate was staring out the side window into the blackness, both legs drumming up and down, hands tapping at his sides in time – a habit he had when his anxiety levels were high.

He spoke quietly now to Seth. He could hardly be heard over the ghostly chanting of Muslim prayers that surrounded them and the strengthening wind. He seemed to be caught up in the surreal nature of their circumstances.

'Am I going to hell Seth? I think I am man, all the deaths I'm responsible for.'

'Honestly bro? I don't know where either of us is headed when the time comes. I just know that wherever it is, we'll be there together.'

Seth used Nate's breaking of the silence to bring up a fear growing in him about his brother's behaviour.

'Nate, we need to talk man, about where your head is. Are you still taking your meds?'

Nate didn't answer, just continued strumming on his legs. 'Nate, the meds, man.'

'No I ain't taking 'em no more Seth.'

Seth was shocked. But not surprised.

'But you've got to keep them up Nate; the Doc explained to us what would happen if you don't.'

'I can't sleep with them Seth, the nightmares are just too creepy, man.'

'Creepy? Explain creepy.'

Nate went silent again.

'Nate, you have to tell me.'

'OK, OK. It's like there's this great grizzly after me, with teeth like knives and claws that could tear you in half with one swipe. And the eyes, Seth. Big round glowing red eyes filled with blood, just staring down at me. It comes for me, man. Every night. I can't move. I'm stuck there in the dark on a lonely shit road on my own with the grizzly thing in front of me. I can't move and it gets closer until the moon is blotted out. Its breath, its whole body stinks of death. It talks to me Seth. Honest to God, it talks to me. It says it knows me, knows who I am, what I am. It says I have to listen to it and do what it says. And then I feel it, right there in my dream man, feel its teeth bite down on my neck. How is that possible, that I *feel it* Seth? But I do, I feel it breaking my bones, its teeth scraping against my torn skin, its dirty claws disappearing inside of me, the hot blood running down my back. I have no weapon and I'm alone with it. Sounds crazy I know. It's the meds that do it Seth, it's the goddamned meds and I ain't taking 'em no more.'

He spoke all of this in one continuous gush while staring down at his trembling knees.

'OK Nate, calm down man, let's drop the meds for now. I'll talk to the doctors again when we get home.'

Nate just nodded and kept his face down.

This was new to Seth. Nate had never mentioned the night tremors before although the doctors had explained that this could be a side effect of taking the meds for his mood swings. Seth spoke again, gently.

'How come you never mentioned the nightmares to me before now Nate? I could've gotten you help, changed the dose or something.'

'Because I didn't want you thinking I was a sissy. Look bro, it's over, I didn't want to take 'em no more and I flushed 'em down the pan back in Ram. That's the last of 'em and that's how it's gonna stay. That pill you slipped me in the cell? Don't do it no more Seth. Please man; get rid of your stash.'

Seth held his own small supply of Fontex for Nate in case of emergencies. He let it go, for now. But they both knew that they would have to face it again sometime soon. Without the meds Nate was unpredictable, unstable, dangerous.

They drove on silently past potholes and misshapen concrete slabs and the occasional dimly lit vehicle heading in the opposite direction. Seth's eyes were like laser beams tracking for trouble.

LAKE FEAR

The night-time sky was decorated with a billion stars but a dense cloud was already travelling towards them in a hurry, seeming to rub out the stars like a giant eraser as it progressed eastward. Gusts of sand streaked across the windshield like a dirty veil forcing Seth to slow down. The leading edge of the storm was approaching. Seth tried to lighten the mood that had built up.

'Might get me some new tats when we're stateside, Baby Bear, maybe a golden eagle on my back. Feel a little underdressed with just these to show for my life in service.'

Seth held out his right arm to show a pair of rolling dice as he said it. One was black and one red, both showing six up.

'What say you; fancy a big-ass ink or what?'

'Mmm, might give that a miss Daddy Bear, you know I don't like pain.'

They both laughed like donkeys as they drove on into the teeth of the worsening sandstorm.

They had been driving for a couple of hours and Nate was dozing. His earlier recall of his Mother had unnerved him. It had been a while since he thought of her so vividly. His mind went there again unbidden.

He was the one that had found her, propped up against...

As now, the image had come back relentlessly when he was younger, sharp and clear and debilitating. When he was taking lessons in class... BAM. When he was hanging out with Seth watching a football game... BAM. But mostly when he was laid curled up in his bunk at night, blankets tented over his shoulders, holding his little flashlight, reading his DC comics... BAM, BAM, BAM. And the stinking video would play again in his tortured mind.

...Home after school, lets himself in to the little timber

framed bungalow…
Seth's planning on coming home later. Nate calls out to Momma but gets no answer, threadbare floral curtains, strangely, still drawn in the living room in the middle of the afternoon creating a dirty mottled half-light, TV news anchor droning in the background, kitchen door wedged half closed by a pair of sprawled legs. He gently pushes the door against those legs to get inside and he cringes because he recognises them in their colourful flowery leggings. His brain is already calculating why they might be there on the floor. And there she is, sat with her back leaning up the kitchen wall with her head hung sideways resting on her shoulder at a painful angle. Pale blue lips, dribble and worse hang out of her mouth and nose in knotty strings reaching all the way down to her chest, empty wine bottle lies in her lap, washed-out ratty nightgown still on and open to the waist, eyes half open, reddened and veined, looking down but seeing nothing, reminding Nate of the chipped and dirty plaster Madonna perched at an angle on a stand in a corner of the room at Sunday school. His Momma, his Momma. Her image seared into his brain now, blotting out all else, and Nate knowing that the image would be his to carry forever, seeping into every corner, waiting, ready to jump out at him, his mind no longer his own, not completely, not any more. His beloved Momma reduced to a Kodak moment, his anger at her leaving him, and at a world that would let her go, stoked to a burning rage.

A massive jolt brought him round as the car righted itself from the deep pothole.

'Sorry man, didn't see it.' Seth had one hand on the wheel, the other holding his flashlight pointing at the map.

'You did me a favour.'

'Listen, I've been thinking about how to get through the checkpoints, Nate. They'll be looking for two soldiers, so we have to be smart.'

'Smart is what you do Seth.'

'I'm thinking we pay a visit to the supply depot Christo told us about, acquire an ambulance that will get us through the checkpoints easier than a town car. They won't be looking for an ambulance. According to the map the depot is just about ten kilometres ahead. I figure once we trade you play hurt from an IED. I'll have to beat you up a little, draw a bit of blood to make it convincing. I'll say we're heading for the nearest military hospital along the route.'

'I like it Seth, especially the bit where a big brother beats up on his younger kid brother. I'm sure they have laws against things like that even in Iraq.'

'Since when do we pay attention to details like the law?'

They drove on as sand whipped and beat against their windshield like small arms fire.

'Jeez man would you look at that?'

Nate pointed forward as the headlights caught fleeting glimpses of the burned out hulk of an AC-130, the lethal flying gunship originally deployed in Vietnam and now operational in Iraq to counter the resistance. It rested half-buried in sand, an ugly monument to death.

'Yeah, how about that.'

'Remind you of anything?' Nate asked.

'No, not a damned thing.'

'Oh, really? Come on man, got the medals to remind us y'know? You remember. Like me carrying your old and broken body back to base.'

'Nope, don't recall that at all man. You sure of your facts? Think all those spliffs must've addled your brain.'

Nate playfully grabbed Seth's knee giving it a squeeze and Seth yelped like a puppy.

'Think it was this leg wasn't it Seth. You know, where I removed that chunk of metal before I wrapped you up like a baby and carried you home.'

'Alright, alright man let it go. So, you saved a man in distress. I was your commanding officer, you had a duty to me.'

The jeep was filled with laughter again, barely heard over the moan of the wind.

That incident had happened in 2006, a code red operation: *aircraft down in enemy territory.* Taliban had downed an Apache helicopter during a night raid by US forces in Kandahar. Seth, Nate and two more Special Forces soldiers had gotten their orders and had been airborne within one hour of the stricken heli hitting the ground. It was a search and rescue mission for the two pilots and one navigator.

Fast air support from a US A-10 jet had already been despatched to destroy the damaged asset so that enemy forces couldn't cannibalise any remaining high tech equipment on board.

Nothing had been heard from the aircrew but Intel indicated that they had been taken to a nearby Taliban safe house. Seth's team had to move swiftly before they were sold to the highest bidder; history showed that negotiations were concluded within the first four hours and then they were lost down a long, dark rabbit-warren until their captors wanted them back in play, or dead. The rescue team had been dropped in the desert under the cover of darkness a half mile from the target.

They'd quickly covered the ground and all four had lain motionless on a sandy mound evaluating the target through infrared night scopes.

A single guard had been stationed at the front door and two more on a flat roof of an adjacent outbuilding. Nate had the front entrance covered, Seth the rear, with the other two soldiers hanging back to give cover. One of the soldiers had fitted a grenade launcher onto his M16 for the first wave assault. Seth had given him the signal and he'd fired at the front door, blowing it out along with most of the surrounding stonework. He switched trajectory and fired another grenade onto the nearby roof, taking out the guards and creating a firestorm of smoke, dust and flames. The soldiers had then laid down bursts of fire as Seth and Nate went in fast and low, charging at the house. Nate crashed through the still burning front entrance, blazing death at eight rounds per second from his rifle. Seth had gone in through a back window shooting out the glass and timber frame before diving shoulder first into the chaos. The Taliban were heavily armed and the small smoke-filled room had become a deafening fire-fight.

When the firing stopped and smoke had cleared, four Taliban lay dead and Seth was nowhere to be seen. Nate had raced back out onto the streets, spotted the wounded Seth being dragged down an alleyway, and had given chase. Seth had been shot in the thigh and was unconscious now. One of the Taliban had turned and fired at Nate hitting him in the arm, but he went on following them down the narrow, winding alleyways, leaving a blood trail of his own as he did. The alley opened up onto a small square, illuminated by the lights from apartment buildings above. Nate stopped, steadied himself, and aimed, hitting one of them in the back of the head with a single shot and sending him spinning onto the rubbish strewn ground. The other dropped Seth and ran.

Nate sprinted forward to Seth and quickly tied his belt around his still bleeding leg as a dozen silent faces watched them from the balconies above.

Then the phosphorous bomb lit up the square like a firework, burning flakes raining down on the two of them. Nate covered Seth's prostrate body with his own, the Kevlar doing its job, but a few tiny pieces found the back of his neck, back of his hands, some drifting on the heat haze, landing on his cheek, his chin, sleeves, setting off tiny flares on his combats that couldn't be extinguished with the frantic flaps of his hands, that ate through the layers like acid until they reached his skin and then continued on until burned out.

He shrugged off his backpack, searching in the darkness for the small pot, fingers grasping it as he held Seth, then unscrewing it, digging his fingers into the Vaseline, slathering his incinerated skin, spreading a layer on Seth's face.

He oriented himself through the smoke, lifted Seth onto his back. He had carried him like that, non-stop, all the way back to the pickup point a quarter mile away. He had given Seth some of his blood on board the helicopter on their way back to base, even though he'd left some of his own on the streets of Daman.

In the end the mission had been a dud. One of the team had found the pilots and navigator in an upstairs bedroom, shot dead.

All four soldiers received silver stars for their bravery, but in truth, Nate didn't give a damn about his medal or the lifelong scars. What mattered to him was getting Seth back to safety, that and the enjoyment of bragging rights over his brother for years to come.

7

The hospital supplies depot was set back off the road. They drove fifty metres or so past the site, pulled over, killed the lights. Seth glassed the building, steadying his hands on the roof of the car against wind gusts. The place looked dead. There were no guards, no activity, just a dull, rust-red glow emanating from lights hung from cables that criss-crossed the site. Seth got out and leaned back in through the open door. Seth had to raise his voice just to be heard over the noise of the wind.

'You wait here Nate and switch on your squawk box. I'll recon the place.'

'Belay that order Bro, I'm coming with.'

'No Nate, we might need a quick getaway. If things go toe up, I'd like you here waiting behind the wheel.'

'OK but any longer than fifteen, I'm coming in behind you.'

'Fair enough. Get all of the kit ready for transfer, and stay alert.'

'Taking a gun?'

'No Nate, I don't want a shoot-out, just a quiet in and out, that's all.'

Nate gave a full salute to his brother who smiled and saluted back. Nate seemed to be calmer now.

Seth handed Nate the glasses and walked quickly toward the depot. The sandstorm was intensifying by the minute and his outline blurred in Nate's lens within a handful of strides as he tracked his brother's progress.

The depot was a single story building with a three metre high, rusted wire perimeter fence. Two low power spotlights attached to the roof were trained on the front gate. A lean-to structure was attached to the western wing covering a dozen or so vehicles: town cars, four by fours and two small ambulances were parked up in neat rows. A single light was on in one of the ground-floor rooms.

Seth slipped around to the side, pulled out his tool bag and took out a pair of wire cutters. He was inside the compound in seconds and heading towards the south side of the building, keeping to the shadows.

He dropped below a small window and peered through the wire-mesh grill into the room beyond. Two men in bright orange overalls were talking and laughing together with no awareness of the security breach.

Seth balanced on his heels, his back resting against the building, head turned watching the two men and whispered into his walkie-talkie.

'Nate, copy over?'

'Copy Seth, over.'

'Nate, just a couple of lab techs here plus they have what we need. See you in short order, out.'

The two men inside the depot had broken up their conversation now and one of them was headed for the front door.

Seth crept around the corner of the building waiting for the man to appear, hoping he wouldn't but prepared if he did. He waited five minutes and figured the guy wasn't coming outdoors after all. He was about to head back to the carport when he heard the front door being unlocked. He dropped low and peered around the front of the building. Both men stepped out and lit up, shielding their faces from the wind. They were speaking in Arabic and Seth could only make out a few odd words. He checked his watch. He didn't want Nate losing his patience waiting back at the car and deciding to come see. He was about to call Nate once more when a cell went off, a jangly tuneless ring-tone, and one of the men wandered away from the other into the compound to take the call. His movement triggered a set of floods that lit up the whole site. Seth crept further into the shadows of the building, rested himself against a low storage chest, and waited. His own handset hissed and he fumbled for it, to turn down the volume.

'You trip the floods Seth? Over.'

'No. One of the lab boys on walkabout. I'm still good man. Stay put Nate, out.'

Seth didn't wait for a response.

He eased himself to the corner of the building on his belly to check on the two men. One had gone back indoors now, the other sat perched on the edge of an upturned oil drum, still shouting into the mouthpiece of his cell. Seth checked his watch. The bodies would have been discovered by now back in Ram. He didn't like that they were wasting time here. He checked it again. Couple more minutes and he would abandon the idea of the vehicle switch, take their chances with the car. The floods suddenly extinguished, the timer tripped, plunging the site into darkness, then back on as the man stood and waved his hands at the sensor fixed to the front roofline. Seth repositioned himself, got ready to withdraw, nervous that the lightshow would bring Nate charging in. Suddenly, the man ended the call and headed back into the building. Seth took a few deep breaths of relief, gave it a few more minutes, returned to the carport and picked out one of the ambulances.

It was a small personal vehicle that had seen a lot of action, just a converted station wagon with stick-on lettering and a blue light jerry-rigged to the roof. Seth tried the door and found it unlocked. He climbed in and dropped the sun visor. A set of keys dropped into his lap. Seth smiled and saluted the empty vehicle, appreciating the good fortune.

He reached round to survey the rear of the vehicle. A single gurney was bolted to the floor, two white coats were hung on hooks battened to the side panel on each side and a large white plastic chest with a red cross rested on the floor at the foot of the gurney.

He hoped the din from the wind roaring across the desert would mask the noise of the engine and fired it up. He backed up and headed for the gap he'd cut in the fence. He eased the van through and got out to make good the damage to the fence.

Nate was sat in the driver's seat, his foot wedged against the open door, as Seth appeared from the darkness. Seth wound down the driver's window letting a swathe of hot air and sand blast in.

Nate got out of the car and leaned in, smiling at Seth on seeing the ride.

'Nice work mein kapitan.'

Seth reached out the window and high fived Nate.

'Follow me a few klicks down the highway and then pull over and we can transfer the stuff. Pull the hood; make it look like a breakdown.'

Within twenty minutes, they had made the transfer and were heading South on Highway 8 in their newly acquired ambulance.

The first rolling check-point appeared out of the darkness as they neared the outskirts of Karbala and Nate scrambled over the passenger seat and lay on the gurney. Usually the checkpoints were doubled up, an Iraqi first line followed by the U.S. a few hundred metres further on. But here the brothers faced just two young Iraqi soldiers stood smoking at the back of their jeep, trying to shield themselves from the wind behind the '*stop or you will be shot*' sign. A spotlight connected to a huge car battery was trained up into the night sky. Seth shook his head and pointed at them; both soldiers had leaned their guns upright against the sign. They reached for them now as the ambulance neared.

'We got Tweedledumb and Tweedledumber looking after

business Nate. Looks like they're both still concussed from *Shock and Awe*.'

Seth slowed the ambulance to a stop and one of the guards walked over and shone a flashlight in his face. Seth was dressed in a white doctor's coat now and was about to reach for his papers when the guard waved him on. Seth smiled; one down, just a dozen more to go.

'Hey you back there, you can rest easy soldier and stop groaning so much, we're clear.'

Nate climbed up and over into the passenger seat, picked up Christo's map and shone his flashlight up and down the route.

'And don't get your blood on my map.'

Nate gave Seth the finger.

Fifteen minutes earlier Seth had torn a gash in Nate's sleeve and casually flicked the blade of Nate's own knife across his upper arm to draw blood, wiped it across a stretch of bandages. Then he had cut the piece in two and had wrapped a piece around Nate's upper arm and one around his thigh.

'I figure we've got about three hundred and fifty plus miles to go before we hit Kuwait.'

The brothers cheered out loudly together as they sped along the highway hoping the remaining checkpoints would be this easy. The cheering spread into a Conway Twitty song that their Momma loved so much, the one about living hard and dying young.

8

Byrd sat uncomfortably in the co-pilot seat of the heli as it was buffeted by the wind. The cabin was hot and sweaty and noisy. The bitter taste of exhaust fumes clung to the back of his throat. He caught his own reflection in the Plexiglas and stared at his dishevelled image for a few seconds before looking back at the tracker. The boys were down there in the gloom on Highway 8. They had stopped off at the military med-supply facility and switched vehicles, all in accordance with the intelligence he had secured from a call to one of the techs holed up there, and from Seth's partner in crime Christo. Loyalty only went so far with the threat of seven to ten behind bars and an empty bank account to greet you when you got out.

He checked his watch. Another ten hours or so of journey time for the brothers in these conditions, and a few checkpoints to navigate. He pulled the mic nearer his mouth, straightened the earphones, shouted across to the pilot.

'Sandstorm likely to catch us up?'

The craft was violently tugged sideways again as he spoke. Sprays of sand blasted across the windshield.

'Figure it's already here wouldn't you say? I'll try outrunning the worst of it but if the wind gets any stronger up here I'll have to bring her down, do the rest of the journey by road.'

Byrd didn't want that. He needed to reach Kuwait International ahead of the brothers, track their movements all the way to their aircraft seats.

'Need you to do your best to keep me up in the air.'

The pilot nodded and looked ahead as Byrd stared back down at the tracker.

9

The brothers had travelled another seventy miles or so. Nate was fidgety and hot.

'Pull over, I'm busting to pee.'

Seth slowed and pulled off the road onto a stretch of sand. He took the map from Nate as his brother hopped out of the car. The sandstorm seemed to be easing a little, allowing glimpses of milky light from the early morning sun between wind gusts.

Seth studied the map again to pinpoint their present position. According to Christo they would be coming up on another checkpoint soon.

He climbed out of the car and took out his binoculars. He looked back as Nate stretched and wandered a little further away along the sandy apron, then he swung around and walked along the road the other way to get a better view beyond a couple of sand dunes immediately ahead of them. He spotted what he was looking for and turned, heading back to the car. He shouted across to Nate, 'I can see the checkpoint Natey. Just behind these dunes, couple kilometres ahead, lit up like a Christmas tree. We need to get closer.'

He spun slowly on his heels and scanned the whole valley that was revealing itself through billowing waves of sand and dust.

The flapping of tent canvas east of their position drew his attention. A large Bedouin tent was pitched between two large dunes, sheltering from the wind. He spotted some of the tribe, maybe up early to check their belongings were still intact: father, mother, two children, perhaps more inside the tent. A handful of goats and donkeys were tethered to stakes a little distance from the tent. The kids were playing, running around dragging something behind them.

Then he saw the dogs. Three huge, lean hounds, like Salukis but bigger, heading towards them, kicking up tiny sand clouds as they raced across the desert, rapidly closing the distance between them.

He shouted over to his brother.

'Nate, suggest you close up your flies man and get over here, we're about to have company.'

Nate came jogging up behind Seth who pointed to the dogs and the camp site that seemed to float in the strange emerging light, drifting in and out of view through skeins of sand.

The family were stood staring their way now and whistling and shouting to their dogs. Nate reached into the car and pulled out a rifle.

'Want me to take them out?'

Seth turned to his brother.

'The dogs?'

'Yeah, the fucking dogs.'

'No, I do not want you to take them out. We don't need any more trouble right now, man.'

Nate lifted the rifle anyway and aimed at the dogs, making three popping sounds with his puckered lips then he looked across at Seth and smiled.

'All dead now.'

Seth shook his head at his brother.

'Let's go.'

They climbed into the car and Seth drove back onto the highway. Nate grabbed the binoculars, leaned out the window and looked back at the dogs. They had stopped running toward them now and stood circling and snapping at each other. Then they headed back to the camp.

Seth cruised slowly along the road for another couple of kilometres, then he pulled over again. He got out and leant against the roof of the car to steady his glasses. He thumbed the magnification until the checkpoint came into view.

'It ain't the goon squad this time; I see U.S. Gonna have to draw some fresh blood from yer.'

'You enjoying this man?'

'Nope, your thick skin blunts up the knife,' Seth said as he scanned the whole area. The sun was climbing, reflecting dully off the fast moving sand clouds, intermittently piercing through with thin laser-like rays that looked like giant prison bars across the whole valley floor.

'Jesus, storm ain't finished with us yet Natey.'

Seth pointed west of their position. A wall of dense sand blotted out the horizon. Maybe six, seven miles distant.

'Come on man, let's go before we get swallowed up.'

The checkpoint was just north of Diwaniyah. It was fixed and organised. The handful of Iraqi troops waved them on as they approached. Seth waved and continued forward at a slow and steady pace toward the group of U.S. soldiers. Two of them broke from the pack, rifles raised and aimed at Seth through the windshield. One stayed at the head of the vehicle, the other came forward and around towards Seth. He raised a hand, pointed at the engine and pulled his hand across his throat. Seth stopped short of the barrier and switched off the engine. He waited in his seat, hands resting on the wheel fully in view, until the soldier reached him and put his head into the vehicle. The whole area was illuminated like a film set by four magnum light towers, each carrying a thousand watt metal halide flood. Seth spoke up first, tried to take the initiative.

'Hey soldier, got an injured back there.'

Seth pointed to the rear of the ambulance.

'Road accident. He'll live but I need to get him to Adder as soon as.'

Camp Adder was a military airbase located near Nasiriyah, about ninety miles south of their position.

'Can't fly 'cause of the conditions.'

'Where's your escort, sir?'

'Lost him about five miles back, engine trouble, the sand y'know?'

'Mind if I take a look at your patient?'

'Go ahead, but I prefer it if you didn't wake him; I've given him a shot of cyklo, need to keep him sedated and his pressure down.'

Seth got out and walked the soldier round the back of the ambulance, opened the doors. Nate was laid on his side, a little blood appearing to bloom from bandages wrapped around his thigh and arm. Seth spoke up again.

'It's nothing this big ugly ain't seen before.'

The soldier waved for Seth to close the doors.

'Wait here OK?'

Seth stood leaning against the body of the car, one hand covering his eyes as sand whipped at him from all sides. Two soldiers climbed into a jeep and sped off down the road that Seth and Nate had driven in on. A wave of dread flushed through Seth as he watched the jeep leave. The soldier returned a few minutes later, gun secured.

'We've arranged for an armed escort to get you to Camp Adder. There's a lot of bandits around here. They see an ambulance unescorted, you're liable to be attacked for any drugs you have on board. I've despatched someone to rescue your escort in the desert before they get buried in this shit.'

Seth nodded, smiled in appreciation.

'You see that?'

The soldier pointed west.

'Gonna get worse before it gets better, you need to make progress as soon as.'

'Yep to that soldier.'

Seth held out a hand to the private.

'Thanks man.'

'My pleasure, sir.'

A soldier raised the barrier as a jeep approached at Seth's side, and then it took off at speed. Seth jumped back into the ambulance, gunned the engine and followed. He turned and shouted to Nate who was raised on his elbows waiting for the news.

'We lucked out Natey boy, we got us a couple of U.S. cherries up front. They're gonna take us practically to the doorstep. Just kick back in your pussy-pad back there and enjoy the ride.'

10

Byrd's cell vibrated in the chest pocket of his sweat-stained shirt. He took it out, lifted off his earphones and jammed it hard against his ear to be heard over the noise of the helicopter and howling wind. He nodded absently to himself throughout the four minute conversation.

'Copy that Captain, out.'

He checked his watch, shone his pencil light down at the map. He reckoned it was around two hundred miles straight line to the border, a lot more for the brothers down on the highway. He reached over and tugged at the pilot's jacket sleeve.

'This heap of shit go any faster?'

11

Seth focussed on the rear of the jeep, gusts of wind knocking both vehicles sideways in unison like they were connected by an invisible tow line as they sped down Highway 8. Nate sat on the gurney with his back against the side of the vehicle, knees up around his chest, reading a dog-eared paperback that he had found inside the med chest.

'Hey sleeping ugly, this escort thing has given me an idea.'

'Can you watch out for the damn potholes, man?'

'Gotta keep up with our boys up front. Listen, you want to know my idea or not?'

'Tell me when you've done it, and I'll give you a big-ass round of applause.'

'Hey, you got all the jokes today. Well put the book down for a second and listen up. Once our escort leaves us, we get to Abdaly and wait for the next military convoy. We sneak in line and stay with 'em till we're over the border, then dump the ambulance and get to the airport.'

'Aren't we gonna stick out like a sore thumb in this Seth? Suppose they think we're carrying a bomb and decide to take us out?'

'They won't. They'll see our faces, we have papers, we talk our way in.'

'But if they do?'

'Everything's a risk Nate. I think this is doable.'

Nate threw down the book and gave Seth a dig in the back, brought his face up close to Seth's ear.

'Well guess what 'bro? I have a better idea. How d'yer like that from your dumb-ass little brother?'

Seth twisted round and put a hand to Nate's smiling face,

pushing him backwards onto the gurney.

'OK Nate, so fucking surprise me.'

They had travelled seventy five miles, running ahead of the centre of the storm and sailing through three rolling checkpoints unhindered, courtesy of their armed escort. They had less than fifteen miles to go before hitting Nasiriyah.

'You got any ties Nate?'

'Yeah, a few, in my ruck.'

'Ok, dig 'em out, gonna need 'em soon.'

Seth put his hand on the horn and flashed his headlights at the jeep in front. The jeep's brake-lights came on immediately.

'You ready Nate?'

'I'm ready.'

Seth pulled up behind the jeep and got out. He ran head down to the driver's side, white med coat flapping, and peered through the glass as the driver wound down the window.

'Fuel line problem. All this sand. Take the weight off for a few minutes, guys, while I clear it, OK?'

Both soldiers were turned to Seth. The driver reached across himself and unfastened a pocket stud on his uniform.

'Need to radio in and …'

Nate appeared at the passenger side then and yanked open the door, rifle trained inside the jeep.

'Really sorry fellas but we need your ride.'

Nate stared into the shocked faces of two Iraqi soldiers.

'Jesus bro', these ain't no cherries.'

'Yeah? So maybe we should just rely on good all-American boys to get us home?'

A single vehicle passed them going in the opposite direction, a battered truck stacked high with broken furniture and scrap held in place with a tattered tarp, as Seth and Nate stripped the soldiers of their weapons and equipment and secured their hands behind their backs with plastic ties. Seth took off the white med coat and bundled it up.

'Here, drop this in the ambulance and get rid of your bandages.'

Nate led the soldiers to the back of the ambulance and steered them both inside. He gave them both a stare and then kicked both doors shut and joined Seth in the jeep.

'Nate, I have to try to reach Christo again. I need you to take the ambulance a little deeper into the desert, peel the stickers off of it, take off the blue light from the roof OK? Put your knife through a tyre, make it look like a blow-out. In these conditions, I'm hoping we'll be over the border and in the airport lounge before they're found.'

'On it.'

'And Nate, leave the soldiers alone, OK?'

Nate didn't answer.

'Nate, you heard me when I said that, right?'

'I heard you man.'

'And let's hustle; we're a sitting duck out here.'

Nate trotted back to the ambulance. He had been shocked when he discovered Iraqi soldiers were escorting them. He didn't like that one bit. He navigated the ditch and drove thirty or so metres into the desert, switched off, got out. He snatched the white letters off the doors and wrenched the blue light from the roof, went round the back of the ambulance and flung open the doors. The soldiers were sat at each end of the gurney. Nate reached inside his jacket and pulled out more ties, prodded the leg of the nearest one with the back of his hand.

'Legs together.'

The man closed his legs and Nate hitched a tie around his ankles.

'You, here now.'

The soldiers awkwardly swapped positions in the confines of the vehicle. Nate tied the second soldier's ankles. He slapped at the legs of the soldier when he'd done.

'Long you been serving?'

'Two years.'

Nate turned to the other.

'You?'

'It's my first year.'

'Why'd you join up, for the fucking boots?'

Neither answered.

'Maybe spying on our boys, passing intel back to your desert friends. Do any of that? I'm betting you did, I'm betting you make calls to your friends all the time. Y'see I don't like this one bit, but I promised my brother, y'know?'

Nate ducked and climbed in to the cramped space. All the while he'd been talking he was pulling out more plastic ties and looping them together. He pointed at the nearest soldier who was getting ever more agitated.

'Need for you to stand up now, friend.'

The soldier looked at the other, alarm in his eyes. He said something in Arabic as he scrambled up from the gurney.

'And be careful with the mouth; I speak the lingo pretty well.'

Nate placed a tie over the neck of the soldier stood in front of him, hitched it a little. The soldier started to shout and curse.

'Gonna ask you to be quiet now or I'll pull on this thing until your fucking eye balls pop out.'

The soldier on the floor spoke up.

'He's shouting that we are on the same side now, why do you do this to us?'

'No friend, we'll never be on the same side.'

Nate held the narrow bony shoulders of the soldier and lifted him like he was hollow. He manoeuvred the plastic loop over a hook bolted onto the inside of the vehicle. The soldier had to stretch and rise on his toes a little to stop the tie cutting into his neck. Nate kicked at the second soldier.

'You next.'

When he had done he pulled out his knife and waved it in front of the two soldiers, cutting a figure of eight in the air less than an inch from their faces. Then he stepped down from the rear of the van and reached back in, slashing at the soldiers' feet, slicing their boot laces in four quick, clean blows.

'Step out of the boots.'

They quickly followed the instruction.

'All you gotta do is stay on your feet until they find you and you're all good. Till then, embrace the suck.'

He tied the boots together, kicked the doors shut, pulled up the collar of his jacket against the scarifying blasts of sand and jogged back to the jeep.

Seth was closing the call to Christo as Nate climbed in the jeep.

'Good to go?'

Nate nodded. Seth stared at him for a few seconds, then down at the boots cradled in his brother's arms, but Nate just looked ahead.

'You planning on taking those along?'

Nate looked down, seemed surprised to see the boots there. He got out of the jeep, dropped them where he stood and got back in. Seth started up the jeep and took a long look behind, back along the road. Vision was down to fifteen metres now. He squinted, trying to gain better focus. A blur of movement caught his attention.

Two dim headlamps appeared at the side of the road, just at the edge of his range of sight, then the ghostly outline of a truck with a tarp whipping wildly from the roof rack.

Nate was reaching down into the foot well for a bottle of water one of the soldiers had left when Seth spoke up.

'You see that Nate?'

He pointed back down the road. Nate turned and looked back.

'I see it. Maybe just sheltering from the storm?'

'Maybe. I spotted a truck heading the other way earlier. Looked just like that one.'

Nate grabbed his binoculars for a closer look.

'Can't see dick with all this sand around.'

He looked more intently trying to make out any movement, any distinct shapes.

Abruptly he screamed, long and loud.

'Let's move, we got hostile.'

A strafe of automatic gun fire flashed across the desert and hit the side of the ambulance, then a heavy burst slammed into the back of the jeep as Seth floored the accelerator and fishtailed across the highway. Nate reached for one of the soldiers' rifles and climbed in back of the jeep. He rammed the stock of the gun against the rear window shattering the glass, great swirls of hot air and sand blasting inside the jeep as he did. The outline of the truck wavered in and out of vision like a mirage through an undulating curtain of sand. Nate glassed the vehicle again. It was on the move.

'Shooter on the roof. Jesus, looks like he's fixing an RPG. Take evasive Seth.'

Seth snaked across the highway as a huge explosion tore up the tarmac just feet away. Nate screamed a stream of obscenities as he was thrown across the back seat hitting his shoulder against the roof support. He scrambled up and leaned on the back seat to steady himself, switched to automatic, took aim.

'Steady Seth.'

'Take the fucking shot man.'

Nate squeezed the trigger and a river of bullets tore into the shooter knocking him backwards. The man was thrown around as the truck weaved left and right. He slid off the roof of the truck and hung there, his belt somehow lodged in the roof bars, his lifeless body crashing into the truck like a bronco.

Nate whooped, lowered his sights, sprayed the truck's windshield and engine block until his gun clicked empty. The inside of the truck's cabin lit up. It veered violently across the highway and turned end over end as it hit the ditch at the side of the road. Nate watched from the back seat as the truck exploded into a searing fireball illuminating the back of the jeep and Nate's snarling face as they sped away.

'What the…?'

Nate was still knelt on the back seat one hand grasping the bulkhead the other holding up the glasses trained on the truck when the thick curtain of sand and black smoke suddenly seemed to shift forward and part, like it was on a drawstring. Then the front fender of a Toyota truck appeared.

'We still got company. Two shooters.'

Nate quickly turned and reached forward into the passenger foot-well, grabbed a second rifle, repositioned himself by hooking his left arm through a canvas loop attached to the bulkhead.

Two men wearing goggles stood in the truck's open flatbed behind the driver, leaning over the roll cage. They already had their guns raised and targeted at the jeep, but Nate was first to the trigger, taking out one of them with one pull. The man fell sideways across the other shooter, disturbing his aim just as he loosed off his shots. They were near enough now for Seth and Nate to hear the sharp cracks of the automatic weapon, but the man's aim was high and wide.

Nate instantly refocused and unloaded at the second shooter as the man tried to steady himself. The bullets tore into him and he dropped out of sight below the backboard. Nate lowered his rifle, the driver now in his sights, but the driver swerved and slammed on the brakes. Nate followed the trajectory of the truck as it violently swung left and he emptied the magazine into the cab. The sand storm swallowed up the truck as it slid sideways and dropped heavily into the ditch.

'Fucking A.'

Nate stared down the road, eyes wide, ready for more trouble, more shooters, crouched that way for another five minutes, then climbed back into the passenger seat.

'Random bandits Seth?'

'That'd be my guess. And I don't think they just wanted batteries for their boom-boxes. They see a stationary army jeep, they get a hard-on.'

Nate reached across and curled his hand around his brother's neck as he rocked backwards and forwards in his own seat, still high from the action. Seth was focussed on the road ahead, wiper blades on high speed trying to clear the sand from the windshield but only managing to cut two wide arcs into the glass.

'Do not fuck with the Stone boys, not ever. That right man? That right Seth?'

'Yeah man, that's right. We beat those dice again.'

It had been less than a quarter of a mile when Seth began to slow, pulled over, and stopped the jeep.

'We have to go back.'

Nate looked baffled, alarmed.

'We do *what*?'

'We go back. Check out those soldiers.'

'Tell me you're joshing Seth.'

Seth looked up and down the road, engaged gear and u-turned. Nate grabbed hold of the wheel and pulled it violently to the side forcing Seth to stop.

'I vote no to that idea man.'

Seth turned on him, shouting spittle in his brother's angry face.

'Listen to me Nate, we have to go back there.'

'Nope we don't Seth. We don't owe anyone shit.'

'I'll walk if I have to, you want that?'

He grabbed the keys from the ignition and threw them across at Nate.

'Here, take off on your own but I'm going back.'

Nate picked up the keys and held them in front of his own face, staring at them.

'Don't tempt me man.'

Seth went to get out of the door but Nate pulled him back.

'OK, you made your fucking point.'

He handed the keys back to Seth and they set off back down the road, past the SUV and still burning truck, and pulled up close to the bullet ridden ambulance. Seth went to get out.

'No Seth, I'll go, you turn the jeep around and be ready to go.'

Nate jumped out of the jeep and ran to the ambulance as Seth fired up the satphone and made a note of their coordinates.

Nate went to the rear doors and flung them open. One of the soldiers hung lifeless from the hook, his face purple and swollen from the pressure of the tie biting into his neck, the left side of his body shredded by bullet impacts. The other soldier stood shaking and bloody. Nate climbed in and lifted the man off the hook and laid him on the gurney. He pulled out his knife and cut all of the ties then tore open the med chest and reached in, grabbing bandages and surgical spirit. He quickly wiped away the blood. A bullet had torn clean through the man's thigh. Nate balled a piece of gauze up and tied it in place with a strip of bandage, covered the man with a med blanket.

'Just lie still soldier.'

He turned and lifted the dead soldier off the hook and lowered him to the floor of the ambulance, cut the ties away. He took a second blanket and laid it over the dead body. He dropped down onto the sand and closed one of the doors. The soldier stared across at Nate, went to speak, body still shaking like a drunk. Nate reached, gripped his bloodied arm.

'There's help coming man.'

Nate slammed the door shut and sprinted to the waiting jeep.

'One dead, one safe, for a couple hours.'

'OK Nate, good job. I called Christo, gave him the map ref. Said he'll make a call, get someone to bring the soldiers in.'

'Yeah man, just what I would've done.'

The two brothers stared ahead without speaking again as Seth pushed the jeep to the limits of his vision and beyond in the blinding storm.

12

Byrd looked out the side window as the heli dropped from the thick yellow sky, unaware that bandits had come close to closing down his mission for him.

They lowered onto a concrete apron within the heavily secured confines of Camp Eastern Angel, a US military base close to the Kuwaiti border. He reached behind him, grabbed a small leather bag, dropped his lap full of kit inside. A Mercedes sedan with blacked-out windows was idling nearby waiting for him. He saluted the pilot, dropped from the craft and ran to the car. The driver was leaning against the open rear door and Byrd handed him a letter-headed note. He dropped his leather bag onto the seat as the driver read. Before climbing in back he barked at him, 'I want to be through the border in ten minutes tops, no shit. You got a problem with any of that, you tell me after you've got us there.'

The brothers were close to the border town of Safwan, just north of their target. Nate was using a rag he'd found to wipe up a handful of dried blood spots on his hands and face from flying glass.

'I got Intel from the call to Christo. Movement of military across the border. If we time it right we can join a convoy at Abdaly. It's due at the border at thirteen hundred. That's a couple hours from now. If we're stopped we say we're on leave, going home for some R and R.'

'And when they see the jeep shot to shit?'

'We say we got hit by bandits, managed to outrun 'em.'

Nate nodded and smiled, grabbed at Seth's neck.

'My idea Seth. Don't forget this was my idea man.'

'Yeah, so I'll drink to you in the airport lounge. We get across the border, head straight to the airport, jump on the next flight home.'

'Sounds beautiful man.'

Byrd held the cell phone in the crook of his neck, speaking to his office as he studied the tracking device on his lap. The brothers were an hour away, maybe less.

The driver was still talking to two Kuwaiti soldiers and waving the note at them both. He could see the CIA eagle emblem on it from where he sat. He closed the call and hung his head out the open window.

'Guys, I got low battery on my cell but still just enough to make one call to the number on that paper you're holding, so let's hustle, OK?'

Seth checked his watch. They were in Abdaly, parked up off the main highway on a side street. According to Christo the convoy was shipping large quantities of obsolete electrical equipment and other supplies back to the U.S. That meant lots of trucks, light armed protection. The convoy was travelling from Tallil. Seth checked his watch once more. U.S. Army worked to fine margins. They'd be here. He fired up the jeep and crept forward to the edge of the street, turned the corner onto the highway and pulled in, engine idling. He watched for traffic in his mirror, turned and checked with his glasses.

A Humvee appeared, twenty metres or so ahead of the convoy. One more led the line of trucks. Seth quickly scanned down the emerging line of vehicles. He counted five trucks, travelling in tight formation. A Humvee followed up the rear.

Seth slammed the jeep into gear and pulled out behind the leading Humvee. He wound his window down creating a howling draught of hot sand through from the shattered back window. He waved theatrically at the drivers in front and behind, making sure he and Nate were clearly seen. The driver behind flashed his lights.

The convoy sped on through the checkpoint and into Kuwait City.

'Map says we need to peel off and head east as soon as, Seth. The airport is about forty kilometres from here.'

Seth pulled left off the main highway and slowed to watch the convoy as it drove on ahead.

'Like clockwork, bro'.'

They touched fists and whooped.

'OK, man, we're in the end zone.'

13

Byrd sat in a huge white overstuffed leather chair sipping a long glass of ice tea. He slowly swivelled, looking around the airport lounge, absently playing his favourite game of *friend or foe* as he spoke to the border crossing patrol. He reached the usual ten-ninety mix.

He closed the call, emptied the glass and headed upstairs to the private offices overlooking the check-in desks.

Seth drove up the concrete ramp of the car park at Kuwait international and parked up in a quiet corner.

'Just the papers Nate, papers, wallet and your dog tags. I'll carry the satphone for now. Everything else we leave in the jeep.'

He slung a holdall at Nate; it held the civvy clothes Christo had acquired for them. Both men slapped away the last of the sand which clung to their hair and faces and began changing.

Nate grabbed at Seth's sleeve and howled as he changed. 'Jeez man, where did Christo buy your douche-wear? All that black. You look like a porn star, man.'

'Yeah? Well guess what, Nate: I'm looking straight at a gay school-teacher, so eat me.'

The brothers stuffed their combats into the two holdalls and rammed them under the seats. The rifles were stashed under a tarp in the back of the jeep. Seth spread the documents on the driver's seat and went through them.

'OK, we're good to go.'

The temperature dropped from forty centigrade outside to a cool twenty two as they walked through the terminal building and into the main concourse. Seth scanned the huge ceiling-mounted displays. He was looking for the earliest flight out of Kuwait with the quickest connections to Bangor, Maine.

'Looking like we fly United.'

They headed for the information desk. The brunette behind the counter confirmed it. United Air to Dulles, nineteen twenty hours. Enough time to wash up and grab a burger. From there they would fly to La Guardia and then on to Bangor, around thirty hours of flying time. They walked across to bookings with Seth all the time discretely scanning their fellow passengers.

'OK baby bear, let's go home.'

Byrd watched the two men as they stood at the United Air check-in desk He was in a small private office overlooking the airport concourse. They were big. Mighty big. Solid. It would be like felling oaks taking those two down. He thought of the line in Jaws, about needing a bigger boat.

A young man sitting at his side read from a computer terminal, then turned to Byrd.

'Sir, their final destination is Bangor, Maine, via Washington and La Guardia.'

Byrd answered without taking his eyes from the brothers.

'OK son, get me on those flights.'

Seth looked across at Nate who was sparked out with his head leant against the aircraft porthole. He had almost done it, got his brother home like he said he would. They were on the final leg of their flights heading for Maine. The transfers at Washington and New York had been uneventful, tedious, just what Seth had hoped for.

Nate twitched, murmured quietly, flexed absently, trying to get comfortable in his sleep.

Seth stood, eased off his jacket and stashed it in the overhead locker. As he stretched up, some of his shirt buttons opened up, revealing his dog tags. They were heavier than usual, a small key spot-welded to the back of each of them. The tags also contained an extra string of numbers engraved on them, hidden amongst his NI number and blood group details. He quickly fastened his shirt and tucked in the tags to conceal them again, a habit he had hardwired since he'd had them done. The key and numbers opened a Chase security box in Vegas. The box contained a cell phone. The cell was his personal insurance. It held a recording: eighty six seconds of chatter from a dying man.

He sat back down and considered the faces of his fellow passengers he'd mentally logged whilst stood up. He'd done the same on all three flights. There were mainly businessmen on this flight, a few families, a group of rowdy teenagers wearing matching sports kits. Further along the aisle a man, sports jacket and flannels, face concealed behind a newspaper. He wore a watch that looked familiar, a Tag Heuer Monaco -limited edition. Seth had worn one once but had lost it in a twelve hour card game in Helmand. Odd. He'd spotted a passenger wearing the same model Tag on the Washington to New York flight. That passenger had been a thirty-something male, tall, lean, in good shape with a fresh tan, dressed in sweats. Maybe he'd changed the duds at the airport for an appointment in Maine, just coincidence that he'd picked the same flight as he and Nate. Only Seth didn't believe in coincidences. He would keep an eye on Tag-man.

He checked his own watch: less than an hour flight time to landing. He reached inside his shirt and twisted the tags slowly on their chain. He lowered his head against the seat, still fingering the tags and thought back to dangerous days.

Seth had led three other special-forces soldiers on a black op codenamed *Cleankill*. Its mission was to take out a regional warlord and his retinue of protectors who had been responsible for several bombing atrocities in Kandahar. The mission had begun with a hellfire missile strike that took out most of the outer walls of the target building, leaving a dozen broken bodies and a heap of smoking rubble and timber. Seth's orders were to go in afterwards, two-man protocol, make sure there were no survivors. He and one other of his team took footage with head-cams as they moved from room to ruined room. The footage included spontaneous commentary as he and one other soldier covered the ground floor and the other two swept what remained of the second. Seth had come across one of the wounded targets sat leaning against a partially collapsed internal wall. The man was hyperventilating from his leaking lungs as Seth leant down towards him, gun aimed at his temple. The man had raised his hands in front of his face then and screamed out a name over and over in stilted English. The name stopped Seth in his tracks. He had reached up and switched off his head-cam, then dug out his own private cell phone, balancing it on a nearby piece of masonry and begun to record.

He had taken out his water bottle and gently dripped water onto the man's cracked lips, coaxed him to continue his story as Seth filmed the explosive footage. The name the man had repeated was of a U.S. three-star General; the man told of weapons-for-drugs deals, other unknown names, places. The man spoke of a *godaam*, Pashtun for *storeroom*, in a place called Dand just off the main Kandahar-Herat highway, where the exchanges took place. Seth didn't know the named General personally, but he knew of him. The dying man's words had become slurred, incomprehensible. Seth had pocketed his cell and switched the head-cam back on.

Then a second US missile hit.

Seth was the only survivor of the operation.

It changed the game.

He finally nodded off, briefly, sleeping fitfully like his brother until touchdown, unaware that Tag-man had been waiting for this moment.

Byrd walked the length of the aisle and back, looking the brothers full in the face as he passed. Then he went back to his seat, quietly pulled out his cell and placed a call to DC while the brothers slept.

14

Maine's Bangor Airport, was quiet save for the hailstones beating against the windows of the concourse and exit corridors leading onto the car park.

Seth and Nate, large and heavily tanned, stood out amongst their fellow travellers.

'I need to pay a visit to the boys room Nate. Here's my card. Go to the cash dispenser over there and max it out. Yours too. We need as much cash as we can get. I don't want anyone tracing our cards once we're away from the airport. I don't want to use them again until we've built new identities.'

He grabbed at Nate's sleeve.

'And you'd better start thinking of a new name bro', something in keeping with your new threads. Cecil maybe.'

He laughed at his own joke.

'And get us a map of Maine. Places could've changed a lot since we were here last.'

Seth still wasn't out when Nate returned. He reappeared a few minutes later.

'Hell you been doing in there man?'

'Later,' Seth said without looking up.

They walked out of the airport and into a bitter cold Maine evening, Seth setting a quick and steady pace.

They kept their heads down as they passed the last of the CCTV cameras fixed over the exit doors and headed for the car park.

They needed a ride away from the airport and out of the City, to where Seth had planned their next rendezvous.

The cold wind was merciless as it hit them at the exit, but the brothers welcomed its relief from the endless stifling heat they had endured in Iraq. They headed for the car park's higher floors scanning for cameras. They were hard to avoid.

Seth began casually trying a few door handles as he passed the line of cars until he finally found one that was unlocked and he quietly let himself in. Nate got in beside him and immediately searched around for the car park exit ticket. He found it under the passenger sunshield and held it out wordlessly to Seth who seemed preoccupied.

'Nate, we got us a problem. We're being followed. That customs guy with the bad rug? He must've planted a bug in the satphone when we were going through security so we can be tracked when it's switched off. I found it when I visited the john. It was interfering with the signal when I made a call. Those things are tiny but I found it attached inside the casing of the phone.'

'Oh man, you're a regular Jason Bourne.'

'It confirmed a few concerns. Didn't any of this strike you as a little suspicious? We navigate through four airports without a single snag?'

'Suspicious? That we got lucky? I thought maybe we were due some luck, y'know? Plus I trust your plans.'

'Yeah, well, you make your own good luck, and I'm wondering who's making ours for us right now. Who the hell is running interference for us Nate? Who is tracking our moves?'

'I don't know man, but the sooner we get away from here the better. What did you do with the bug?'

'A suit heading for Florida is now on some evil fucker's radar. Evil with a nice watch I'm guessing.'

Seth described the man with the Tag.

'That should buy us time to disappear. I dumped the satphone too after I called ahead to Manny.'

'Manny? The hell you call that piece of shit for?'

'Because we need equipment and he's the local boy. We don't have to like him Nate, but we need him. And I trust him. I've already sent him inventory and wired his account. I've arranged for us to meet him on route to Fear.'

'Could've called Anton instead of that asshole.'

'Anthon is way out in Philly. We need local.'

Nate looked out of the car window onto the street below. Union Street was almost deserted save for a few travellers queuing for taxis.

'The hell are you sulking for Natey boy, we're home aren't we? Come on, lighten up man.'

'He's a Judas, Seth. That Manny? He's a goddamned Judas. You don't wanna trust him, that's all I'm saying.'

He didn't elaborate but he looked troubled. Seth reached under the dash and tore away the ignition wires. He nodded to Nate and stared past him out at the night sky.

'Seems like we swapped a sandstorm for snow. We need to motor before this shit starts to stick.'

He twisted bare wires together.

'Well, we're home and dry Nate. Didn't I say it? Didn't I tell you I'd get us home safely?'

Nate's mood brightened.

'That you did and I'm grateful man, truly. I would still be lying on that prison floor in Ram if it wasn't for you.'

Seth dismissed his words, carried on with the wires until he connected the last pair and fired up the Accord. He wound the window down and drove past the last of the security cameras, heading for the neon exit sign. He began humming to himself. The hum became a song as Seth dug his brother in the ribs and sang out loud into Nate's face. They drove away from the airport into the stormy Maine night singing loudly in unison, Nate drumming time on his knees.

March along, sing our song, with the Army of the free,
Count the brave, count the true, who have fought to victory

MICHAEL WILLETTS

We're the Army and proud of our name!
We're the Army and proudly proclaim…
They were home now and they sang their hearts out together.

'Monkeys are on the run Mark; the brothers went off plan, pulled a switcheroo on me in the airport. I had a bug put on 'em but they must've found it. I've been chasing down a car-parts salesman heading for Florida. I should've suspected it before now; Miami doesn't fit their profile.'

Byrd was sat in a rented Toyota Avalon parked up in a bay at Bangor airport, talking to Slater. The heater was dialled to maximum, distorting his words. Byrd had delayed the Miami flight and had the unhappy salesman dragged from his seat. He had left it to local officials to apologise once he realised the screw-up. But he had temporarily lost his targets. He had raced back to airport security and ploughed through a mile of CCTV footage looking for the brothers. The last image captured of them was of a smiling Seth, head hung out the stolen car's window, flipping his middle finger at the camera.

'No Mark, I haven't lost them, I just need to recalibrate my plan. I'll have them back on radar within twenty four hours. They know someone is after them now though and that makes them more dangerous. I may need resources.'

Byrd held his cell away from his ear until the voice at the other end calmed down.

'I know all of that Mark, I'm on it right now. I'll call in within twenty four hours– OK twelve hours with an update. Yes sir… yes sir I do… I will sir, goodbye.'

Byrd was pissed from his balling out by Slater. That Poindexter wouldn't last a day in the field but the little shit had the power to trash Byrd's career with one phone call.

He had to get those maniacal brothers found and dealt with.

LAKE FEAR

And quickly.

So they knew someone was tracking them but they didn't know who or why, which still give him an edge. But he would have to be careful.

Byrd stared out the car window and spotted a Papa John's across the street. He u-turned, parked up and collected the file from the passenger seat. The café was almost empty save for a teenage couple sat at the counter whispering together. He ordered an espresso, found a corner booth and opened up the file on the table. He hated the shit these places served but he needed the hit.

He had read the file twice already in the past twelve hours: army records, family stuff, other titbits. But he sensed the answer to where they would be headed lay in their earlier life. It nearly always did. It wasn't random that they were in Maine. People had a habit of going back when they were under threat, when they needed a place of safety. He'd read somewhere the homing instinct was learned in the womb. That's what *he* would do too. Hunker down on his own Colorado cattle ranch with Aspen peaks on the horizon, a hundred thousand square miles of plains and mountains where he could see anyone coming for him a hundred miles away. That was *his* place, where *he* felt he was home. Now he just needed to find the brothers' favourite place. That's where he would find them. He was sure of it.

He re-read the newspaper clippings and accompanying photographs in the Washington Post and the Army Times of the brothers receiving their silver stars. Brave sons of bitches. He was beginning to like them.

A small discoloured clipping partly peeled away from the back of the main papers as he thumbed the pages. Byrd hadn't spotted it before, held between the sheets. Some of the ink had stuck to the sheet above, and it tore as he pulled it loose.

It was both brothers stood next to one another in Cougar uniform, stood slightly apart from the main group, ignoring the camera. He recognised them straight away. He wasn't even sure why something like this would be in the file – clearly someone else had been looking into their past.

Jeez, what were they? Fourteen, fifteen? Byrd thought they looked big mean bastards even then. He looked closer at the storyline under the photo, a story about the group achieving some kind of Cougar award. Seth was facing forward but Nate was side on, showing the Cougar emblem on his shirt sleeve. Neither of them was smiling. There was some lettering beneath the outline of the big cat but Byrd couldn't make it out. He needed an eyeglass.

He called out to the waitress as he drained the last of his cold coffee and put a five on the counter.

'Is there a public library in town Ma'am?'

'Sure is. Small one, just two blocks down on the right, at the junction of Northern Maine and Odin.'

Byrd thought he was on to something. He pulled up the collar of his jacket and walked the couple of blocks to the library.

The building was pure seventies architecture, featureless, dark, dismal. A faint whiff of body odour greeted him as he pushed his way through the heavy double doors. He figured this was where the homeless gathered for a bit of warmth. He approached the old girl behind the counter. His looks and attitude got him immediate attention despite his damp, dishevelled appearance from the walk.

'Do you have an eyeglass I could borrow Ma'am? I'm trying to make out some tiny detail on a newspaper article I have here.'

'We can do better than that young man, we have a mag-reader. Here, let me show you.'

She took him to a small table with a squat little device that was covered in dust and fingerprint smears. She plugged it in and switched it on, smiling vacantly all the time, and then returned to her station. Byrd lifted the top and placed the clipping on the bed of the device and moved the handle around until the image of the Cougar was centred. He increased the magnification. *Cougar Troop – Rumford division* was just visible now. He spoke to himself quietly.

'I've got you now. You're on your way there right now aren't you boys? I'd put my pension on it.'

He removed the paper and tucked it inside his jacket.

'Ma'am, you have been a great help. Could I impose on your patience a little more? Do you have a current map of Oxford County that I might get a copy of, and could you recommend a hotel close by?'

He had decided to lay over for the night, get some sleep, clear his mind, and start the hunt afresh in the morning.

Seth and Nate had been travelling a couple of hours and were hungry. They had decided to stop to eat and refuel.

They also needed a couple of new cell phones and some provisions. They were sat outside the 7-Eleven store now just outside Brunswick, studying the list under the dull glow of the car's interior light.

'This is one brutal shopping expedition little brother. Now do as daddy bear says and behave while I'm gone OK? And keep your dirty feet off those seats.'

Nate gave him the finger.

Nate was humming a Twitty song when the tailgate opened forty minutes later.

'Little help here?'

Nate climbed out and helped Seth load up the cans and boxes of food and drink and other supplies.

'No more near-beer for us Natey boy. From now on we're

suppin' the real thing.'

Nate looked across at Seth and smiled.

'Been thinking Seth, we good for a brief detour? I'd like to visit Momma's grave, lay some flowers. It's been a while since we've been. Thinking then maybe hire a bit of female company before we hibernate?'

'Not the grave Nate, not yet anyway. They could be watching it.'

Nate stared across the dirty windswept car park and nodded, face blank. Seth reached across and grabbed at Nate's arm.

'Hey, man, I didn't say we could *never* visit, just let's settle in a little, see if anyone is tracking us, OK?'

'Yeah man.'

'Now the dancing girls are a different proposition. Dare say I could put that in the schedule, but only if I get first dibs on the best looking pie.'

Nate turned and grabbed at his brother, got him in a headlock and knuckled his shaved head.

'Good enough man, but you're gonna disappoint a lot of girls when they see me versus your uglies.'

Nate released Seth, dodged his swinging arm, jumped into the passenger seat.

Seth got in beside him and reached for the map, studying it for a few minutes in the half light.

'Was thinking of heading to Lewiston for a layover, give Manny time to assemble the stuff. We could maybe find that company for the evening. What say you?'

'Amen to that Seth.'

'Just be a minute Nate, I'm gonna call Manny again, tell him we'll be hitting Buckfield around noon tomorrow.'

Nate curled his lip and spat out a stream of phlegm from the open window.

'Tell him hi from me.'

15

Byrd felt hung-over. He had booked a room at the Marriott and had taken a half bottle of Ballantine to his room after dinner and emptied it as he read the brothers' files one more time. He was developing an unexpected affinity with them.

He had phoned in as instructed but Slater had been in a meeting. He left a brief message saying that he'd called and that he would call again in twelve. His cell had two messages from his office: one with a weather warning for the region, the other confirming details of an appointment his secretary had made for him at his request later that day to see the good folks of Rumford Cougar Troop. He made some notes and then switched off his cell. Wasn't his fault that Slater was in one of his endless backslapping meetings with some of his chinless drones. He'd promised to ring in and that's what he'd done.

He had read the files enough times now to be able to put together the fragments of their history. The records presented a Shakespearean tragedy if you cared to piece it together. Absentee father, druggy mother, school-board expulsions for them both for violence and long term absences. Their mother had passed away when the brothers were young teenagers and they had been placed with children's services.

The boys had enlisted in the army together just as soon as the younger brother had been old enough. Head-hunted by Special Forces. Two years' Service in Afghanistan, then four in Iraq. Both had several bravery citations but Nate had been busted out for *patterns of misconduct*. Lot of baggage. Seth had walked away with him, straight into the waiting arms and big bucks of Stygian Private Security.

The record of abodes for the brothers was patchy, a lot of gaps in the timeline. Moving from their home City of Portland when they were around ten, the trail going cold after their last known address, a rental on Avalon Street in Stoneham. He figured that they'd had some dirty little secrets that they'd been running away from. He also figured they must have moved to Rumford at some point, and stayed long enough for the boys to join the Cougars. Byrd closed the file and rubbed his neck, reflecting on what he'd read and what he knew from his own sources about his targets. There were strong parallels with his own life.

Fact was, he felt for the brothers. They had been bad and they would pay, but he truly felt for them. They had put themselves on the line like no one else he knew. Except perhaps himself.

He had over ten years of combat service, the last five with Delta Force. He'd drawn his first blood on Operation Gothic Serpent in Somalia and risen to captain. He'd sweated blood on the front line until one day he'd got taken to lunch by a couple of suits and within twenty four hours he had his own office and small staff in DC. Timing was good for him, or so he'd felt at the time. Back in theatre he'd had command of a hundred hard-as-nails men who clawed metre by metre, mile by mile, in forty-degree desert temperatures, to capture territory from the enemy – and for what? The treasure wasn't worth the blood anymore, if it ever had been. He understood the strategy well enough: win the hearts and minds of the citizens, suffocate and terminate the enemy, disrupt supply lines, build native leadership and policing and security capacity amongst the indigenous population. But he knew deep down that they were rowing against a vast and powerful tide, just 'mowing the grass` as his CIA colleagues would say. Centuries of tribalism, vested interest and corruption were deeply hard-wired. He didn't see any high ground anymore, just deep-dark sinks in a boiling sea. The politicos, war lords, weapons manufacturers, private armies, religious blocs – he couldn't separate them out anymore. And where was he in this? Right there in the middle of it all, pulling long strokes across the roiling surface, trying to stay on top, pulling ever faster to save himself from getting caught in a whirlpool and being dragged under in a moment. What the hell had he become? Was he any different to Seth or Nate? Other than having his instructions come from an asshole in a suit? Oh yeah, the brothers were terminally dangerous and he had his orders, but Jeez they had taken it up the ass, firstly for country and then for money, and boy did he wish he could buy them a bottle of Bud and sit right down with them, talk over old soldiers, maybe share a joint or two, then smile and tear up their records, drop them in the trash, stand and give them both the world's strongest handshake and see them on their way.

Then he could walk away, let someone else handle it. Only he couldn't. You only walk away when the suits want you to. He realised that much now. *They* played the tune and the Byrd's of this world danced until they dropped, until they couldn't pull hard enough across the surface and the water seeped in, until the dirty poisonous water closed over their heads and they sunk without trace leaving nothing but a stream of tiny bubbles that quickly burst, then nothing. But he had been trained to *live in the now.* That was what one of his commanding officers had taught him and *now* meant following his mission, tracking down the brothers and quietly terminating them. No matter the morals of the argument, it wasn't *his* argument. That way lay chaos when the Byrd's of this world became judge and executioner. You can only be one and he sure as hell wasn't the judge.

He refocused, pulling out the map of Oxford county and drawing a random ring around Rumford. It embraced several small towns but mostly forest and fresh water lakes. They were in that circle somewhere, he knew they were, and he'd sniff them out because that's what he did, that's what he was best at.

He collected his stuff and checked out. Three hours to make the journey to the Cougar offices in Rumford, a hundred and seventy kilometres of slick highway. He wiped away the layer of snow that had accumulated on his car overnight, climbed in and cranked up the radio. He switched it to channel WKIT for some heavy rock and began singing a tuneless accompaniment to Motorhead.

16

It was just before noon when they arrived at a remote car park off Highway 95 in the Oxford County Town of Buckfield. Both brothers felt brittle from the previous evening's events. They'd sunk a lot of beer and hired two lap-dancers, finally rolling into bed at four am in a Super 8 just off the Maine Turnpike.

The car park was mainly used by truckers and for pit stops in summer. It was deserted now save for Manny, who was waiting for them, sat behind the wheel of a Chevy Tahoe with a flatbed trailer hooked up to the back. He jumped down as Seth approached the back of the vehicle and held out his gloved hand.

'Hey Seth, welcome back friend, you and Nate tire of Iraqi hospitality?'

'Just home for a nice long fishing trip Manny.'

'You plan to blow those mothers out of the water, man?'

Manny laughed out loud at his own joke as he dropped the tailgate of the flatbed and threw off the tarp revealing several large crates, a snowmobile, and a motorcycle. He jemmied the lids off the crates and pulled out a clipboard. Nate came round the back of the truck and silently looked over the kit. Manny gave him a single blank nod and turned back to Seth.

'Let's go through the inventory Seth. I want to get back to Dexter before we get snowed in man.' He tapped each item with his pen as he spoke.

'OK, we got one Arctic Cat snomo with a couple extra gas tanks, two Browning hunting rifles with sights, one colt peacemaker and ten boxes of ammo, three M84 flash-bang grenades, one Excalibur hunting crossbow with fifty bolts, one Bowtech Guardian hunting bow with fifty carbon arrows, two Buck hunting knives, couple Fenix flashlights, two RP vests, med kit, pair of voyager night-vision glasses, cell and GPS jammer, pound of plastic, dets and timers – that stuff is in the silver case just here.'

He looked up at Seth as he mentioned that last item and pointed to a small aluminium briefcase. Seth didn't respond.

'Two walkie-talkies with base, one Tosh laptop and dongle, good for ninety days web surfing, four high-intensity floods with motion sensors, two sentry wi-fi cameras and, two sets of cold-weather clothes and boots size four X.'

He pointed his gloved hand at the motorcycle.

'The Honda's mine. Oh and the fishing tackle is in the case on the back seat. The Tahoe is all gassed up and ready to rock.'

'Appreciate it Manny. The money is already in your account.'

'Yep, got it, counted it, spent it. Plan to order myself a new explorer, plus my current girlfriend just loves to surf for new handbags and shoes. Well, it's been a pleasure to do business with you man…oh…almost forgot.'

He reached inside a pocket and pulled out a baggy, handed it to Seth.

'Mary Jane. Good grade, smoke it myself.'

'Thanks. Listen Manny, I don't need to tell you that all of this is strictly private OK?'

'Same as always Seth, same as always.'

Nate hadn't said a word as the two other men transacted their business. Finally he spoke up.

'How's your sister Manny, she out yet?'

Manny's pleasant demeanour soured.

'Fuck you man. There was no need to treat her down and trampy the way you did. She's better off in Bolduc than with you.'

Manny pushed past Nate, pulled out a plank from the back of the flat bed and dropped it to the ground, resting one end on the tail gate. He carefully steered the Honda down and climbed on.

'Enjoy your fishing trip Seth.'

'Intend to Manny.'

Manny fired up the motorcycle and roared off.

Seth turned to his brother who still had his middle finger raised at Manny's back.

'What's it with you and Manny, Nate?'

'It's history Seth, just ancient history.'

Seth secured the flatbed and covered the back with the tarp while Nate transferred the boxes from the stolen car and then drove it to a far corner of the car park behind a row of bushes, out of sight.

'Well Nate, as our favourite Buck Jam might say, *get the wheels goin' sqeelin', 'cos the natives won't be reelin', forever.*'

They tore out of the car park, all lights blazing, raking holes in the darkening sky. They were on the final leg of their journey. They were heading for Lake Fear.

17

It was still snowing in patches from a filthy leaden sky when Byrd pulled up at the small single-storey building and parked up. This was a long shot, he knew, but he guessed that Cougar folk tended to be in it for the long haul and that maybe they had records, or better still someone there who remembered the boys. The snow lay down an inch thick now and the path was slick as an ice hockey rink. He carefully picked his way to the door and let himself in. It was straight from All American Boy: pictures of kids swinging on ropes, paddling kayaks, playing ball games, they covered every inch of the walls.

The single reception desk was cluttered with papers and posters and a stack of key fobs. It was unoccupied but he could smell a coffee pot somewhere close. He walked around the desk and knocked on the nearest door, opening it as he did.

'Hello, I have an appointment?'

The place seemed deserted. Byrd walked further into the room and looked around. Half a dozen desks were positioned around the room, papers strewn on most, all were unoccupied. He heard hammering then and he walked back out of the building to track down the source of the noise. A tall slim man stood at one of the rear windows fixing battens to the frame.

'Mr Hamis? My secretary fixed an appointment?'

'Ah yes, Mr Byrd, Walter Hamis, sorry about the reception, sent everyone home early. I'm securing the place; we're in for some real bad weather from all accounts.'

Hamis was taller even than Byrd which put him at Six four or five, but thin with it. He looked about early sixties so Byrd figured old enough to know the brothers. He showed Hamis his badge.

'Yes, we were awful anxious when we got the call from

your secretary Mr Byrd, we don't take calls from the National Government every day.'

'Nothing for you to worry about Sir, I just need a little confidential information if you have it.'

Hamis directed Byrd back indoors and through into a tiny office. One complete wall was taken up with a map of the Rumford area and surrounding forest and lakes. Byrd stood taking the map in and mentally comparing it with his own map of the area. He took a notepad out and scribbled a few lines. Hamis stood behind Byrd now, following Byrd's interest, pointing at the map with his chin.

'That's our backyard so to speak. It covers around a hundred square miles.'

'What're the little red squares Mr Hamis?'

'Walt, please. They're our little outposts. Just tiny one-room cabins really, for short lay-overs or protection from the elements – it can get mighty fierce around here in winter. Our Cougars use them mainly when they're on assignments, just a couple of bunks, a stove, toilet. Some have running water.'

'And these?'

There were a few larger boxes scattered throughout the map.

'Private cabins, mainly vacationers. We put them on the map for emergencies. We have arrangements with some of the owners to use them if we're in dead trouble so to speak. Most are probably secured for the winter now.'

Something clicked with Byrd. The Cougar cabins seemed a little too small to accommodate two big men for any length of time, but the larger ones – they held promise.

'Mr Hamis, Walt, how long have you been here at Rumford?'

'Oh let me see, since two thousand and two, so just over eight years now. Why'd you ask?'

Byrd felt disappointed but hoped it didn't show.

'I have to confide in you Walter, I'm chasing two brothers, two felony suspects, who I believe may have been members of the Rumford Cougar Troop around the early nineties. I was hoping you might help me with some background information that I could use in tracking their whereabouts. I have a photograph of them in a newspaper article here.'

He pulled out the piece of paper and showed it to Hamis who made a show of studying it intently but shook his head.

'Nope, can't say as I remember seeing 'em, but they were quite a while before my time.'

'Do you have any records going that far back?'

'I could take a look but I doubt it. We introduced a computer a while back but we didn't bother loading all the historical stuff.'

Hamis switched on his desktop and searched the system for any details of the brothers.

'Sorry Mr Byrd, nothing here. Latest records go back to 2001.'

'Did you keep any of the paper records dating before that?'

Hamis looked awkward.

'Think Dorothy shredded them. We couldn't afford the space you see.'

'Who's Dorothy?'

'She was my secretary up until a couple of years ago. She retired on account of her Alzheimer's.'

'Would you know if she was here about the time of the boys?'

'Pretty sure she would have been. She was always telling me about the old days.'

Byrd pressed at his temples and persisted with the conversation, hoping his next question wouldn't run into a wall.

'She still live local?'

'She's in a nursing home in East Andover, about sixteen miles west of here.'

'Do you have any contact details?'

Hamis reached inside his jacket and took out a small pocketbook. He shook his head as he flipped through the pages, then nodded and jotted down the address and number on a slip of paper and handed it to Byrd.

'Yep I do, but I don't think it will do you any good. Most times when I visit she can't remember me. Why, she can barely remember her own name.'

Byrd hadn't called ahead, just flashed his badge when the receptionist pointed to the visiting hours timetable on the wall. He was escorted now down a long brightly lit corridor by a pleasantly smiling nurse, towards Dorothy's room.

'Are you family Mr Byrd?'

'A friend.'

'Oh. You know she might not remember you? Although somedays, well, she can recall the details of a cleaning bill from a spilt drink at a dance in the fifties.'

Byrd decided not to use the badge in case it scared the old girl off. He tried a different approach.

'Hello Dorothy. Remember me?'

She was sat in a winged armchair, hands in her lap, staring out the window. She came alert at the sound of his voice. Byrd lowered himself onto the end of her bed facing her. He smiled broadly.

'It's Ben, Dorothy, from your Cougar Troop.'

She turned and faced Byrd, leaned forward and got a hold of his face, held it in her trembling hands.

'Of course I remember you, I remember all of my boys.'

Byrd wasn't sure if this was a good sign or not.

'How are you today?'

She let go and sunk back into her seat, went back to staring out the window.

'Cold. They make me keep the window open.'

LAKE FEAR

The room was stifling hot, a feint smell of lavender permeating the room along with something else, medicine maybe.

'Want me to close it for you?'

'They'll only open it again.'

'Want me to talk to them, tell them to keep it closed?'

'I'm not sure they'll listen, dear, but you can try if you want to.'

'I have a picture from the old days Dorothy, want to take a look?'

She seemed to come alive at that.

'Am I in it? My hair was red when I was younger you know.'

'No, not this one, just two more of your boys.'

'Which boys?'

'Well that's the thing. I can't remember their names and I'd like to say hello while I'm in town.'

'Do they live here, the boys?'

'Could be.'

This was likely to be a real test of Byrd's patience, but he liked her. He felt an asshole playing her like this, but what else did he have?

Dorothy went quiet again, started to rub her hands together; it was like the sound of paper being folded.

'So cold.'

'Let me get that window for you.'

Byrd stood and she reached for him as he brushed past her in the tiny room, felt the material of his jacket.

'I like your suit, I like the worsteds best. But you should only buy the high twist.'

Byrd took care not to harm her out-stretched hand as he reached up and tugged at the small window. It seemed to be jammed.

'Have you brought the boys to see me?'

'No Dorothy, like I said –'

'Oh.'

She seemed disappointed. She looked across at the bedside table.

'Nearly tea time, you'll have to go soon.'

Byrd gave a final pull and the window slid into place.

'There we are Dorothy. I'll tell them to leave it that way.'

'You'll have to leave now, they'll wonder where I am.'

'Would you take a look at the picture, see if you know my friends?'

'If you leave it on my bedside table, I'll have a look after tea dear.'

She stood awkwardly and reached for the door handle, then turned and looked at Byrd.

'I remember you, you were a good boy back then.'

She opened the door and shuffled out of the room leaving Byrd alone and pondering his next move.

He had decided to stay for one more shot. He didn't have much else planned and he was sat in the armchair when Dorothy reappeared an hour or so later, accompanied by the same nurse. The nurse's pleasant demeanour was gone. Byrd figured word had gone round about the badge.

'You really have to leave now. Dorothy needs her rest.'

'Oh it's alright Ruth, he's one of my boys come to see me.'

The nurse turned to Byrd and looked straight at him.

'Fifteen more minutes.'

Then she turned and left them alone.

Byrd stood and steered Dorothy to her chair, picked up the clipping and put it in her hand. She looked up at Byrd apologetically and reached for her glasses hung on a chain around her neck.

'My eyesight isn't, well, you know.'

She refocused on the picture, read a little of the article and spoke up almost immediately.

'Oh my yes, that's Seth and Nathaniel Stone.'

Byrd's senses leapt.

'They were trouble if you know what I mean. Sad boys really, what happened to them I mean, but trouble.'

Byrd nodded at her sympathetically, conspiratorially.

'Nate at least. Always causing trouble with the other Cougars, but we thought that they were better off with us than on the street. Don't get me wrong, they were good Cougars. Very bright. And they were…'

She hesitated, searching for the right words.

'Poetic. When you listened to them talk to each other. The younger one anyway.'

'Poetic?'

Byrd seemed puzzled by the description; it wasn't what he was expecting.

'That's the best word I can find for it. Always seemed to be writing things down in his little book.'

Byrd wrote the word down in his own notebook but wasn't sure how he could use it.

'They earned every badge going. Nate was the local hunting-bow champion. But they were bad. No father you see and a mother that was… so-so if you know what I mean. She was found dead in… unfortunate circumstances and the boys were taken into care for a while. They carried on with us though, I'll give them that. They both joined the army just as soon as they were able. Never saw them again after that although I heard they were posted to the mid-east, one of those foreign places you see all the fighting in on the television?'

Byrd nodded again, urging her on. She was up and running now, just how Byrd liked it. He knew there would be a nugget somewhere in all the dross. There usually was.

'They were always together those two. Never seemed to make

any other friends from what I remember; I quite felt sorry for them at times. They loved the outdoors, the forests in particular. If it wasn't for their meanness, they would have made troop supervisors, maybe higher. There was an incident back then. Nate had a fight with another boy, damned near, well...'

She seemed to dry up at the thought of the incident.

'Did they have a favourite place you might say, you know, Dorothy, a place where they hung out a lot together?'

'Well, they lived in Rumford, but beyond that I couldn't say.'

Byrd felt his hopes fade.

'Were they in the same Cougar team?'

She paused. Byrd wasn't sure if she was thinking or else slipping away.

'Did you say you had a picture of me? People thought my hair was red at the time but it wasn't, not really, I used to put henna on it, every Friday, leave it on all night. I watched Moonlighting and ate my way through two layers of chocolates with a silly bag on my head.'

'No, sorry Dorothy, just this one.'

He cupped his hands around hers and gently steered the picture back into view, trying to get her back and focussed.

'Ah yes, I remember now, the brothers were assigned to Hanover and Newry Troop. It's mainly forest and fresh water lakes. There are quite a few rocky trails and steep gorges. It's very isolated up there. I think that's what the boys loved about it. And I remember we had a conversation about the name of the nearest town. That appealed to them too. It's called Lake Fear. Don't know why, it's perfectly pleasant on a summer's day.'

Byrd smiled inwardly and thought to himself, *Yep-there's the nugget right there.* So now he had a drop zone. He liked the name a lot too. It fitted their profile and that's what mattered to him.

There was a knock at the door and the nurse came into the

room. Byrd turned to her.

'Just leaving ma'am. Well, it's been nice seeing you again Dorothy.'

He reached and took the piece of paper from her then gave her a gentle hug. She smiled and whispered to him as he stood close. Byrd smiled back and nodded at her words.

'Thank you for closing my window. You know, it's a pity you weren't one of my boys, I think I would have liked that.'

Byrd called Hamis from his car as he travelled back to the Cougar building and explained the conversation he'd had with Dorothy. Hamis was waiting for him with the copy of the map he'd asked for. They stood over it as Hamis pointed out the cabins surrounding Lake Fear.

'That's still a big area to cover, Mr Byrd, and the weather reports and all. I suggest you find a guesthouse here in Rumford for the night and hire yourself a four-wheeler in the morning. You'll need it to tackle the terrain instead of that town car you're driving. Byrd thanked him again and returned to his car, his earlier footprints already covered over with fresh snow. He decided to take Hamis' advice and find a place in town to stay that he could use as a base. He Googled vacancies in Rumford, took down the zip code for the first hit, and fired up his satnav. He would also get himself a four-wheel drive vehicle for the rest of the search.

18

It was four pm and almost dark. Seth cruised slowly as Nate scanned the surrounds with his binoculars. They had turned off the highway and were on a two-lane blacktop now, within the confines of Lake Fear. They passed a small road-sign announcing that the town was four miles north of their position. Nate pointed it out as they passed it and spoke with a sing-song voice.

'See it? Home again, home again, jiggetty jog.'

The lake's shoreline was just visible as they skirted its Eastern edge, sleet beginning to turn to heavy flakes of snow, instantly transforming the landscape into an ashen, cadaverous wilderness.

They were looking for something secluded with just a single main route in and out.

He drove on, stopping every quarter mile or so to survey the countryside. They were pulled up at the side of the road now, Seth leaning on the open door of the SUV, glasses to his face.

'See that, Nate?'

He handed Nate the glasses and pointed towards a small timber building stood in darkness at the edge of the lake.

'Looks like a boathouse. Not gonna be much by way of facilities in there, not for sleeping anyway. Gonna be cold man.'

'I'm thinking maybe we could just spend the night undercover that's all Nate, and carry on searching in the morning. Can't see dick in this light.'

Seth drove down a rutted single track and emerged at a small gravelled turnaround. The boathouse was set back from the lake on a slight rise, sheltered under the thick branches of two huge black cottonwood trees. Seth reversed the SUV and positioned it to face back in the direction of the track.

'Just for tonight man, then we start up again in the morning.'

Nate nodded and got out. Seth grabbed a flashlight and a cardboard box from the flatbed and followed Nate. They both headed for the double doors and Nate grabbed a hold of the two handles. The doors swung out freely and Seth shone the flashlight into the large open space, his breath sending clouds of vapour across the beam in the cold air. The acrid smell of spent oil hit them as they walked into the gloom. It was occupied by an upturned rowboat balanced on several large timber blocks in the centre of the room. A heavy oak workbench ran along one wall, oily tools scattered across every inch of its surface. An old sink and a bathtub with an overhead shower jury-rigged above it lay in a corner, a greasy La-Z-Boy in the other.

'Nobody worry about security round here?'

The boat was in the middle of a repair job.

'We clear out first light Nate; I don't want to come across whoever is fixing that boat.'

Nate pulled the doors closed as Seth balanced the flashlight on the flat of the boat. He handed Nate a pre-packed sandwich, a snickers bar and a can of coke. They both sat down and ate on an old dirty bedspread that had been hanging from the jaws of a bench-vice.

'Almost there Nate, almost there man.'

He reached across and squeezed Nate's shoulder. Nate nodded, only half listening, staring ahead, his eyes following the sharp angles of the shadows.

'You wanna get some early kip Nate? I'll keep watch.'

'No Seth, you get your head down man. I'll cover.'

'OK, wake me at midnight.'

But Nate seemed distant again. He got up and wandered across to the tub. He sat, balancing on a timber support holding it in place and played a hand across the rusted rivets, wiped away some of the crumbling enamel from its side, sat in the semi-darkness and drifted back.

...Nate heard his name shouted out...
It seems from a distance away. His brother's voice. He stumbles out of bed like a drunk, along the landing to the source. Seth has their Momma in his arms, holding her upright in a bath of blood, screaming instructions that echo in the tiny bathroom.
'Call 911 Nate, call for an ambulance.'
Nate stands silent, motionless. Seth kicks out but the impact barely registers. Seth kicks again, screams again. Nate has been calculating the blood loss, wondering how much a body can lose and survive. Seth is manhandling her now, raising her arms above her head. It is her left wrist, a two-inch slice, skin pale and puckered around it. The voice again, screaming his name, his brother in his face, the neat wound still weeping, bar of soap with the blade embedded, bloody, balanced on the side of the tub. Then Momma groans, one eyelid trembling, lips curling back showing bad teeth, and Nate finally moves, like he has wings, flies down the stairs to the phone, drops a penny to the authorities, unlocks the front door and opens it all the way for when they arrive, back to the bathroom to help Seth bind her wrist with a towel, cover her body with another, both talking to her until help arrives.
Nobody speaks about it afterward when Momma returns with her wound treated, she just gathers her boys around her and pats them for hours. Nate notices that she has switched her watch to her left wrist and takes to wearing long sleeves even on hot days. And they moved on north.

The sound of Seth stirring on the floor of the boathouse brought him back to the present. He looked across at his brother, waited for him to settle, then stood and walked to the doors and inched one open. It had stopped snowing now and the heavy clouds had parted revealing a full, bright moon, its laser light shining on the lake, seeming to split the lake in two. A bitter wind forced its way through the gap of the doorway but Nate didn't seem to notice, or care. He stood that way, staring at the lake, losing himself in its darkness, its depths, until the moon slid from view.

19

They were on the road again, Seth stopping every quarter mile or so to glass the scene. Snow covered the landscape, the sun flashing off every surface. Seth pulled over again and they both got out. Seth scanned east to west all the way to the horizon.

'Why didn't you wake me Nate?'

'Figured you old 'uns need your rest.'

'You stand at the door the whole friggin' night?'

Seth had heard Nate moving around the workshop, had watched him standing there before finally falling asleep.

Nate didn't answer. But he hadn't stood there all night. At some time past midnight he had quietly closed the door and walked over to the workbench, playing the flashlight over the tools there, looking for particular things. He'd found a coiled-up piece of electrical cable in a drawer slung underneath the bench top. A box-cutter, hacksaw and hand-drill were amongst the random mess. He'd cut two short lengths of the wire, stripped off the insulation layer, twisted and knotted the pieces. Finally, he'd found a length of wood that he'd cut down in the dimming beam of the flashlight to make four small end pieces that he'd drilled, then threaded onto the ends of each wire.

He had dropped the waste fragments in a waste bag hanging from a hook on one wall.

He'd pocketed the wires and returned to the door, opened it a fraction to stare back out onto the lake.

'There.'

Seth had spotted what they were searching for.

The overhead power line gave the cabin away.

Seth handed the glasses to Nate and pointed about a half mile ahead.

'You see it?'

'I see it.'

'You like it?'

'Yeah, I think I like our new home. Let's get a little nearer, make sure it's vacant.'

Nate reached inside his pocket and pulled out one of the wires. He handed it to Seth.

'Made you this.'

Seth looked at it, admiring the handiwork.

'Thanks man, bet you have one just like it.'

Nate took it back and threaded it through Seth's belt loops.

'Keep it here.'

They drove further along the road and glassed the property again.

'Don't see any smoke Seth.'

'Look for the access.'

They pulled off the road and followed a single track for a half mile or so, and then they both got out and walked the rest of the way.

Nate saw it first. It was almost completely hidden from view by bog rosemary bushes and button brush. The cabin was side on to the road giving it a narrow profile, positioned that way for protection against the worst of the prevailing westerly winds.

'That's her Seth, don't you feel it?'

Seth nodded and smiled at Nate, enjoying the moment, Nate's more than his own.

No smoke, no lights and he could see shutters in place at the windows as they neared the timber cabin. The neat garden with timber play furniture meant that the place was probably a family holiday retreat, secured for the winter. Perfect.

'You flank left and go round back, Nate. I'll meet you there from the other side.'

Seth was still cautious even though the signs were good.

The rear was completely enclosed by tall red and mountain maple trees, with a flat lawn and small goalposts positioned at each end. A lean-to outbuilding and carport were attached to the single story structure of the cabin – probably a workshop or storage. A small up-turned rowboat and trailer were parked under one end of the carport. Seth spotted the bars of an old snowmobile wrapped in tarp and pushed up tight against a low wall of straw bales. He figured that might come in handy if it still worked.

Nate was stood at the back with his hands on his hips looking up at the darkening sky, snowflakes beginning to fall again, beginning to cover his close-cropped head.

'Check under those pots Nate; I'm betting there's a key here someplace, don't want to trash the door if I can help it.'

They both began turning over the collection of plant pots that had been arranged on each side of the front door.

'Bingo.'

Nate held the key up to Seth.

'You want to carry me over the threshold bro'?'

Seth smiled and swiped the key from Nate.

They let themselves into a large, tidy, single room with white covers draped over all of the furniture. The room led off to two bedrooms, a kitchen and a bathroom. The smell of burnt wood permeated the whole cabin making it feel welcoming and familiar.

'Hunt for the power and water supply and get a fire going. I noticed a log pile out front. I'll go bring the ride up here and hide it around back.'

Thirty minutes later, the power and water were on and a fire was burning in the grate. The light was fading and the two of them were unloading the SUV and trailer under the light of a small halogen above the rear door.

'Jeez Seth, I thought we were thinking of holing up for the

winter not re-enacting Desert Storm.'

'Just caution Nate that's all. Until I know who the hell is on our tail, I want full site security.'

20

Byrd was sat on a high stool pulled up at the bar, sipping a Coors and chewing a handful of salted peanuts in the Boardwalk Inn just off Route 120. He was alone. He unfolded the map that Hamis had copied him and laid it across the bar top. He leaned over it now, taking in the town of Lake Fear and the surrounding countryside. Then he studied the small red squares; there were maybe a hundred cabins within the town's boundaries alone and many more beyond in neighbouring towns. He rubbed at his neck, easing the tension away, thinking, *hoping*, that this hunch of his would pay off or he was royally screwed.

He took a pen out and drew an outer ring around his imaginary drop zone, then an inner ring around the town itself.

He thought about the terrain he had encircled, the densely wooded areas, the lakes, and he imagined them there, imagined them hiking along rocky paths through undergrowth, hunting down their next meal, hauling their dead prey back to some remote cabin clung to the side of a hill. He imagined them hanging the carcass out on a line to drain, opening a couple of cans, sitting down together on a huge log, talking and hacking off the mud and gore from their boots. All of this he imagined as if it would somehow make his plan a reality.

He finished off his beer, folded the map and went to his room to make a call to his boss.

This time Slater was in and very unfriendly. Byrd had to be bullish if he was to get a result from him.

'Mark, I'm gonna need aerial intel of the neighbourhood. I've tracked the boys to a wilderness here and I need to narrow my search. Yes sir, I can guess how much that might cost but I'm close sir, very close. Plus the isolated location works for us.'

He told Slater about the location of the search and that he needed to focus on any *occupied* cabins. A low-level high-res drone sweep would tell him which of the cabins were giving off a heat signature – he figured the brothers would have a fire going in this freezing temperature. Snow on the roof would block the reading but thermal leakage through the windows would tell him what he needed to know. Visible images would tell him about any vehicles at high value targets, and routes in and out of them. He didn't tell Slater that all of this was one huge gamble based on a twenty year old image of the brothers in Cougar uniform and wishful thinking. Slater listened to Byrd's plans without interruption. He finally green-lighted the operation, followed by some very clear and specific threats to Byrd's career trajectory should the operation prove what he called *erroneous*. Byrd wasn't sure what the word meant exactly but he had the feeling that it wasn't all good.

He'd promised to call again once the results of the fly-by were in. The second call was to his office.

'Donna, I've just got the approval from Slater for a Reaper flyby. I need a detailed aerial map of the drop zone here and I need it tomorrow, next day latest. I need thermal and visible images taken at midnight and midday local time. Two cycles should do it.'

'Yes I know Ben, I've got Mark stood next to me right now. He's already briefed me.'

Byrd lowered his voice.

'Yeah? Did he tell you how expensive that's gonna be yet?'

'No, not yet.'

'Oh, he will, and when he does, tell him I already know and don't give a rat's ass. I'm already living out of a hole in the ground here, so take it out of my expenses.'

'Why didn't *you* tell him that?'

'Hell no, that's what I pay you for honey, do all my dirty work for me, you know that.'

They both laughed conspiratorially.

'Listen Donna, I'm about to send you a map of some pretty trees and lakes and a whole bunch of hillbilly shacks. I've circled the location I need sweeping. It's around fourteen square kilometres excluding water, with lots of little biddy boxes. They're quaint wooden coffins that outdoorsy types apparently stay in when it rains or when they want a sly skim of penthouse. But I'm only interested in the bigger cabins that I've marked on the map. I need to know if any of those cabins are giving off a heat plume, maybe showing two adult heat signatures in the grounds if we get lucky. I'm hoping most won't. If they've seen the weather report you sent me they'll have left. Then I need you to mark up the map and send it back to me with the images within twenty four hours of you receiving the intel.'

'Jeez Ben, I'm not sure we can get the drone in position that quickly.'

'That's why I'm dealing with you and nobody else, 'cause you're my go-to gal. Plus there's dinner at Maggiano's in the deal. You, me, two steaming plates of Mom's Lasagna, couple bottles of St. Jean.'

'Do I get the zuccotto?'

'Two slices with ice cream, but that's gonna cost you a little more. I need the usual suspects picking up and questioning in Oxford County – there can't be too many in this wilderness. The brothers must have collected supplies somewhere en-route from Bangor. Third, I need the names of local agents; I want some sites watching for a while. I'll brief them directly via telephone conference.'

He closed the call, switched his cell to photo-mode, began taking pictures of a section of Hamis' map, six images in all, then uploaded them to his laptop and fired them off to Donna. He sat back then and rested his back against the bed-head, rubbing absently at his chin and staring down at the map, trying to bring it to life again, trying to sense by sheer willpower where the brothers were holed up. He spoke quietly, unselfconsciously to himself in the confines of his room.

'You're here aren't you boys? I can sense you, and it's getting stronger. Well now I'm here too and I'm genuinely looking forward to finally meeting you both.'

21

The brothers woke early on day one. Seth wanted security in place, tested and operational by the end of the day. Nate had jogged the full circumference of the property to scope all of the access points. Just a single dirt road in and out, capable of allowing four-wheel vehicles. A narrow trail at the back of the cabin led off into the forest. A small hand painted sign in the shape of an arrow flint said *Lake Fear – 2 miles.*

They positioned motion sensors twenty five metres out on each corner of the property; they'd trigger a couple of high intensity lights rigged to wooden poles that they had found in the storeroom and had lashed to fence posts.

Closed-circuit cameras were installed at the front and rear of the cabin, and covering the access road. Seth had fixed a small ball of Semtex to a tree at the side of the access road with a remote detonator, just as a delay in case they needed emergency evacuation. He had then configured all of the devices both to the laptop and to a couple of small handhelds for them to carry with them when they were on site. They lit up and gave out a series of beeps when the sensors triggered. By late afternoon they were up and running and Seth felt more in control. He had also prepared a *ready bag* that held all of their papers – passports, driver's licenses, other stuff – ready to grab in case of an emergency evacuation.

Seth had been tracking the web on the laptop for any stories of them back in Iraq. Sky, Reuters and Al Jazeera all carried short pieces about the street shooting but nothing about their escape. Even the shooting was quickly overtaken by newer stories.

Someone had to be shutting the incident down. Who? Why? But they had to be safe enough out here in the middle of nowhere while he planned their next move

LAKE FEAR

They were sat eating steaks and watching a football game that evening when both handsets triggered. Then the floods lit up in front.

Nate was up first, handgun out of his leg holster in an instant. Seth ran to the light switches, throwing each in turn, plunging the cabin into darkness. They had rehearsed this. The flashlight was on a cabinet near to the door and Seth reached for it and switched it on. Nate had positioned himself at the back window and was easing the slats open to see out onto the floodlit lawn. Seth ran to the laptop and studied the images from the cameras.

'You got anything Seth?'

'Nope, you?'

'Nope.'

They waited. Seth spoke up quietly then.

'Four o'clock. Got some movement on the edge of the screen.'

Nate dropped below the window ledge, crawled along the floor to the other side of the window, opened the shutter a tiny crack.

'Deer.'

He lowered the shutter and ran to the front door.

He crept forward onto the porch, steadied his aim and flipped the safety off. The noise spooked the deer and it bolted away before Nate could get a shot off. Nate came back inside to a round of applause from Seth.

'Where'd you say you learned how to hunt? Friggin' deer comes all the way up to the front door and practically knocks and you don't so much as get a shot off?'

Nate looked embarrassed.

'Caught me cold.'

'Oh come on man, you were like Mister Bean out there. I could've walked over to it, wrestled it to the ground, carried it in here on a plate.'

'That's because you're too damned mean to spend your money

on ammo. Besides I had to let it go, man, it was way too small, it was just a baby.'

Seth walked back to the laptop still laughing and reset the security.

'Least we know the kit works in these temperatures.'

Late afternoon on the second day they had dragged out the boat and trailer, hitched it to their SUV and headed to the lake. They had thought it safer fishing late in the day to reduce the risk of encountering any locals. It had stopped snowing but a frozen crust covered the raw wilderness. The lake was empty as far as the eye could see, water and sky seeming to mirror each other in blue-grey wonder.

'This good enough for you Natey boy?'

Nate had his feet up on the side of the boat, rod in his lap, staring at the hypnotic sway of his lure on the surface. He trailed a hand in the cold clear water.

Seth was sat at the other end of the boat concentrating on tying a new lure on the end of his line.

They had a small collection of blueback trout and perch on a stretch of tarp at their feet. Nate looked across at Seth and smiled. He looked like a kid again.

'It's all good man.'

The boat slowly crabbed sideways, pushed by a cold breeze. Seth looked up as they neared a small plastic buoy bobbing on its chain.

'What d'yer make of that?'

Seth spotted a small photograph that had been sealed in plastic and lashed to the side of the buoy. It had a date written underneath but he couldn't make it out. He pointed.

Nate reeled in his line, grabbed the oars and rowed closer. They both looked across at the picture of a young boy. The date was 2008 but it was a fairly new picture; somebody took trouble replacing it to keep the memory alive. Nate studied it more intensely, the image unsettling him. Seth spoke again but Nate was only half listening.

'Accident maybe. Damned shame, young kid like that.'

Nate seemed lost in his thoughts and spoke in a strangely distant way.

'How old d'yer think he was?'

'Seven, eight maybe.'

The boy was dark haired and handsome, with a wide easy smile. He bore an uncanny resemblance to Nate; a younger version of him. Nate was mesmerised. He couldn't help it. He did the arithmetic.

Leon would have been in his twenties now, *if he had lived*.

This kid, this *Zach Cooke*, would have now been just a young teenager.

Seth had said something else but it was lost on him; Nate was retreating into memory, going back to Leon's bedroom over twenty years earlier, replaying his Momma's heartbroken words that night, about the death of their baby brother Leon at the hands of his Dadda.

'Oh, he didn't mean to...' He recalled her saying. *'...Your Dadda, he let the devil in that night.'*

But it wasn't like she said it was that night.

Not like that at all…

…Nate has silently let himself into baby's room…

He stares down for a full ten minutes, not moving, just watching the baby sleeping in its cot. Its tiny chest is heaving up and down, a quiet hiss as lungs fill and empty, tiny bubbles appearing at the edges of the mouth, eyelids fluttering, arms, legs occasionally twitching, the shadow cast by the nightlight producing a larger distorted copy of it all on the damp stained bedroom wall behind them.

Baby has stolen his Momma away from him.

She no longer comes to watch him play soccer, not that this had been a regular thing. She never asks how he's doing in class any more, she never even bitches about the mess in his and Seth's bedroom. Nothing. Just the baby now. Just the fucking, thieving baby. He has to fix that. Make it like it used to be. Just him and Seth and Momma.

He gently lifts baby from its cot and holds it in his arms. The baby is warm to the touch, soft, its smooth pearlescent skin reflecting the glow from the nightlight, tiny red, pursed lips like miniature rubies, long dark eyelashes, almost feminine, just like Nate's own. He shifts baby and reaches up and across with his free hand, all the time looking at it, looking at life, feeling something like electricity in his veins, then placing his fingers over the baby's mouth and nestling them there, and extending them so that they lay against the bottom of his nose at the same time. Baby hardly moves, just a single awkward jolt and a gentle puff of air escaping between Nate's fingers. Its eyes open, slowly, just briefly, looking straight at Nate. They close again, but Nate has captured that briefest of moments and something comes loose inside him.

He lays him back down in the exact same spot he found him. A small stool lies at the head of the cot; Momma uses it when she sits for hours coaxing Leon to sleep. Nate pulls it around and sits at the side of the cot. Looks down on the lifeless form. Bile rises in his throat at what

he's done. He chokes it back down. He reaches down, wipes away a tiny trace of blood from baby's nose with a finger, brings it to his own trembling lips.
It wasn't his fault. Not really. Not if he wanted his Momma back. Baby's fault. He leans into the cot, whispers to baby.
'You gave me no choice. D'you see that? I'm sorry. I'm sorry. You gave me no choice.'

He returns to his own bed. Seth is still sleeping soundly, turned away from Nate. Nate is glad that he doesn't have to look Seth in the face even though he is sleeping. Later that night. Dadda comes home drunk as a fool, playful. He goes straight up to see his youngest, as always, creeps into the bedroom. But he trips on the unseen stool, Nate hears it clearly, Dadda loses his footing and stumbles headfirst onto the crib. It collapses instantly under his drunken deadweight, crushing the already dead baby. Momma rushes in then just in time to see Dadda turn around to her, his mouth a perfect 'O'. She scrambles to pull him away, shouting the boys to help her, him still trying to help himself up but can't, taking an age to stand, Momma finally scooping Leon up off the floor, pretending that his floppy head and flattened chest don't really matter because everything is going to be alright with a bit of loving care isn't it? The boys finally arrive, Seth wondering what all the commotion is about, Nate already knowing but joining in with the tragedy being played out. And it works for him, his plan. It works that night, and only he knows the truth. And he isn't telling. Not even to his brother. Not ever.

And the terrible truth is it doesn't work, not really, not in the way he had imagined, not in the way he wanted. He doesn't get his family back. That has been destroyed for ever. And something else is also lost forever, something warm to the touch, soft, his smooth pearlescent skin reflecting the glow from the nightlight, tiny red, pursed lips like miniature rubies, long dark eyelashes, almost feminine, just like Nate's own.

And that fateful night was the start for Nate, the real start. That was when Nate became lost.

Seth slapped at his brother's leg a second time as they bobbed up and down in the boat.

'Hey, Nate, you still in the land of the living, man?'

Nate rubbed at his eyes and looked up at Seth.

'Sorry bro', just thinking of the boy there.'

'Yep well, let's go. We've got us a good catch here and it's getting damned cold.'

Nate grabbed the oars and pulled hard, occasionally looking across at the image of the kid gently undulating on the buoy, seeming to nod at Nate, smile and nod.

A figure sat unseen overlooking the lake, a layer of snow scraped away into a small mound beside him on the bench, coffee flask at his side, collar up, huddled against the cold wind. He'd been staring out onto the lake and had seen the two strangers row out to the buoy. They'd seemed to study the photograph. He absently wondered who they were, but he had witnessed many people row across to it to take a closer look over the years. It comforted him to know that people cared enough to make the effort. He got up and stretched, rubbing at his arms for warmth. He emptied the remains of the flask onto the snow and pocketed it, climbed onto his Quad bike and headed home. He thought no more of the two strangers out on the lake.

The first days back in Lake Fear were uneventful and disorientating for Seth and Nate. They'd enjoyed passes from war zones throughout their service but only brief ones, and they'd known they would be back in action before their scars had healed. This time they knew there would be no going back. They felt strangely adrift, freewheeling, waiting for their gears to grab onto something meaningful. They spent most of the time eating, sleeping, reading from the small stock of books the owner kept, the occasional target practice in the yard with their bows. Seth's crossbow was no match for Nate's longbow and Nate won the ten dollar pot every time. They had discussed their future a few times; ideas were emerging.

One evening they were sprawled on the big sofa, cans of Bud in hand, watching a basketball game, when Seth mentioned going north in the Spring, to Canada, out of security business altogether.

'What say we head up to the Canadian oil patch bro'? We're ghosts in the security business now. I read they've found new reserves at Bakken and are hiring. Plus Canadians are very hospitable according to Leno.'

Nate laughed out loud at that.

'Never figured myself as oil trash, Seth. I've only ever pointed a gun at things for a living.'

'Yeah, well I'm done with all that shit. Think maybe it's done with us too.'

'Guess I could do that.'

'OK man, I'll hit the web some more and get the full story.'

'Good enough.'

Nate thought of his brother looking out for him one more time. If Seth was headed to Canada then so was he. He stood and grabbed two more cans from the table, pulled the tab on one and handing it to Seth.

'Momma would be proud of you,' he said, 'getting us back here safe. She said you would look after me and that you have.'

He reached out and tapped his can on Seth's.

'Forget it man,' Seth said.

'No Seth, I'll never forget it. And I'll pay you back one day.'

They emptied the cans in one swig and smashed them together.

'Gonna hit the sack Nate, all this doing nothing is tiring me out. Hey, how are you sleeping? Had any more of those nightmares?'

He had forgotten to ask Nate until now.

'Nope, like a baby, sleeping just like a baby.'

But that wasn't true. The nightmare had returned the previous night, the first in a while. It only seemed to last a few seconds but it was enough to wake Nate in a rush, leaving him sweaty and spooked. The bear was back and bigger than he remembered it, its mouth an open gash, and when it spoke blood and spittle bubbled through its massive hooked teeth.

It had appeared at his side as he walked alone along a narrow path and had roared down at him, just a single word, over and over, before it had reached for him, swallowing him up. *Timesup, Timesup, Timesup.*

22

Byrd lay on the bed, one hand propping up his head, the other flicking ash absently into an empty coffee cup on the bedside cabinet. He squinted at the no smoking sign fixed to the wall, right next to the disabled smoke detector that now dangled from a wire above it. His mind circled the reports he had just read.

He stubbed out the remains of the cigarette and picked up a faxed report from a bundle of papers received from Donna that morning and that were spread out around him on the bed. He had set up a secure office in the small bedroom of the B and B courtesy of the FBI field office in Portland.

The report was three pages long and consisted mainly of a list of items. Manny had been picked up the previous day and had actively volunteered the inventory to avoid trouble for breaking his parole order. At least Byrd knew his hunch about the brothers' whereabouts was good. Byrd's attention was drawn to the C4. That frightened the crap out of him. *What the hell did they want with that?*

He picked up another note from the pile and reread it. It was an instruction from Slater, just seven short lines. Unusual for him. He liked long reports and longer words: *shit-speak.*

The note read:

Following location of targets, you are to obtain whereabouts of a private cell phone containing images of interest to us taken in theatre. Do not attempt to retrieve the phone personally unless in their possession, just its location and manner of its safe recovery.
THIS IS PRIORITY ONE in your engagement with the targets BEFORE completing your mission.

He smiled to himself. So, now he knew. The boys had the dirties on someone and Byrd had been sent on a sanctification mission. Now he liked the brothers even more and his capture-kill mission even less. He would get Donna to do a little quiet digging back at the office, try to find out more about these cell images that Slater wanted so badly.

He dropped the papers on the bed and went back to studying the map Donna had annotated for him. There were six cabins that she'd marked up as *strong possibles,* plus a further eight *maybes* and a whole lot of *who the hell knows?* She had signed off the accompanying note with a hand drawn smiley face.

The weather conditions had played havoc with the drone sweep, but this was all he had. He transferred the locations of the six primary and eight secondary targets onto the full map from Hamis. It would take three or four days at least to stake them all out, but maybe he would get lucky. He folded the map into a holdall along with a pair of field glasses. Then he pulled on the cold -weather gear he had bought from Sears in town. Finally he placed the handgun on top and zipped up the bag.

As he pulled on his parka he looked up at a poster fixed to the wall above the bed: *Visit Maine in the fall.* It was a fabulous palette of golden hues topped by a cloudless azure sky. He snatched it off the wall, balled it up and dropped it in the waste bin on his way out.

Act 2

It is in the shelter of each other that the people live
Irish proverb

LAKE FEAR, MAINE, USA
November 22nd, 2010

23

Sheriff Gene Cooke was guiltily smoking a rollup and looking down at his outboard that lay in pieces on a stretch of tarp spread across the end of the jetty. A small mound of snow lay to the side of it where he had scraped it away with a boot.

The jetty, complete with flagpole, was one of four constructed on the south side of the lake. Jack Hancock of Hancock's Lumber Mill had gifted the wood and anted up the previous year for the building work to celebrate his family's 150th year of trading in Lake Fear. Cooke was being careful not to spill oil on the new timber.

A picture of this particular jetty and the lake beyond, cable-car in the middle distance, was the centrepiece of the town's summer house-letting flyer since it seemed to best capture the town's natural beauty and heritage.

Cooke's fingers were getting numb from the cold and fiddly nature of the repair work. He'd been fixing the ancient Honda on and off for about three years and he knew it was time for a new one. He might get one more season out of it, but right now winter was just around the corner. The lake would be frozen over within the month meaning he'd get a couple more fishing trips in before he hauled his boat into the boathouse until spring.

His cell rang and he left a smear of engine oil on his parka as he fished it out of his pocket. The caller ID confirmed what he suspected – it was his secretary Jessie Parker.

'Jess, I am on leave this morning remember? I need to work on my boat.'

He answered with just a hint of impatience.

'I know. I'm sorry Sheriff, this isn't exactly business. I wanted to know if you and Mary were firm in coming to the double-centenary party next Saturday night is all, what with Mary's mother still in Rumford General.'

Cooke felt a little awkward now at his impatience.

'Guess so, Jess, Mary had me buy provisions this morning for a casserole she plans to bake for the occasion.'

'Sounds good Sheriff, I'll mark you down as a cert. By the way, you've received a weather alert from Portland Met. Says a heavy snow storm could be on its way. From my reading of it, could be 1998 all over again.'

'Let's hope not.'

Cooke absently toed at the thin layer turning to mush underfoot.

'Seems to be getting earlier each year. You can forward the message to me at my home email. And copy Eddie would you? Ask him to alert the council and Kate at *The Mariner*.'

Lake Fear was a tiny rural community of just a couple of hundred residents in winter which bloated to five times that number in the summer from visitors, mainly from Lewiston and Newport and Portland. It was a magnet for the hunting and fishing fraternity. It lay around thirty miles inland of Portland, Maine, surrounded by the lake that gave the town its name and whose kidney shape seemed to fold around the tiny community like giant protective hands. Access was via Ellis River Road, a two lane blacktop off Route 8. Its economy was built on fishing, hunting and logging. Most of the visitors had gone now, motivated by the weather forecasts trailed in recent state news broadcasts. Locals were left bone-weary but with enough visitor dollars in their bank accounts to keep them going until next season, plus the funds for a decent winter break in the Florida sunshine or maybe Europe for the more ambitious if they chose it. Most didn't. Some got casual winter jobs at the lumber yard and on environmental maintenance projects, some sunk their income and time into home improvements, and some prepared for the following season and plain relaxed with a dozen or more good books.

A few visitors had hung around for the extended archery season through to December, introduced by the Maine regulators to handle the excess deer population causing domestic grief on neighbouring residential estates.

Two hours and a lot of cursing later and Cooke had the engine reassembled and in place. The engine fired up on the second pull and he slowly followed the shoreline of the lake for just a few hundred metres before heading back, satisfied that she was seaworthy again.

He had headed east. He only ever headed east, along the shore, or north, into the centre of the lake, never west, never down that dark stretch of water toward Gifford Point. Mary went there, but not him. That was where they had eventually found the body, caught up in tangle-weed, at the bottom of the lake.

Cooke had gone fishing with Zach his eight year old son one beautiful spring morning five years previously. They had been fishing for whitefish and splake and had run out of bait. He had rowed back to shore just briefly, to restock from the fishermen's cabin on the west shore, and had left Zach on board the small rowboat. The boy had somehow untied from the jetty and the boat had drifted west pushed by the prevailing wind. Cooke had only noticed when Zach had stood up, still holding an oar, and had shouted out for his father. The boat had already drifted twenty metres from shore. And then he saw that Zach had taken his life-vest off and had placed it on the seat next to him, despite his father's scolding when he had done this once before; he'd said it chafed at his neck. Cooke had dropped the provisions at his feet, run, dived off the end of the jetty, just as Zach lost his balance and fell into the lake. As he'd dived, Cooke had heard a sharp crack as Zach's head clipped one of the metal rowlocks hard. When he surfaced from the dive there was no sign of his son.

By the time he'd swum out far enough the boat had drifted further still, confusing him about the exact location that Zach had entered the water. He dove time after time, searching in the freezing gin clear depths of Lake Fear, , shouting out each time he surfaced for air, shaking uncontrollably, limbs cramping from cold and panic and the sheer effort, but diving anyway. A rambler had seen Cooke, heard the cries for help, had phoned the local emergency services.

Divers had found the body later that night, under the glare of spotlights rigged to a half-dozen bobbing boats.

The town council had built a sitting area on the lake's shore and they'd fixed a buoy out in the lake in memory of Zach. Cooke never took his boat near there, but often sat alone on the bench staring out at the spot on the lake and blaming his own stupidity and thoughtlessness, going over and over the events in his mind like a penance.

> *...tying the rope tighter this time...*
> with a double hitch or, better still, taking Zach out of the boat and walking hand in hand to the cabin, buying a bag full of live wax-worms and getting Zach an ice cream they'd keep just between the two of them because Mary thought that Zach ate far too many sweets. And then walking back to the boat that they had christened Dr Doofenshmirtz, from Phineas and Ferb, Zach's favourite TV show. And both laughing out loud,

ice cream dripping off Zach's tiny chin, his little hand lost in Cooke's big calloused one and Cooke wiping the boy's face while secretly working open the bag of squirming worms with his other hand behind his back and getting ready to whip it around and stir up a scream from Zach as he thrust it under the boy's nose.

And the screams did come, but not of mock terror. The screams were real, real and never-ending for Cooke.

This reworking of events he did so often and so convincingly that he was shocked again and again when reality returned.

Mary hadn't blamed him, but he had wished she had. He began to resent her understanding, her compassion, because he needed to suffer. So he had picked fights with her that had no substance, just for the friction it caused, and so he could work it around to their boy, his carelessness and recklessness that had killed. But she wouldn't have it, and the fighting continued until late one night he found himself parked up on Amy's Ridge in his police truck, sat in the dark, looking down onto the town, engine off, radio off, eyes swollen and bloodshot, handgun in his lap, fingering the criss-cross pattern of the colt's grip, enjoying its heavy solid feel, watching the lights of Lake Fear flicker below, looking at the lake beyond, glistening and beautiful and deadly. Almost time. Time for the fairy lights around the town square to wink out. Wiping sweating hands on the sleeves of his jacket and it was almost time.

Until a gentle knock on his side window shocked him alert, a flashlight played inside his truck and he fumbled the gun from sight, lowered his window to stare into the creased smiling face of Lou Tennent, a local hunter, a friend. And a simple honest to God conversation changed everything.

'You still on duty Gene? Still looking after us at this time of night? Need to be home in bed, friend. We can cope until morning.

But tomorrow? Well that's another day and I guess we'll be needing you all over again.'

And he had gone home then to Mary, lain still next to her in the darkness, trembling, hating his own selfish heartless behaviour back on the ridge, but still realising he wasn't yet fixed.

They'd tried for another child but it never came. Cooke convinced himself that he was being further punished, and they both sleepwalked for the first few years unable or unwilling to give focus to their lives. But gradually they committed to the community that had helped them through it all. Lake Fear was their family now, the children were *their* children, and slowly loving and caring supplanted some of the pain.

But it wasn't enough for him. Yes, Lake Fear had become home for them, but it had also taken his son, and how could he live with that?

His cell rang again as he was tying off.

'Hey Eddie, what can I do for you?'

'Sorry to bother you Chief but I just got a copy of the weather report from Jess. It looks pretty ugly.'

'Yeah, so I hear. I asked Jessy to circulate to you and the town committee, and to Kate at *The Mariner* so she can get a flyer out.'

'It says here that we could be in for two feet of snow, that can't be right can it? This early? Have they got their charts right Gene?'

'I don't know Ed. Judging by this early fall I guess anything's possible. Why don't you call them? Better still, get Jessy to call them and you bring round your copy of the FEMA weather ops plan. I'm still at the lake but I'll be back home within the hour.'

'OK, later Chief.'

Cooke finished securing the boat and headed back home. He had been in Lake Fear in 1998 when three of the locals had been lost. Two had been killed by falling trees collapsing on their homes, and one of the elderly residents was lost to hyperthermia when he'd fallen in his own back yard and lain there all night unable to get back up again. A storm that bad, this early, could catch a lot of folk out, and he was damned if he was going to have any more grieving in Lake Fear.

Cooke and his Senior Deputy Eddie Lister sat at the dining table poring over the FEMA plan. It spelled out the operational necessities for a storm level five. It had been twelve years since they had needed to familiarise themselves with its details. Their coffee was cold in their mugs before they finished. Mary poured them some fresh.

'From the look on your faces, you boys look awfully concerned.' Cooke looked up at his wife.

'Could be. If those guys at the met have their forecasts right, we might be headed for one helluva a storm.'

'We just need to plan is all Mrs Cooke. So long as folks have plenty of your pastries and steak pies we should last out just fine.'

Lister smiled at his own wit but Sheriff Cooke hadn't noticed.

'Eddie, it says here that communication is the vital first step. We need to call a council meeting for first thing tomorrow morning, followed by a session with as many of the townsfolk as we can muster. I want you and Jess to start making phone calls to the community representatives and committee members. Mary, would you call ahead to Bobby Whit and book the community centre for ten am sharp.'

They nodded and left Cooke at the table still studying the plan and making notes.

24

Nate stood looking at himself in the full length mirror fixed to one side of the wardrobe in his bedroom. He'd gone there to read once Seth had gone out to check the security. He rarely spent time studying his looks, just perfunctory glances as he shaved, but he did so now. He had his Momma's eyes and high cheek bones, her defined chin. He couldn't discern much of his Dadda, except maybe his thick eyebrows. The half-light coming from the lamps in the living room made him look haunted as he continued to stare at his reflection in silence. He remembered a saying from his childhood, that if you stared long enough you would see the devil.

Your Dadda, he let the devil in that night.

Perhaps that's why he didn't use mirrors too often.

The hunting knife lay on the bedside cabinet and he reached for it, began cutting a pattern in the air before him, a habit he had developed from his teenage years, a smooth, hypnotic mobius that seemed to soothe him. The dull light seemed to dim further, leaving just his outline in the mirror like a corona. Then the outline danced. Jagged shadows swarmed around him.

And the bear came.

He immediately took up an offensive stance and thrust the blade forward and upward again and again, grunting with the effort. The knife swished through the air just in front of the bear, then Nate leaned into the blows and impacted, tearing through fur and muscle, and the animal roared. He wrenched the blade loose and went again, aiming for the same ragged entry point, burying the blade deeper, feeling the warmth of still-pumping blood, feeling splinters of bone break away and enter his own hand and wrist, but still only dimly aware of the pain it caused, going deeper, slicing a cavernous hole at the centre of its body which seemed pinned in front of him, still howling, panting but still erect with a hole at its centre. A new sound at his side, close yet somehow distant, a familiar voice, and then a hand grabbing at his arm, the bear's entrails and gore hanging like knotted rope, swaying then dropping away from him. Nate turned to face the voice, to tell whoever it was that he mustn't be stopped, not now, because he finally had it, but the voice was insistent, and then a powerful blow came down on his arm knocking the knife out of his hand and he was unarmed, powerless before the bear, and he carried on using his fists until he was wrestled away, almost slipping on the gore collecting on the floor, and then the scene was flooded with light and Nate had to shield his eyes with the hands that had worked on the bear moments earlier.

But there was no bear.

Just his own lacerated hands sliced open with broken glass, and the shattered remains of the wardrobe door.

Seth steered Nate to a chair in the kitchen and sat him down, ran cold water into a bowl, retrieved the med kit and began cleaning Nate's hands and arms, carefully removing the splinters. Several deep gashes criss-crossed his knuckles and fingers.

'Flex them for me.'

Nate held out his shaking hands and flexed them.

'OK, no broken bones or damaged tendons. Could have been in trouble there Nate, if we'd needed help.'

Nate didn't answer, just stared down at his swollen, lacerated hands.

'Want to tell me what that was all about?'

Nate went pale and shuddered involuntarily.

'Here, hold that.'

Nate held a piece of gauze that covered the cuts on his right hand as Seth wound a piece of bandage around it. Then he went to work on the other hand.

'They hurt like a bastard.'

'Yeah? Well smashing them through glass and wood will do that.'

Nate seemed to be coming round, colour returning to his face.

'Thanks man.'

Seth looked up at Nate and nodded as he finished off the dressings.

'You gotta tell me, Nate.'

Nate slowly shook his head and looked away. Seth reached across and gently pulled Nate's head until it faced his own. He spoke so quietly that Nate had to strain to hear. He spoke with sadness in his voice.

'Yep, you do man, you have to tell.'

'It was right here, in my room.'

'The bear?'

'Yeah, the bear. I don't get it, Seth, I stopped taking the meds weeks ago.'

Seth stood and began clearing away the kit.

'Think I must be losing it Seth. Beating the crap out of the furniture, that can't be a good sign, man.'

'We've been through a lot of crazy stuff lately Nate. It's just your way of adjusting, that's all.'

Seth reached down and helped Nate to his feet.

'Come on, let's get some sleep, talk some more in the morning.'

Nate stood and looked toward the bedroom where blood stains and splinters of wood covered the floor.

'Think I'll sleep on the sofa tonight, Seth. I'll clean up in the morning.'

Seth nodded, walked over to the bedroom, pulled the door shut.

He listened out for Nate most of the night but there were no more disturbances, just the sound of Nate quietly sweeping up the mess from the bedroom floor in the early hours. Next morning

Seth had gotten up early and gone for a run, leaving Nate asleep on the sofa. A layer of snow covered the path, muffling his footfalls as he pounded his way down towards the lake.

The sky hung heavy with impenetrable dark cloud, mirroring his mood. The events of the previous night had unnerved him. He slowed and trotted towards a big oak trunk that lay on its side and sat there staring out at the million tiny breakers working their way across the lake, water and sky an unnatural aluminium hue. He thought of his brother, his mood swings, his meds or lack of them. It felt like he was somehow in a race. Maybe, once they settled in more fully, he could seek out some help for Nate, get him back on the meds. The more he thought of it, the more he realised that it *was* a race, one where there were only losers.

He walked from the shower into the living room, still towelling himself off after the run. Nate was sat on the floor with his back to the door; he hadn't heard Seth come into the room. He'd surrounded himself with photographs like a little kid with collector's baseball cards. Seth watched him pick up each photo with his bandaged hands and stare at it, then carefully place it back down like it was made of fragile glass, pick up the next. Seth knew these pictures, had seen them a thousand times. Nate took them with him everywhere.

A few of them were of the two of them dressed in combat uniform in theatre. But most were them in younger days, together, and with their Momma.

Nate focussed on one in particular. It had been taken at a local fair in Portland by their Dadda. It was of Seth, Nate and Momma, sat on a bench, Momma with a small smile, not looking at the camera at all but looking to the side at something or someone. She was heavily pregnant with Leon. Nate was leaning forward looking down at the ground in front of him as Seth stared at the back of Nate's head, unsmiling. The backdrop was of a shooting gallery stall, a few battered BB guns chained to a counter top, tin cans arranged in pyramids. A trick of the camera made it look like some kid was aiming at the back of Momma's head as she stared away into the distance, but he wasn't of course. Seth had only noticed that a few years later. Something about the photo made you stop and think. Everyone seemed preoccupied. Not even pretence of happiness. Not a family picture at all really. Images of strangers in their own capsules of thought. They had talked about it for hours over the years. Neither liked it that much. But it meant something to both of them and they couldn't destroy it. Their Momma had got sick a few days after that photograph was taken. She'd suffered in her own bed because they couldn't afford health insurance. They had both shared the cleaning up of the blood and the vomit, bathing their Momma and taking her clothes and bed linen out into the yard to hose down before washing them in the sink.

Not a good memory to have. But it was theirs and they knew they couldn't change it.

Nate suddenly looked up and across at Seth, who felt awkward at being caught this way.

'Sorry man, I … I know how you like your privacy when you look at those.'

'I ain't bothered about that no more Seth. What's done is done.'

He gathered the photos up and carefully put them back into their plastic wallet.

'How're the hands?'

Nate looked up with a question mark on his face as though the previous night's scene was all part of his private nightmares and no one else should know. Then the reality seemed to dawn on him and he smiled and flexed his hands.

'Healing already.'

Seth was about to ask more about the night before but Nate spoke again like he needed to diminish its significance, draw a line on any further discussions.

'Think you're right Seth, we both been through a lot lately. Best to leave it there man.'

They both knew they couldn't, not if Nate was ever going to conquer his demons. But Seth let it lie for now.

He was leaving the room when Nate spoke up again, hesitantly.

'I'd like to visit Rumford, Seth, visit the old place, see if it's still standing.'

Seth didn't answer, just stood in the doorway. He knew there was more to come from Nate, and that he was powerless to stop him despite the risks. He had been waiting for the time his brother would want to visit the place where he had found their Momma lying dead. He knew at some point he'd have to let him go.

'Maybe it's been built over by now Seth, y'know, but I'd like to go see anyway.'

Seth turned and came back into the room. Maybe it was time.

'Yeah, OK Nate. Why don't you take a drive out there on your own? Have some time to yourself and I'll keep watch here in case anyone shows up. The weather seems to be easing up a little .'

Nate seemed relieved, tension draining from his face as he realised that he wouldn't have to battle Seth over the idea. A smile lit up his face.

'Yeah, maybe I will Seth. Think I'll take off first thing tomorrow. Won't take long and I'll come straight back.'

'Just the house, Nate, and just a drive by, OK? Don't stop. Plus, don't go to Momma's grave.'

Nate nodded but without really listening. Seth walked across the room, crouched and took hold of him by the shoulders, staring into his eyes, raising his voice to make Nate understand.

'Nate, I mean it. Not the grave. If we're being tracked they could be watching that.'

Nate pulled away from his brother, all trace of the smile gone.

'Yeah OK, OK, got it, Jesus man, I just wanted to see the place is all, just, you know…'

His voice trailed off and Seth felt bad that he had intruded on Nate's innermost thoughts, spoiling them. Seth's voice softened.

'I know Nate; I'm just trying to keep us both safe, that's all.'

25

Six am next day and Nate was quietly heading out the door. He had left the coffee pot on for Seth, and a note reminding him to re-engage the security system. He cleared the windshield of the latest fall of snow, ignoring the flashes of pain from his hands, and headed off for Rumford, a journey of twenty five miles and nineteen years.

He'd decided not to visit the kids' home in nearby Bethel, even though he and Seth had spent almost three years after the death of their mother. The home meant nothing to him. Precisely zero. They had both just ate and slept and studied and played the occasional game of fuss-ball in a small graffiti-covered room that stunk of sweat and beer and stale food. The other kids had been scared of them and stayed clear. The staff ignored them. Their contact officer had called in weekly to supposedly check on their progress, but in truth she just stood talking to the tutors and ticked a few boxes on her clipboard. Then she'd leave, sometimes without even sitting down with them. Seth had said to Nate once that he thought of their lives at the home as living in a zoo, the zookeeper throwing scraps of meat at two dangerous animals through the bars of the cage. They had both laughed out loud at that and had made growling noises like they were tigers or bears, and they had chased some of the other kids around the corridors, bringing them down like prey.

They had stayed together, that was the main thing. And Seth had made plans. That was where they had first talked of joining the army together. Seth's idea. It had set Nate's imagination alight. For the first time since Momma had died he could see a life together that had a purpose. They'd thrown themselves into reading up every scrap of information in readiness for the day they would leave the stinking home.

Nate had covered the distance to Rumford in less than an hour and was parked up now opposite their old house on Romney Street. He stared across at the small whitewashed bungalow. *Jesus but it looked tiny*. The front door was a different colour now. Of course it was. What did he expect? It was no longer the shiny, lipstick-red, solid timber one with brass hardware, but a white, soulless UPVC. The small, square front lawn where he and Seth had occasionally played football together had been partially dug up and planted with roses that had turned into brown, intertwined sticks. A covering of snow made it all look bloodless and brittle, like he could take the place in his huge hands and crush it all to dust. The wind played at a weathervane tied to the chimney, an image made out in tarnished brass of a farmer bent to his toil, a new addition maybe because he didn't remember that. Nate felt his eyes being drawn back to the front door.

He had fought them there. All those years ago.

...Seth is trying to pull him away but not able...
Two paramedics and a cop are carrying the body bag that is zippered up with his Momma inside, carefully manoeuvring down the narrow hall, out the front door, and Nate loses it, grabs at the black shiny slippery bag, pushes one of the medics to the ground by accident, the young woman trampled in the melee, bag half drops, one end of his Momma falls, hits the floor, he winces, cries, screams for them to let her go. Seth and the cop finally prise Nate loose and hold him as he continues to fight, second cop sat in his patrol car parked up behind the ambulance talks into his radio, looks across with a disinterested weary expression, like he's seen it all before. Hatred for his brother flares in Nate for the first

time, just briefly, then gone. He pulls at his own short hair, bites his own arm in panic and terror, begs Seth, implores him to help, help him free their Momma so she can escape that terrible airless bag and walk back into the kitchen with them somehow, make them something to eat, sit down with them both, all laugh out loud at something stupid on the goggle box like Alf or Family Ties.

But they hold him tight, trying to soothe him while he keeps shaking his head violently from side to side like a tied animal lashing out trying to get free of them. Still they hold him until the red wash from the emergency lights of the ambulance no longer bathe the front door, finally fade to nothing. Nate finally pulls free and runs into the street, runs after the ambulance, but it's gone. He slows and drops, sits cross-legged in the middle of the street, cars steering round him, him not caring if one does run him down.

Strong arms are lifting him to his feet, someone speaking his name, Seth gently coaxing him to move, and the two of them walk back home arm in arm like wounded soldiers. But these injuries won't heal.

Nate sits in the doorway for hours, staring down the empty street where the ambulance drove away with his Momma inside, staring and praying that it will reappear, that it was all a terrible mistake, that she is fine, that it was just in his head, but he is staring at nothing, hearing nothing, feeling nothing, and the red door is not a warm welcoming kiss from his Momma anymore but the threshold of a different life, dark, empty, without meaning.

LAKE FEAR

The grief that came to him afterward was total and blinding, the pain visceral, like razors in his blood. It hollowed him out. Seth had suffered profoundly too but he internalised for the sake of his brother, giving Nate his full attention, helping him through with infinite patience. But nothing Seth could say or do worked those first few months. The counsellors and social workers that came and went were like ghosts to Nate, indistinct and faceless, just voices echoing in his aching head. He would grind his teeth and stare at them unblinking if they came close to him, touched him, for he blamed them all, every last one of them. Where were they when they were really needed? Where were they when his Momma was alive but barely hanging on?

He had counted them up once during that terrible time: fourteen. Fourteen ghosts, fourteen lives that he would have traded in a heartbeat for just one more day with his Momma.

Life after that period had had few interludes of happiness. The ghosts had stopped visiting. Nate's self-harming habit spiked. He had been like a slow-motion tsunami, being engulfed from within.

He'd risen early one morning, careful not to wake Seth. He'd dressed in his running gear and headed for Tacoma Park, running until his lungs burned and his legs stiffened and spasmed with pain and cramps. He'd finally dropped down onto a stretch of damp grass and looked up at the cloudless blue sky. It had been spoiled by the spreading criss-cross pattern of jet contrails. And that's how he'd lain that late spring morning, staring into the eye of the sun, counting the seconds before each blink, longing to burn out his eyes, his memories, staring, unreachable, hiding in a narrow dark seam between *before* and *after*, unable and unwilling to move on, guilt spread over him like a suffocating blanket. He could have hidden the drugs, the hypo, emptied the booze down the pan, *talked to her.* But he hadn't, not really, just silently cleaned her up when she messed herself and watched, waited for the next time, until there was no next time.

Seth had appeared and stood over him, covering Nate's face with his shadow. Then he had reached one hand out to pull his brother up, the other hand contained two little pills to calm him, bring him back. Nate had spent a week wearing eye patches. His sight returned but his thoughts had never left.

The months merged into one long procession of desolate days and fearful nights until the day finally came when he and Seth packed their few personal items into a holdall, left the children's home and boarded a Greyhound for Fort Jackson.

Nate rubbed at his tired eyes and finally dragged his attention away from the house. He started up the engine and crept slowly past the lifeless bungalow. Once it was out of sight he made the short journey to Rumford cemetery.

Agents Patrick Cole and Joseph Eastoe had been watching the cemetery for seventy two hours, in shifts with two other local agents, and were cold and fidgety. Cole sat in the black Chrysler sedan with the heat cranked all the way up. He was covering access to the grounds from a discrete corner of the car park. One way in, one way out. Eastoe sat on a wooden stool, binoculars hung round his neck, in an old shed within the cemetery grounds. It was used for storing garden equipment, and had a good view of the target gravestone.

He was flapping his arms against his sides to generate warmth and occasionally peering out the dirty window to scan the headstone and surrounding grounds. They had been briefed directly by Byrd via a telephone conference call a few days earlier. He'd impressed on them the need for discretion, but above all for extreme caution.

'Your orders are not to approach the targets but to track them back to their current address.' Byrd hadn't been able to see the agents as he spoke, nor they him, but his voice had made it plain that they shouldn't dick with him.

Eastoe, the younger of the two agents, had frowned at this and cut across Byrd's discourse.

'We don't take them down if we get a chance?'

'You don't take them down, you don't approach them, you don't let them see you. You call me immediately if they show up and you follow them home. Period.'

'But if we're made do we –'

'Don't get made.'

Cole had said nothing during the call. He had studied the short briefing notes and images emailed to them by Byrd just before the conference call; he'd read enough to know that he'd just as soon track the brothers and hand the case back over to Byrd. But he worried about Eastoe. He had worked with him before. Young, ambitious, impetuous. He didn't like that last thing about him. It could get you in trouble, especially with the Byrd's of this world, but they were the nearest agents to the targets and Byrd had needed them in the drop zone within twelve hours. Cole had the engine running, listening to the radio tuned to nostalgia coming out of Ellsworth, when the Chevy Tahoe cruised through the cemetery gates. The four-wheel drive had blacked out windows but he sensed something about the vehicle, about its hesitancy. He made a call to Eastoe.

'Josh, it's Cole. Potential suspects driving toward your position in a blacked out Tahoe. It should be in view within five minutes. Confirm ID, over.'

'Copy that. Out.'

Eastoe watched the access road that circled and criss-crossed the cemetery grounds. His binoculars shook a little as he waited for the vehicle to show up. He withdrew a handkerchief from a pocket and dried his hands, withdrew his handgun from its shoulder holster, placed the gun, in the handkerchief, on a small wooden table in front of him. The vehicle stopped in front of the headstone, engine still running, billowing a steady stream of exhaust clouds into the cold still air. The driver's door opened. A huge tanned man with shaven head, dressed in black, got out. He looked round the cemetery grounds, eyes flashing momentarily, then past the shed where Eastoe stood in darkness. Eastoe slowly brought his handset to his mouth and spoke quietly into it without taking his eyes off the man.

'Positive ID Patrick, I see the younger brother, I see Nate. He's gotten out of the vehicle … gone round to the passenger side … opening the passenger door … bending down … turning … looks like he's talking to someone near the gravestone.'

'You see the brother?'

'Negative, but I guess that's who he's talking to.'

'Don't guess. Know. What's he doing now?'

'Still bending down behind the car door talking, maybe planting flowers on the grave or something. I need to get closer.'

'Negative! Make your way back here and we can wait for them to pass back out the exit. Then we follow them. Over.'

'I just want to ID Seth, then I'm on my way back. Out.'

Eastoe clicked off his handset before Cole could come back at him, picked up his gun, dried his hands once more on the handkerchief and let himself out of the shed door in a half crouch. He eased around the tall headstones, keeping Nate in view. Car headlights on a distant highway looked like a cheap gold necklace hanging just above the grounds of the cemetery, momentarily distracting Eastoe as he picked his way round the graves.

Nate still appeared to be talking but Eastoe couldn't see anyone else. He wondered whether the guy was talking to his dead mother. Grief does that sometimes.

No, the brother must still be sat in the car. That's who he's talking to. Work round behind and take them both down, easy does it, creep up on them as they're lost in conversation about their precious mother. What're they gonna do with a gun covering them? They're not superhuman. A charge sheet with these two on it'll look just fine on the resume.

He quietly closed on Nate, stealth aided by the dampening effect of the snow. Just a couple of large headstones between them now, and the cover of the open vehicle door.

And then he would just walk out in the open, tell them to lie face down, call his partner who'd arrive when it was all over to help him make the arrest and to witness the charge sheet. Eastoe's *charge sheet.*

He had gotten close enough now to hear Nate's muffled words, and then another voice, slight, seeming older.

God almighty, was Seth kneeling down next to Nate? Had he slipped out of the passenger side unnoticed as Eastoe had been manoeuvring around the gravestones?

Eastoe took the final few steps, aimed the gun at Nate's back and barked his order to *freeze* as he came from behind the vehicle but his feet slipped just a little on the slush giving Nate the briefest of time to rise from his haunches and grab the old man tending the grave next to his Momma's he had been talking to. Eastoe froze; *Jesus Christ where had the old man come from?*

Then Nate had a knife at the old man's throat and whispered something in his ear. Eastoe flashed a quick look into the passenger side of the vehicle, hoping he would find Seth sat there, maybe use him as leverage. *Empty. Jesus, but I'm in trouble.*

Nate's voice boomed in the silence of the cemetery.

'Throw the gun underhand over here asshole or I cut the old timer's throat.'

Eastoe was shocked by the suddenness with which he had lost control. He looked at Nate, then the old man, then back at Nate.

He was thinking of his next move, but he already knew, knew that if the old man suffered, he would be bumped back to desk duty.

'You've got five seconds, then I cut him and use him as a shield. You'll never hit me with that thing son. Then I'll reach you and cut off your balls and hang them over that headstone. Now fucking do it!'

Eastoe threw the gun into the snow next to Nate and raised his hands in compliance.

'You got a partner, Agent Dipshit? The suit in the black Chrysler in the car park?'

Eastoe nodded.

'Call him. Tell him you have me trussed up like a turkey and to bring the car round. Keep it brief. Tell him not to call back to base yet until you speak to him here. Send him a warning signal and I'll kill all three of you.'

Nate picked up the agent's gun, still holding the old man close, but he had loosened his grip and was speaking quietly to him again, calming him. Then he let him gently go and the man moved free and got into the passenger seat of Nate's SUV, his bony arms wrapped around his midriff. He was shaking a little, waiting for his next instruction from Nate.

Eastoe pulled out his handset and made the call.

'OK, good, now we both hunker down here and wait for your partner.'

Within a minute the black sedan sped towards them along the path. It came to a sliding stop on the wet snow. Cole got out, ran to the side of the car, and into the barrel of the gun in Nate's hand.

'Nice to see our law enforcement officers are as smart and brave as ever.'

Nate stood them apart and patted them down, removing Cole's gun and both agents' mobile handsets. Then he opened the trunk of their car, leaned in and smashed the handle of the gun first against the interior light and then the trunk's internal safety release switch.

'Figure you can keep each other warm while you're in there.'

He waved for the two agents to climb in and slammed the trunk shut once they were in. Cole hadn't said a word to his partner throughout, hadn't even looked at him.

Nate emptied the magazine from each of the guns, pocketed them, dropped the weapons onto the back seat. He pulled the keys from the ignition and dropped them into the snow.

He banged on the trunk as he passed it.

'Hey, you two behave in there.'

He left the cemetery grounds and made another brief detour to drop the old man at his lodgings before heading back to the cabin.

It was already turning dark. Heavy steel-grey clouds were being driven like a conveyor across the sky as Nate swung into the grounds of the cabin. The SUV's headlights cut two golden halos through the murk, lighting up the misty droplets that hung in the air like weightless spider's webs.

Once he'd reached the bottom of the dirt track he had called ahead to Seth to turn off the security. Seth stood at the open door now, shielding his eyes from the headlights and watching for any movement behind in case Nate had been followed.

Nate killed the engine and stepped out holding a large brown bag that gave off puffs of vapour in the cold air. He shouted across to Seth.

'I've brought you a present. Couldn't resist. Not that I don't like your cooking bro' but I figured chilli dogs would be highly welcome on a cold night.'

Seth walked out to meet him and they touched closed fists in a greeting.

'Miss me?'

'Yeah Nate, like a sore head.'

They went inside and Seth locked up and reset the alarm.

Nate spread the small mound of dogs on two plates as Seth pulled the tops off two Buds. They both dropped onto the sofa with their feast.

'So, tell me.'

'The old place is still there Seth, but it's different, y'know? Like it's had a makeover. Not good, man. All the life's been sucked out of it.'

'That's 'cause we're not there no more.'

Nate smiled when Seth said that.

Then he looked down into his lap, his eyes blinking.

'I visited Momma, Seth. I know you said not to but I did.'

Seth took the news calmly, just nodding as he ate. He knew there was nothing that would have stopped Nate visiting the graveside, not even the instructions of his big brother.

'And you were right, they were there waiting for me.'

Seth stopped chewing, his eyes narrowing, anxious to learn more.

'Two of them, but don't fret, I didn't nix 'em, they're keeping each other warm now in the trunk of their company rental.'

Seth's demeanour changed. He set the remains of his food back down onto the plate.

'I need to know everything, Nate, everything. Jesus, didn't I say…'

He had raised his voice but Nate raised his higher, drowning him out.

'Yeah man, you said. But I wanted to see Momma and that's an end to it.'

Nate spent the next ten minutes telling Seth the full story and Seth listened without interruption. At the end they both avoided eye contact at first, sat in silence, until Seth leaned across, placing a hand on Nate's arm and spoke quietly.

'You have a good talk with Momma?'
'Yeah Seth, I did.'
'Good for you Nate. Good for you.'

The next twenty four hours were spent reviewing and tightening security and intensely studying local news items on the web. Whoever was tracking them now knew they were likely to be close by. Seth considered moving on, or even up into Canada, ahead of plans. In the end he decided that they were just as safe where they were, for now.

26

Lake Fear community centre stood on an incline overlooking the east side of Lake Fear. The building dated back to 1906, its position chosen to give a view of the lake in the distance but escape the threat of flooding. Its lowly clapboard construction belied its importance to the community. It was the focal point for almost all social and civic events for the people of Lake Fear. It was full now. Sheriff Cooke and Earl Adams, the town mayor, stood talking while the crowd settled. Adams was the first to his feet.

'Alright folks, can I have your attention. Thank you for attending at short notice and please don't be alarmed. We are just being cautious. We have received a weather report from Portland Meteorological Office and Sheriff Cooke would like to outline a few measures we plan to put in place to make sure you all stay safe. Sheriff…'

'Thank you Mr Mayor.'

Cooke stood tall, and greeted them with a broad smile.

He spoke up with confidence; he knew many of them personally since he had been in the Sheriff's department at Lake Fear for over twelve years: eight as Deputy and four as Sheriff. The job had come naturally to him although taking up the post had been against all the advice he'd gotten from his colleagues back in Boston.

He had been in law enforcement since leaving college, moving quietly up the ranks until he announced to astonished colleagues that he was submitting an application for the Deputy spot in some tiny backwater called Lake Fear. He'd reached the stage in his life where he wanted a different challenge from chasing down drug-addled low-lifes. He wanted to raise a family in a community without the threat of teenage gangs and pimps and crime lords. He wanted to make a difference. He'd been following the vacancies posted in various places and had spotted the Deputy's job in a tiny box at the bottom of the Jobs77 website. He'd looked up Lake Fear on a map and he and Mary had done more research. Then they'd visited the small hamlet one weekend, and stayed over in a B and B overlooking the lake. They'd both loved what they saw and had decided that weekend that he would put in a serious application.

Four weeks later he was serving his notice and packing boxes. The change of pace and nature of policing had taken a while to adjust to and they'd both giggled like kids the first time he'd wore the three cornered hat to work. Inside six months Mary got pregnant with a son. They began living out their dreams, day in and day out.

'Friends, as Mayor Adams said, we received an alert yesterday from Portland Met concerning the forecast weather pattern for the next week or so. They've been playing around with all of that computer wizardry down in Casco Bay using a stack of our tax dollars and they reckon we could be due some early snow. Well, honestly? I reckon I could've told 'em that myself when I had to scrape a couple of inches off my truck this morning.'

Gentle laughter permeated the room, a reaction Cooke had been hoping for; it eased the tension.

'Bad as '98 Gene?'

It was Reverend Tate, *Good Jay* to pretty much everybody in Lake Fear. That year's weather event was etched into the memory of anyone that experienced it. The North American ice storm of January 1998 had hit a swathe of land from eastern Canada through northern New York and central Maine, laying down ice eight inches thick. It had knocked out power lines and phone lines, roads had been blocked, it'd brought the region to a standstill. Power outages for millions had lasted for days and for some, weeks. Thirty people had died. Military had been scrambled at the height of the event. But it had also brought people together like never before.

'...cause I've been there and done that one already.'

A few in the gathering laughed at that.

Rev Jay wasn't a native of Lake Fear, or even Oxford County, but after thirty three years the place had seeped into his bones. He loved the beauty of it, the solitude, but mostly the people. He had come from Newark where you could live next door to someone for years and not get to know their second name. In Lake Fear you knew things about people because you *wanted* to know, and then did something about it. Somebody's roof needed fixing, you pitched up with your toolbox and set to work alongside them.

Jay had done his service in Lincoln Park Christ the Shepherd in the seventies and had been ordained in nineteen seventy nine. The *Good* in Good Jay had come from the people of Lake Fear; it suited him just fine. He *felt* good here. Practically the whole town of residents were his congregation, and many seasonal visitors were too for the duration of their stay. The church elders had asked him more than once over the years if he wanted to move to a bigger parish in Oxford County but he had turned them down flat every time, until they had stopped asking. No, he had made his mind up that this was his home now, until his time was up.

Cooke nodded at Good Jay and smiled.

'Don't know that yet Jay. Met folk aren't sure where it will hit, could pass by north of us with just a little dusting, could hit heavy. Wind direction keeps changing so no one knows for sure. Many of you will remember Ninety Eight as I do but we'll be better prepared this time. I want to run through a few things that we all need to follow over the next few days, maybe a week at most.'

He counted off the points on his hands as he strode across the makeshift stage: mainly stay indoors, stay warm, stay in touch with other folk, especially with the singles in town.

'My Dep' and Kate here from *The Mariner* have produced a flyer for you so that you don't have to try remembering the main points from today, and of course if anything occurs to you afterwards please get in touch at the numbers on the sheet. Jess will be answering calls twenty four seven from now on.'

He nodded toward Jess on the front row and laughed quietly. She made a show of ignoring him all the same. Cooke handed back to Mayor Adams who closed the meeting with another prompt.

'Can I remind you good folk that we are celebrating the double centenary of our little town right here on Saturday evening starting six pm. We've got good food and beer and of course Marsha and the band will be entertaining us for the night.'

A whoop went up which developed into heavy applause and foot stomping.

'So let's not let a little snow get in the way, huh? What d'y'all say?'

The din echoed round the room, and Cooke thought, *Slick Willy does it again*.

But he felt anxious at the Mayor's playing down the risks. If the report was accurate the skies would dump a couple feet of snow all across the eastern seaboard.

The guy was playing to the crowd a little, maybe thinking ahead, planning on extending his tenure.

That wasn't something that Cooke himself felt constrained by. His own four year term was up in a few months' time, and he was thinking more and more of talking Mary into moving on, had even done some research, maybe back to the City, drown out the constant ache of loss, the constant reminder every time he passed the lake.

Maybe it didn't matter where he was anymore, maybe the pain would follow him wherever he went, but it wouldn't hurt to carry on looking.

27

The remote cabin stood at the end of a long narrow track that snaked around a copse of Fir and Acadia bush. Byrd lay still on a crust of snow, binoculars raised, watching thick black smoke from the chimney stack slowly billow and twist in the still dank air. Somebody was home. He had left the four-by-four at the bottom of the track and walked up the steep incline to his third target of the day. The others had turned out to be duds: a young family braving the elements building a giant snowman in the front yard, and an elderly couple packing up, preparing to leave. He was cold and pissed. Movement at the rear of the property caught his attention and he refocused the glasses to a more distant point. The guy was big, his features obscured behind the hood of a parka. He seemed to be un-spooling a length of rope. Then he reached up and tied one end to a cleat driven into the side of the cabin. Byrd studied the man as he attached the other end of the rope to a timber support of an outbuilding. He was six four at least, maybe two thirty pounds, fit looking. This could be either of the brothers but from this distance he couldn't fully ID him. Byrd tried to close in on the man's face but it remained in shadow. The man reached inside a pocket and pulled out a handful of large pegs and attached them to the rope. Then he suddenly looked up and over in Byrd's direction.

Byrd heard it too, behind him, the distant barks and whines of dogs.

Jesus, had the brothers acquired hunting dogs? The sounds were getting nearer but Byrd couldn't risk moving, the man was still looking his way. Clouds parted momentarily and a bright beam of sunshine lit up the grounds of the cabin, reflecting in all directions.

LAKE FEAR

The man lifted a hand to his face to shield his eyes as he continued to stare. Byrd was caught. The barks and yaps could only be a few hundred metres away now. He slowly lowered his glasses and dug his toes into the snow, gradually leveraging them, pulling himself back and away from his vantage point towards a small dip in the ground behind him. The man lowered his hand to his mouth then and gave out a piercing whistle that silenced the dogs, even from this distance. The silence was only momentary and then they resumed, louder and more excitedly. Byrd had reached the dip and he manoeuvred a knee underneath himself, easing his body around and reaching inside his jacket for his gun, ready to somehow defend himself against two trained and alert killers and a pack of hunting dogs. Not what he had in his plan.

The barks became almost deafening as they reached the beginning of the track just fifty metres or so below where Byrd knelt with arm raised, gun aimed. And then he heard voices, at least three men, maybe more. Local dialect.

Wrong targets.

He quickly holstered his weapon and dropped into a sitting position on the snow, nursing an imaginary leg injury, as dogs and hunters appeared in view. Two were dragging a sled with the still-bleeding carcass of a whitetail deer lashed to it, a trail of gore pooling in their boot-prints.

Byrd held up a hand as the hunters and dogs came upon him and circled him cautiously.

'Glad you showed up. Slipped and put my knee out, could use some assistance.'

Two of the hunters reached down and lifted Byrd to his feet. One, a teenager from his looks, spoke up.

'Where you headed Mister?'

Byrd lied.

'Trying to find the town of Mechanicsville.'

'On foot?'

'I got a little disoriented with all the snow, thought I'd get a better view up here, but I just managed to fall on my ass.'

'Disoriented? Hell does that mean? It's five miles east of here. You're some lost mister.'

'Like I say, map don't read right in the snow, can't spot the signs, y'know?'

He consciously mimicked their speech patterns to build favour with the strangers.

'You live there, 'cause you don't sound like you're from round here?'

'No, just visiting. Doing a little business.'

He instantly regretted that last bit, expecting them to ask him what that might be, frantically working up a plausible response, but they didn't ask. The young man asked about something else though, looking at Byrd, then back down the incline to the road.

'That your new Cherokee down below?'

Byrd was getting angry and he subconsciously patted his breast pocket, feeling for the gun.

'Rental. Think you might help me out here?'

The big man in the parka had made his way from the cabin now and all four hunters stood around Byrd. The dogs had fallen silent. The man pulled down his hood and spoke up. It wasn't Seth or Nate, none of them were, just a bunch of hillbillies dragging two hundred pounds of dead meat around.

'Quit yapping and help him down to his car Cam.'

Byrd nodded his appreciation at the man as the hunters lost interest in him and began making their way down to the cabin. Byrd leaned on the young hunter as they navigated back to Byrd's car. The boy was solid and seemed to grip Byrd a little too tightly. Then he spoke, in a quiet sly voice, as they walked out of earshot of the rest of them.

'Might get me one of those when I'm some big shot like you. Some *lost* big shot. Might wear me a suntan in November too.'

Byrd didn't respond. The car was just a few metres below them now.

'Thanks friend, I can make it from here.'

'Nope. Taking you all the way, *friend*.'

He said that last word like he had stepped in something bad.

'Didn't you hear my Pa tell me to take you to your car?'

The boy gripped Byrd even tighter and smiled, seemed to take pleasure in the knowledge that it had to be hurting a little, even through the padded jacket. Byrd sucked it up; he couldn't afford complications.

They dropped down the final few metres and the boy let go and turned away without more talk.

Byrd slammed the car door as the hunter returned the way he came. He could feel his heart beating, despite the gun in his pocket. He pulled out the map while silently screaming obscenities to himself in frustration.

Three more high value targets to go.

28

Car and truck headlights lit up Sheriff Cooke's driveway as their visitors all seemed to arrive at once. He had cleared the drive of snow hours earlier and scattered handfuls of salt down. It had stopped snowing but the sky looked heavy and bruised.

Cooke and Mary greeted each member of the town council, and other friends and colleagues, and steered them into the kitchen. Coffee and freshly baked pastries sat in the centre of the scrubbed wooden dining table. The council often met in informal places rather than the dull council building. Their favourite venue was Appleby's Bakery and Café, directly facing the public square of neat lawns and rose beds on South Main Street. They would carry plates of fresh cakes and a coffee pot outside on warm summer days and transact their business right there perched on the public benches, or else when it was cold they would sit at the indoor dining tables and take in the aroma of fresh baking and enjoy the warmth coming from the ovens. *Democracy in action* was what Mayor Adams called it. Cooke laughingly called it slacking on the job, but it worked in binding the policy makers together and in making them genuinely accessible to the residents who would often throw in their opinions when they crossed paths on meeting days.

Cooke had asked for this meeting to be held at his home since Mary had been feeling unwell on and off for a couple of days now and he wanted to keep an eye on her.

He quietly drifted between the small groups that had formed in the kitchen, shepherded them to the chairs around the large table.

Mayor Adams, Nancy Fisher the local nurse, Cooke's two Deputies Eddie Lister and Jordan Washington, Jessie his secretary, Kate, and Good Jay all sat now but the hubbub hadn't changed any.

Cooke tapped a spoon against a coffee mug and spoke up.

'Friends, can we get started? Mr Mayor, can you call session, we have a lot to get through.'

Adams formally called the meeting to order, then immediately handed back over to Cooke and reached for another piece of cheesecake.

'Thank you Earl. Glad you like the desert by the way.'

Adams licked at his fingers and gave a silent thumbs-up to Mary who was stood quietly in a corner of the kitchen.

'Following on from our session the other day at the centre, I want to discuss the detailed weather preparations before we get to the arrangements for Saturday's party. Now as you know most of the preps are in place, in response to the original weather report from Portland Met. And also, that report was updated thirty six hours ago which suggested that the worst of it would pass a hundred miles north of us. Well those geniuses have changed their minds again. Now it looks like it's blowing back our way and, you guessed it, looks like it's gonna hit late Saturday night or early Sunday morning. Maybe as much as two feet of snow and wind chill of minus ten. Least, that's for now, but there's a great big swirl gonna pass right over us which apparently doesn't make for accurate weather forecasting. Kind've like the eye of the storm. It's gonna come and go, whiteout one minute and clear the next. I'd like us to go through the plans one more time just to be sure, starting with you Kate on public information.'

Kate Miller had been the editor of *The Mariner* for almost fifteen years. Her Father for longer still before that. It often occurred to her that the title *editor* was a little overblown given her usual daily business of interviews, taking photographs, attending council and community meetings, producing copy, and helping Helen, her girl Friday, with the printing. She even manhandled the papers into the vans for distribution sometimes when help was short. Maybe *dogsbody* was a better title. *The Mariner* was important to her though. It was more than a job, it had become her life. She was the glue for the community.

The paper itself had been in production since the early 1830s when the first single sheet covering a flooding event in Lake Fear had been given out freely to the hundred or so residents at the time. It had dispensed advice to farmers, millers and loggers about insurance claims; it had alerted them to the pool of free second hand furniture donated by other residents to replace their damaged stuff. The paper was owned now by a syndicate of locals, businesses and a small insurance company in Farmington.

Kate felt the weight of that history on her shoulders at times and treated her stories with respect and professionalism no matter how lowly. The paper was often used for public information and announcements too, it had become one of the primary means of emergency alerts, like now, that and the town website she kept going. She ran through the plans to the group.

'One flyer has already been distributed to all our residents and copies left in stores, public buildings and voluntary groups. I've got a second one here drafted by Ed and myself and it's ready to go out immediately after this meeting.'

She circulated copies around the table.

'I've also updated the website and copied in some of our neighbours in Rumford, Mechanicsville and Newry, see if we might share a little good practice so to speak. Finally, Good Jay here has done a piece in the flyer reminding people about our buddy system to make sure all the housebound, infirm and singles out there are contacted at least once a day by their nominated buddy during the worst of it.'

Jordan turned and grabbed hold of Good Jay's arm.

'That *singles list* include me Jay? 'Cause if it does, you're way out of date, friend.'

A couple of jeers sounded around the table and Eddie, his partner, threw one back about his border collie not counting.

'OK, good job Kate, Jay.'

He turned to Eddie and Jordan.

'OK Deputies, you're up.'

Eddie pulled a single sheet of paper from his top pocket and then reached for his new reading glasses. Jordan nudged Earl.

'Chairman, can I ask since when did Spongebob Squarepants get invited to join the meeting?'

Eddie ignored him and set to with his report.

'Got a few items here Mr Mayor if the stand-up has finished. First up, snomos. We got all four serviced, fuelled and parked up under tarp in Denis's Yard.'

Denis Curran ran the local gas station and car-repair workshop and he often let the authorities use a spare piece of land that sat back off the main highway into Lake Fear.

'Second, emergency aid. I raided the rainy-day fund and got a couple dozen mobile oil heaters and around twenty cases of food rations. They're stored at the community centre and ready for issue. We've also put a warning in the flyer reminding people to check that their generators are working. Third, we've set up an emergency shelter in the old prefab adjacent to the clinic in case anyone's home is affected or we come across any out-of-towners looking for a place to stay. Last up, Gene, we've set up the 24/7 emergency number with a rota that kicks in at midnight Saturday. Kate has all that covered in the flyer too.'

'What about the Tucker?'

Cooke meant the old Tucker Sno-Cat, an ancient narrow-width snow groomer that they hadn't used in a couple of years. It had been parked up at the back of Curran's garage along with several rusting, write-offs.

'Could get Denis to give it the once over and fuel it up, if you think it's necessary?'

'Think it could be. Ask Denis to bring it around to the car park at the clinic once he's looked at it.'

'Done.'

'Ed, could you contact some of our friends from the hunting fraternity? We need eyes and ears out there.'

'Clem, Lou, Sky? They do you Gene?'

'Yep, they'll do … if they can stay sober long enough. Oh and secure Scarlett, for the duration. We don't need some hard-man trying his luck in these conditions.'

Scarlett was the two-person cable car that ran from the centre of town down to the east side of the lake, stopping off at several levels along the way. It had been installed in the nineties as part of a push for extra visitor dollars. The town had christened it *Scarlett* when it got painted a deep ruby red by the locals in its first year; it had stayed that way.

Cooke finally turned to Nancy Fisher, a former state-registered nurse. They were lucky to have a fully-fledged nurse in such a small haven as Lake Fear. Most rural communities relied on enthusiastic amateurs who received training via the Emergency Medical Services Programme. Nancy, and Janice her young assistant, donated their time voluntarily.

'What about our medical support, Nance?'

'All in order. We've set up four extra beds at the clinic. Janice and I have put together some extra emergency med bags for you to issue to your teams when out on duty during the worst of it. Any serious cases that we can't handle, we can call in air ambulance from Rumford.'

The clinic was an old building, originally built for negotiating and transacting timber and livestock prices and now given over for local health care. It had been re-used that often over the years it wasn't even annotated on the town map.

Cooke nodded and smiled and looked around the table. He caught sight of Mary quietly leaving the room with a hand across her mouth.

'OK, good work. I'm setting up command and control at the community centre as a temporary measure until my office is repaired.'

His small office in town had suffered from a burst water pipe the previous day. It had flooded, leaving him and his Deputies working for now out of their trucks or else at home.

'Let's hope we won't need any of this. Let me hand you back to Earl to cover Saturday's celebratory arrangements and I'll rejoin you later.'

He left the room and went looking for his wife.

She was stood at the sink in the bathroom wiping her forehead with a cloth. Cooke came up behind her and held her closely by her waist.

'OK honey?'

'Just one of my headaches, that's all. I've taken a couple of Advil, I'll be fine.'

'Why don't you ask Nancy for something a little stronger?'

'No Gene, that isn't necessary.'

Cooke turned her around.

'You sure? Maybe you're coming down with something?'

'Listen, I'm OK, really. Go back to your meeting and give me a few minutes. I'll be back in a minute to freshen up the coffee.'

The fact was she knew she was coming down with something, but she'd decided not to share it with Gene. Not yet. Not until the tests came through.

The meeting broke up and Mary had made up some doggy bags with the remaining cakes and pastries and she handed them out as the group left. Nancy came up behind Jay and linked arms with him as they navigated the slippery driveway.

'Jay, can I give you a ride home?'

Jay had walked the half mile or so to Sheriff Cooke's home, enjoying the numbing effects of the wind. Now it was colder still.

'Sure Nance, appreciate it.'

Ten minutes later, they arrived outside his small bungalow. Jay made to get out of the car but Nancy grabbed his arm.

'Not so fast. This happens every time with my dates. Would a hug kill you Jay?'

He seemed reluctant but she pulled him across to her anyway.

'Thought so. The mints don't fool me.'

Jay said nothing at first, just sat listening to the drone of the car engine as they sat parked up outside his home.

'Sounds like your muffler's holed Nancy.'

'Don't do that Jay. How long have you been off the wagon?'

He looked down, hands fidgeting, then looked out the side window toward his house. He had forgotten to switch on his lights before he'd left for the meeting and the place looked empty, abandoned.

He looked away and back down, the darkened sight of the home that he had shared with Grace for over thirty four years too much to bear. It seemed a hostile place now, filled with taunting, pain-filled memories.

'Not long. A couple of weeks that's all. Honestly Nancy, just a short time. And it won't last, I promise you that.'

'Oh Jay, tell me why.'

'You know why. I miss her. I'm lonely and I miss her.'

Jay had lost his wife to cancer the previous year and he had taken to the bottle to ease the pain.

'I mean why go back to it when you came off it? You have been off it haven't you Jay?'

'Yeah I've been off it ... mostly. It blots the memory when I need it to, that's all, but I can stop it when I want to.'

'But we've been through this, Jay, you know the dangers with your condition.'

He held his shaking hands up in submission.

'I know Nance, I know. Listen, I'd better go, my pooch will be bustin' to pee by now.'

He reached for the handle but Nancy grabbed him a second time.

'Will you promise me that you'll pour what's left down the sink?'

He hesitated.

'Jay?'

'I'll do it. I'll do it for you Nance. Goodnight girl.'

But he didn't, not right away at least. He filled a tumbler of his favourite Colonel Lee first, *then* he tipped what little remained of the bottle into the sink. The full case of bottles that he had stored on a shelf in the pantry he left undisturbed.

29

The lake that gave the town its name covered around twenty square miles. The surrounding forest and countryside in which the town was set covered a further twenty, crisscrossed with narrow hunting trails overhung with invasive buckthorn and dogwood. There were clearer routes too for hikers and bikers that often opened up onto picnic areas and camp sites. Timber cabins populated the whole area; they belonged to local hunters or out-of-towners.

Eddie and Jordan had parked up in a small, dirt, car park south east of the lake and had walked the hundred or so metres down a narrow muddy path to one cabin that had been bought and converted into a hunting lodge shared by three local hunter-guides.

Eddie knocked and he and Jordan walked into the cabin. It looked like a Disney set; old, stained deer antlers pinned to the walls, stuffed animals wearing rictus grins mounted on stands and in glass cases, and pictures of all three hunters, in action, pinned everywhere. A fire was crackling and spitting in the hearth adding wood smoke to the stagnant air of Oxford Flake pipe tobacco. A radio dialled to country droned from a high shelf.

All three men, Clem Wade, Sky Noonan and Lou Tennent, were sat sipping coffee and reading their daily newspapers. Two young huskies lay curled up at Tennent's feet got up and went to the deputies, sniffed at their boots and whined for attention.

Eddie spoke up as all three hunters lowered their papers and looked across.

'Morning boys. Hey Jordan, we got Davy and both his Crocketts here this morning.'

Clem put his coffee mug down, got to his feet and arched his back.

'Looking for something deputies? Come here for some help on

how to find your own dicks?'

Sky picked up an old rag and threw it to Jordan.

'To clean your boots – wouldn't want to have to buy you both a new pair from my tax dollars.'

All three hunters barked out loud with laughter. Ed and Jordan grinned and nodded at each other.

'Y'know, I don't doubt your advice Clem, you've a lot of good experience in finding dicks. You found these two well enough.'

The fact was, despite the barbed banter, they were long-standing friends.

Lou poured fresh coffee into two chipped mugs and placed them in front of the deputies. Eddie and Jordan dragged up a chair and all five sat round a huge wooden table. Eddie continued.

'Boys, we're in for some rough weather over the coming days.'

'No shit, Colombo.'

'Not what *I'm* saying Clem, just what *Portland Met* is saying. We could use your assistance – unless you're planning to fly to Miami for the winter?'

Jordan intervened.

'They don't plan to do that, Ed. These three wouldn't get passed airport security with their ugly mugs; they just *look* guilty of *something* nasty wouldn't you say?'

'You were saying, Ed, before your faithful puppy butted in?'

'The Sheriff's office would be obliged if you would be our eyes and ears, so to speak, when the weather hits. Y'know, just snomo round town and some of the other main routes, look out for anyone in trouble.'

Eddie pulled out a map of Lake Fear, unfolded it and smoothed it out on the table.

'Just during the worst of it, that's all.'

'Like a stalker, Ed? You want us to become official stalkers?'

'Something like that, but this time without hiding in the bushes waiting for a pretty girl to climb out of the bath.'

'Eyes and ears? Sounds like something Cookey would say.'

'Yep he said it. Will you do it?'

All three hunters were third generation residents of Lake Fear. They knew every hill, every undulation, and they knew what bad weather could do. They'd all been around in ninety eight, helped with the med runs, circulate food and fuel, helped to stoke fires and clear roofs. And they would do it again. The old boys looked at one another.

'No girls in the bath eh? So, what's in it for us Ed?'

'Well now Clem, I let you carry on driving around on public highways with that pile of shit you call a truck, without having it hauled away as a death trap.'

'Seems fair to me.'

Ed looked across at Sky and Lou.

'You two in?'

Lou spoke up.

'Hell, course we'll do it.'

All five leaned over the map, talked over plans to cover the ground, to keep everyone safe.

Sheriff Cooke and Harvey Munce one of the young technicians from the council offices had been working on setting up a central comms facility within the community centre all morning. Cooke had wanted it located there, at least temporarily, until his office had been fixed; most of the Sheriff's office and other officials would be coming along there Saturday night.

Kate and a handful of other volunteers were there too, decorating the place up in readiness for the anniversary shindig.

Cooke had manhandled a desk and a couple of chairs into a corner of the large room to create a makeshift workstation, wheeled a mobile plastic screen round it.

Cooke stood now, looking over the shoulder of Harvey as he tuned in and tested a dozen or so walkie-talkies with the base station.

'Harvey, can you config them for both one-to-one and one-to-many communications so that I can broadcast to everyone on the line or just reach say one or two of my men?'

'Sure thing Chief. I've used 800 MHz frequency with maximum range. That should give you up to about ten kilometres from handset to base unit and between handsets.'

'OK, thanks Harve. Chances are we won't need them, but we *do* need to be prepared.'

'Party still going ahead then Chief?'

'It is for now but we plan to start a little earlier in the evening, give folk a chance to leave early and get home before the worst of the snow hits. Wouldn't want to have to deal with a crisis on our centenary weekend.'

Mary Cooke walked through the entrance to Rumford General carrying a bag of fruit and a bunch of fresh cut flowers. She headed for the orthopaedic ward. Her Mother was still recovering after hip surgery and was expected to be in for a few more days yet. She checked her watch. An hour with her mother and then she could catch her own medical appointment.

30

Seth was sat at the laptop making notes of roughneck job vacancies on the Kodiak Oil website when Nate quietly appeared at his side. He just stood there looking over Seth's shoulder but not taking any of the information in as his brother studied the oil jobs.

Seth looked up.

'You OK, man? You sleeping OK?'

Nate looked heavy-lidded and pale.

'Been better. Bed's way too small, what are they, fucking midgets living here? All the cabins hereabouts and we have to choose one that's owned by Santa's little helpers.'

'Thought you liked it here?'

Nate rubbed at his neck and eased his head around in a few small arcs.

'Naw, I do man, just a little stir crazy y'know? I feel like a prisoner.'

'We've been over this Nate; I'm none too keen to bump into any locals who might start asking questions about the two of us.'

'Yeah, I get it but I'm beginning to feel like a goddamn vampire Seth, sleeping in the day and going out in the dark.'

Seth didn't answer, just continued to study the screen and fill up his notepad. Nate went to the large picture window and stared out at the bleak landscape beyond the front yard. Occasional flakes of snow drifted down, adding to the ghostly cast on the lawn. Seth had told him about a snow storm brewing along the eastern seaboard. It mirrored his mood. Nate's breath fogged the window. He reached out and drew jagged lines on the pane of glass.

'Am I the bear Seth?'

Seth stopped tapping at the keyboard and looked up again.

'Are you what, man?'

LAKE FEAR

'I'm the bear aren't I? Y'know, in my dreams? That's what I think. I'm the big grizzly, eating everything up in its way.'

The jagged lines became more acute as his finger sped up like a seismograph tracking an emerging earthquake.

'I think the bear means something. How could it not when it won't leave me the hell alone? I think…'

He stopped mid-sentence.

'I'm listening, Nate.'

But Nate just scrubbed out his line drawing and turned and headed for the kitchen.

'Aw screw it bro'.'

Seth caught hold of Nate's arm as he passed.

'Listen Nate, why don't you go catch us some fresh meat later. I'm seeing on the local news that there's plenty of white-tails. But kit up and don't stray too far.'

Nate's mood seemed to lighten immediately.

'Done and done, Seth.'

Rudy Miller had finally given in to Rhya, his sixty five pound three year old Siberian husky, and had taken her out on a run on Eagle trail. He was on his mountain bike, she running free alongside, heading down to the eastern edge of the lake. He had an hour to kill before he planned to shower up and go along to the town party. The day was already losing what little light there was and he had switched on an LED light fixed to the handlebars of his bike. He knew the route, figured he could cover it blindfolded, but the snow had covered the potholes along the path making it risky going at any speed.

A vicious north-westerly ice-laden wind was blowing in from the gulf of Maine, making it hard going. Rudy slowed, pulled his scarf up higher over his face, as Rhya raced ahead. He called out her name; he didn't like to lose sight of her in this desolate spot, in these conditions. Snow had already begun to fall again. Kate's flyer had said there could be a couple feet of snow, unbelievable at this time of year. Still, he kind of looked forward to it.

Rudy had lived here all of his life, attracted by the natural surroundings. He hated the city, only venturing into Augusta or Portland when he had to.

His Father had a small boat repair and hire business that Rudy helped to run during the summer season. It would be his soon if his father's threats to finally retire were true. Rudy had been developing a business of his own, breeding huskies, and Rhya was from his very first litter three years earlier. He'd sold some to local hunters, which had helped pay for food and vet fees. He had a small cabin a mile or so from the lake that he had helped build himself on a piece of land he had bought and cleared with the help of his Father and friends. Leaving home and setting up in the cabin on his own had come easy – apart from the washing and ironing, which he often dropped off with his mother each Friday evening.

He and Rhya lived the perfect life, hiking and riding and hunting and fishing together. So when Rhya had padded round the cabin giving quiet but distinct growls, Rudy had known he wasn't going to get to stay in no matter the weather.

He'd pulled on his weatherproofs, grabbed an extra flashlight, checked his cell battery and opened the door, nearly being knocked down by her as he did. She was already twenty metres down the path by the time he had jumped on his mountain bike and given chase.

Nate felt the power of the elements coursing through his veins. He had walked through a narrow wooded trail and along a path that wound its way between the lake and the town of Lake Fear, and not seen a soul. He had earlier tracked a white-tail deer for about a half mile, but it had gotten spooked and bolted away. The light had almost faded and snow had begun to fall again. He knew he had to head back soon. Seth had given him the speech, again, about steering clear of town and avoiding anyone else that might be out hunting. Nate had taken Seth's crossbow since he had yet to re-tune his own long bow following a string break during target practice. It had been a while since he had handled one of these but it felt light and balanced in his hands. Nate had welcomed the chance to be outdoors on his own. He'd been having the night tremors the last couple nights. The bear had figured in both of them. The bear and the teeth and the voices. *Why wouldn't it just leave him the hell alone?*

Nate was angry. Tired and angry.

The dog came upon him suddenly, in the dim light. A low growl turned into short deep barks, hair raised on its broad back, huge head thrust forward with teeth bared, and then it lunged.

It was reflex action from Nate as he whipped the crossbow off his shoulder, loaded the bolt, fired, all in less than three seconds. The big dog went down onto its side, mewling and snapping at the entry wound, trying to remove the bolt, the source of its pain.

Nate reloaded. He went toward the dog as it lay on its side panting and whining. He aimed the bow at the animal's head to finish it, put it out of its misery, when a shout froze him in his stooped position.

'Hey Rhya, come here girl.'

The wind was picking up and Rudy knew enough to realise the risks of being out here in these conditions.

He was about to call her again when he heard a faint whining just on the edge of his hearing.

'Rhya. Is that you girl?'

He rode hard towards the source of the sound, his flashlight waving left and right across the narrow path, but he didn't hear her any more. He was getting anxious now as the snow blew in more heavily. His yelling sounded flat, like he was in a box somehow, the deepening level of snow damping out the noise. He rode on deeper into the trail, only yards now from the lake edge, and then he saw her, lying still. He couldn't figure it out; why would she lie down on her side on a night like this? He dropped his bike and ran to her, grabbing her huge furry head. He could feel it rather than see it, warm, sticky, even through his gloves. She was panting heavily, an uneven choking sound. Even then he didn't piece things together, just thought that she had somehow got caught up in an oil spill and licked at herself, swallowed some of it. *Maybe from one of the shitty boats that plagued the area, maybe someone moving an outboard had leaked its oil. But why wasn't she responding?* And then her tongue rolled fully out and a gout of blood spilled from her mouth and he knew then she was in trouble. She was haemorrhaging massively. He examined her more carefully now and saw a bolt lodged in her side.

Jesus, why would anyone be hunting around here at this time of night, and how the hell could they mistake a dog, even a big dog like Rhya, for game?

A slow scraping noise pulled his attention away from his dog.

'Hey, who's out there? The hell are you doing? You shot my dog you asshole. You'd better show yourself or I'm going straight back into town to alert the Sheriff's office. You'll do time for this, man, I'll see to it.'

Nate came from behind a nearby bush and stood in front of Rudy.

'Sorry man, I thought it was wild.'

Rudy jumped back involuntarily, shocked by the size of the man in front of him, size bulked up still further by protective clothes.

Rudy played his flashlight onto Nate, onto the high-end crossbow in his hand. He summoned the courage to speak out.

'Wild? Wearing a collar?'

'Didn't see no collar. I thought it was going to attack me, was just defending myself.'

'You defended yourself with *that* thing? I have to report this man, I want your name.'

'No friend, you can't do that. I'm telling you it was just an accident, leave it at that OK?'

'Not OK, she's my dog you –'

'Please son, I have to ask you to walk away and keep this between us. I'll deal with your dog. I can pay you for the inconvenience.'

'*Inconvenience*; are you *serious*? I don't want your *money*. You can't go round shooting pets for Chrissake; you can't just call it an *inconvenience*. Sorry but I have to report this. They'll tear up your license, if you even have one.'

Nate advanced on the boy to frighten him, to intimidate him into silence. That was all.

The dog growled and sprang at Nate then, taking him by surprise as it pounced from his left and sunk its teeth into his arm, its sheer weight bringing Nate to his knees. Nate's body tensed with the pain, pressurising his trigger hand and releasing the bolt. Nate saw the boy drop as he grappled with the dog, saw him clutch at his throat.

Rudy just saw a blur of motion, heard a muffled thud, felt a puff of wind on his cheek. The bolt tore into his neck, knocking him backward onto the freezing ground. Pain arrived in waves that engulfed his head like a huge wall falling down on him, then numbness at his extremities, vision blurring. He had to get up, move, either that or close his eyes, right here, for the last time.

The dog snapped and clawed at Nate, its blood still flowing from the wound in its side, a dark stain spreading down its silvery coat. Nate's initial shock gave way to fury and he reached for his knife and slashed at the dog, its squeals and growls sounding like whistles from its damaged lungs. He caught it finally and buried the knife in its neck. It shivered and howled as Nate pushed its bloodied body off him. Finally it stopped fighting, back legs twitching in time with its final gasps.

Nate got to his feet and raced to where the boy had gone down. He pulled out his flashlight and frantically searched the hedges and undergrowth for him but there was just a bloody smear and cycle tracks leading away towards town. Nate sprinted ahead along the path, expecting to see the boy lying on the ground but the path was clear. He ran for fifty metres more, counting the regular patches of blood, some turned a muddy red mix amongst fresh tyre tracks, with the dawning realisation that the boy had escaped on his bicycle. He shouted in fury into the night.

'The hell are you, you asshole! It was an accident, just an accident that's all!'

He stopped and stood, pondering his next move, dry washing his face with his gloved hands, rubbing at his arm which was bruised but not pierced through his thick jacket.

He caught sight of a small silver object on the ground at his feet in the thin beam of his flashlight. He bent and picked up Rudy's cell phone.

It was still switched on and Nate pressed last number redial and held the phone close. An automated message kicked in.

'This is the Lake Fear Sheriff's Office. The office is closed now until seven am tomorrow morning. If you have an emergency please ring ....'

A sickening sensation flushed through Nate, like falling through space. A fear took hold of him. His and Seth's future were about to unravel before it even had a chance to develop. He had to call Seth, warn him. Then he had to reach town and find the Sheriff's office, delete that message in case the boy had described him. He also had to hope that the boy would die before he could tell his tale. Nate had felled big game with a single arrow in the past; he was shocked the boy was still upright. *No, he had to be dead, or close to it. The chance that the boy could reach town with a hole in his neck, describe Nate, was slim to none. It was that message he had to prioritise.*

He nervously pressed the transmit button on his walkie-talkie.

'Seth, it's me man. We have a situation to deal with 'bro, over … Seth, pick up man it's me over…'

Seth came on the line. He sounded a little drowsy as though he had just woken up.

'Explain the word *situation* to me Nate.'

'I shot someone Seth. Jesus, it was an accident. I shot a kid with the crossbow.'

'Oh man, oh Christ Nate. How is he? And where the hell are you?'

'I'm on a trail close to the lake. I don't know the boy's status Seth; he took off on his bicycle. He dropped his cell phone and I pressed redial. He'd called the Sheriff's office but just got an answer machine. I have to go into town Seth, see if I can delete that message before someone ID's us.'

'No, listen Nate, come back here. We'll figure out what to do when you get back.'

'No man, I've got this. I can wipe that tape before they know it's there.'

'And the kid?'

'Seth, you need to fire up the cell-jammer, stop any calls coming in or out of the area.'

'Nate, what about the kid?'

'I'm on it Seth. I'll call you in a couple hours, out.'

Nate switched off his handset before Seth got the chance to call again. Nate knew what he had to do next; he just needed the time to do it.

Seth tried calling Nate back but just got static. He raced out to the storage room next to the cabin, triggering the floods and bathing the site in white light. He screwed up his eyes against the glare and ran, slipping and sliding on the slick surface. He threw open one of the doors and sprinted inside.

He'd included the jammer on Manny's list to disrupt calls between agents on their tail, if any showed up. He hadn't planned on using it against the locals.

In the cabin Seth's handset picked up movement inside the security perimeter, and buzzed its warning. The device lay balanced on one arm of the sofa. It was loud enough to be heard anywhere in the cabin. But Seth had run out fast. From the storage room he knew nothing of the alarm.

He fired up the jammer and turned the range to max. It gave out a low hum as it scrambled any signals within eight kilometres. He had to get after Nate before all this escalated out of control. If it hadn't already.

Snow lay six inches deep now and was still coming down heavy. Seth lost his footing and slipped as he headed back to the cabin.

A voice bellowed from the shadows by the cabin as he was getting to his feet.

'Get back down on the ground, face in the snow, spread your arms and legs, just like a snow angel.'

Seth froze. He realised, too late, that he had let security slip, just for a moment, but that had been long enough. He dropped down and spread-eagled. His knife was strapped to his left leg, but no gun. He heard a single pair of feet crunch through the snow towards him; he lay unmoving on the freezing ground.

'I've got my SIG pointed at the back of your head and that is one huge target, so please, no tricks. OK?

Byrd recognised this guy, the older one.

'Where's your brother? Where's Nate?'

'He ain't here.'

'That so? Well that much I know already; I watched him take off a couple hours ago. Where to and how long before he returns is what I want to know.'

Byrd was crouching low and spinning slowly around as he spoke, watching for movement from the nearby forest, but visibility was down to just a dozen metres. Even with the floods on.

'Listen man, I need to get up. I'm gonna die of hyperthermia down here. If you want information, I can do that best while I'm still alive. Plus my brother is out there somewhere right now, maybe with your head in his cross hairs.'

Byrd knew he was an easy target should Nate show up and spot them out in the open like this.

'OK, but one step at a time. Do what I tell you when I tell you. One step out of line, I'll shoot you, wait for your brother to show up. Now get up on one knee and keep your arms high and wide. But first lose the knife.'

Seth twisted his head and looked at Byrd, caught sight of his watch, then back at his tanned face. Tag-man.

Byrd slow-walked Seth back into the cabin and slammed the door shut behind them. He bolted it and wedged a chair under the handle. Seth was stood with his arms raised, his back to Byrd.

'Head on through the back there, Seth.'

Byrd took him into the rear of the cabin, gun trained on him as he tested the back door, then he marched him back into the main room and closed the shutters.

Seth stood in the centre of the room as Byrd lowered himself into an armchair, gun raised.

'You two are some pieces of work y'know? From what I've read you're too damned smart for all this bullshit. Now your brother, he's a whole other story, so one question man, why the hell d'you put up with your brother, let him keep dragging you down?'

'You got family?'

Seth answered quietly, conversationally.

'I got an ex that's bleeding me dry.'

'My brother is all I have. He's all I've ever really had. The whole world just ignored us, man, just drove on by.'

'So he's your Huckleberry and you're his.'

'We look out for each other no matter what.'

It was just small-talk.

Seth knew Tag-man hadn't chased them six thousand miles to talk about family ties; the real questions would come soon enough.

'My employers don't appreciate your games back in Iraq, Mr Stone; you and your brother made a lot of noise over there.'

'Who knew, man?'

'They're trying to turn a new clean page out there and you and your brother are one big ugly smudge.'

'We served our Country.'

'That you did, can't deny that, but your files… '

'You think you know me and my brother? You don't know dick.'

'Wrong. I know a lot about the two of you.'

'You know what the files say, that's all.'

'That's all I need to know. That and the fact that my bosses have a very strong and urgent preference for you both to leave the game.'

'You sound like the mafia, nothing personal. It's just business, that it? And that doesn't bother you any?'

'Bother me?'

Byrd hesitated.

'Honest truth? Yeah it bothers me, bothers the hell out of me. But we all got to eat right? And I have my orders.'

'Howd' ya find us?'

'That I can't say, friend. Trade secrets. I tell you that, I'd have to kill you. Sorry, it's what I do. Find bad people, and then take them out of the game. We found the two screw-ups in the cemetery by the way. Made me pee my pants, but it confirmed I was on the right track y'know?'

'We don't get a judge to decide what happens to us? We stopped living in America?'

'Oh grow up Seth. You know the script by now. Listen, buddy, enough of the chat. We have one of your acquaintances, a certain Emanuel Garcia, in custody. Says he met with you a while back. Traded some stuff. You know him Seth? You got the stuff here?'

Seth still had his back to Byrd, still had his arms in the air almost touching the cabin ceiling.

'Manny? Yeah I know him.'

'I need the plastic, Seth. I can't let you keep that. That's a whole lot of death right there. Oh, plus the cell of course. My bosses really want that cell.'

Now Seth knew the reason for the foreplay.

Tag-man knew about the cell phone footage they'd stashed. What he didn't know yet was *how* they'd found out. Seth played dumb until he could think of an angle.

'Wanna enlighten me on what cell you're talking about?'

'I wish I knew. You got me on that one, but I think *you* know which one. Y'see I work for some smart people, Seth. *Very* smart. They say you got a cell they want, I gotta believe you have it, gotta believe it's important to them.'

Seth knew he had nowhere to go with this. He had to play for time. hope Nate was close by and would somehow work up a plan.

'We get into trouble from time to time, me and my brother, so I like to know that people will be on our side when the time comes, y'know?'

'It connected to the so called friendly-fire incident? Kandahar?'

'The what?'

Donna had done her homework and had faxed Byrd a copy of an *eyes only* internal report of the incident in two thousand and seven. Three of the four team members had been wiped out by a second US missile. Only Seth Stone survived. The report referred to head-cam footage found on the dead soldiers confirming the termination of their target insurgents following the first missile strike. It also mentioned images captured on the head-cam found on one of the soldiers containing evidence of further *independent footage* that was taken of events that day and was yet to be retrieved. *Very Mysterious.*

The second missile that levelled the building and took out most of the soldiers with it was recorded as *comms error*. Byrd believed that like he believed in the tooth fairy.

'Operation Cleankill?'

'That's classified.'

'Oh man, you want to see my badge? I've waded up to my neck in the same cess pit you and your brother have, Seth. I know how these things work.'

Seth shook his head.

'Don't know anything about that.'

'Whatever, man, but now's the time to tell. You got the cell here?'

Seth kept quiet.

'Jeez, am I stuttering? I said is it here?'

'Nope.'

Byrd quietly stood and peered out through a gap in the window shutters but all was in darkness. He wondered about Nate, where he might be. He was the sort to come crashing through the windows, all guns blazing, if he suspected anything. Byrd peered out again before pushing the shutters tight.

'Want me to shoot him first Seth? I will, man, and if I have to I'll let you watch your precious brother die. Want that?'

Seth shook his head, kept silent.

Byrd rubbed a knuckle against his stubble. He was running out of time. Nate would show up soon.

'Gonna give you one last chance, Seth. Feel I owe you that much given your blood tours. Where's the cell?'

'It's like I said.'

Byrd had thought about this moment. The moment of truth, when you can't fake it, when you have to take a decision about the path you take. This was the fork in the road; he had to ignore where he'd been, just focus on where he might be headed.

'Listen Seth, let's quit the bullshit OK? I have a proposition for you and your brother. They want the cell, that much isn't negotiable. Honest to God, they'll never stop hunting the both of you down for it now that you're out of theatre. But I don't have to give them *you*.'

'I give you the cell and you'd let us walk?'

'We discuss a plan.'

Seth was baffled by this man. He'd tracked them down and now he was offering a trade. *Was it just a ploy?*

'Why would you do that?'

Byrd sat back in the armchair. *Did he even know the answer to that question?*

He gazed at Seth.

'You just have to trust me. I'm all you have and the alternative isn't good for you. Some of my associates would be giving you a head bath by now.'

But Seth was all out of trust, especially trusting someone that had travelled thousands of miles and traced them to a cabin in the wilderness. That didn't mean that he couldn't play along, though, wait for his moment, wait for Nate to show up.

'OK man. I'm in.'

'Good choice, Seth. Just need you to turn around for me.'

Seth turned his back on Byrd, his hands still raised.

Byrd quietly closed the distance to Seth's back, cocking the hammer on his gun as he did.

'My name is Byrd by the way. I think you should know me by name.'

The handgun made a deep thud in the confined space of the cabin, even with the suppressor on. Seth collapsed like a tall building after a quake. Byrd knelt down and spoke into Seth's ear as he lay groaning, blood spilling onto the polished wooden floor.

'That's Byrd with a 'y', OK? Most people spell it with an 'i', but I enjoy correcting them when they do.'

As he reached the end of the dirt track and entered the edge of town, Nate could see lights hanging like a string of coloured beads. A large colourful canvas was draped high up, between two street lights across the street, advertising the upcoming double centenary dance. He did a quick three-sixty to take in his surroundings. The street was empty. More coloured lights were attached to a small structure to his right and as he concentrated his focus he could make out a two-seater cable car through the window. He traced the direction of the cable and its support stanchions as they ran over a small ravine and down to the lake. He turned and headed into town.

The lights reflected off the fresh snow collected on roofs, tree branches and low walls, creating a magical postcard setting that jarred with Nate's mood.

He hadn't come across the boy, though the tyre marks were still visible. He reached an intersection marking out the main streets of Lake Fear. Here the bike tracks had become obliterated by traffic. He had already memorised the street map of Lake Fear they'd discovered in one of the racks at the cabin. The Sheriff's office was just a few streets away from where Nate was now standing. He had to 'dust' that voice message and then find and disable the landline exchange. He had to stop any comms in or out of the town until he was sure that Seth and he were safe and on their way out of the area; state firepower he did not want to face.

It would take a couple of hours at most, back to Seth, relocate out of the area. Get the plan back on track.

Messy but it could work.

He had to believe that the kid was dead for all of that to work. He didn't want that, not at all, but what could he do? It was an honest to God accident. Why was he such a magnet for trouble?

He didn't have Seth to take charge so he had to stay calm, think straight, act like Seth would. Seth wasn't here, only him.

He was the number one brother now.

Act 3

Sometimes even to live is an act of courage
Lucius Annaeus Seneca

Lake Fear
November 27th, 2010
7.05 PM

31

Lake Fear community centre was almost full now. The music was at its height when a scream went up. Then another. They weren't heard throughout the room over the din of music and laughter and general hum of chatter.
And then a tray of glasses crashed to the floor.
 The front entrance door had been opened and thick smears of darkening blood and slush trailed along the ground after the boy.
 Rudy Miller stood to the side of the dance floor looking on at the revellers with a vacant stare. He shook like he was trying to match the rhythm of the dancing. From some angles he wasn't doing a bad job of it, and then he moved a hand away from his throat and collapsed to the floor. The volume of the screams went up a few notches and drowned out the band. Someone switched the sound system off and screams were all that were heard.
 Sheriff Cooke ran to the boy who was convulsing now, blood pumping down his neck and shoulders. He pushed his knee into the wound and held it there, all the while frantically looking around him for something to stem the flow of blood. Cooke screamed an instruction then to Ed his Deputy who was looking on pained and confused.
 'Pass me that table cloth.'
 Ed whipped the cloth from a nearby table sending drinks scattering to the floor and passed it to Cooke who rammed it hard into the wound in Rudy's neck, leaving the bolt in place. But he

already knew that the boy was lost.

The group cleared a path then as the boy's mother and father went to him, kneeling beside him, mother reaching out and grabbing one of her boy's hands, kneading it, talking to him, wiping his forehead, wiping his long floppy wet fringe away from his bloodied face, as the other townsfolk stared. Then Nancy Fisher appeared and almost wrestled the mother away.

'Get his feet above his head.'

Ed grabbed a nearby chair and manoeuvred it close to Rudy's legs and he and Cooke gently raised them and placed them on the seat. She checked his pulse and gave a slight shake of her head. She turned to the Deputy.

'Call air ambulance right now, the boy has to get to Rumford.'

She had to shout over the rising din of the townsfolk. Ed spun away from the group and pulled out his cell to make the call.

Rudy seemed to be stiffening in their hands, his breaths just tiny puffs of air that bubbled up blood between his grey lips. Cooke took off his jacket, folded it and placed it under Rudy's head.

'Gene, I think we're losing him. I think we're losing our boy.'

Nancy felt Rudy's pulse again but there was nothing. She leaned over him, wiped away the blood and then began pumping his chest, breathing into his mouth, pumping, breathing, the boy's mother looking on, shaking and finally collapsing into the arms of her husband.

Ed ran back into the gathering still fiddling with his cell.

'Can anyone get a cell signal? Mine's out.'

Hands were thrust into pockets and purses to retrieve cell phones but none could get a signal. Cooke got his out and tried firing it up.

'Nope, mine's out too. The transmitter must be down. Try the landline.'

Ed raced to the office at the back of the centre.

Nancy's actions became more laboured but she persisted, wiping away Rudy's blood from her own mouth after each effort.

Ed leaned his head into the main room then, the telephone cradled against his chest as he shouted over the hubbub to Cooke.

'Sheriff, the air ambulance is grounded; the snowstorm's about to hit.'

Cooke nodded and reached across to Nancy, trying to still her actions, but she knocked him away and continued until her arms ached with the effort. Then she stopped and let her hands dangle limply in place on the boy's chest, staring down at him, willing him to breath, willing his heart to start up again. But he was beyond that now. She lifted her hands and walked away from the gathering, walked over to Rudy's father still holding his wife in shaking arms as she lay passed out on a sofa in the corner of the room.

Some of the townsfolk stood around the boy, their heads bowed, others stepped away weeping in each other's arms.

Ed had collected another cloth and began placing it over the boy as Good Jay leaned over the body making the sign of the cross.

'Heck Sheriff, is that a hunting bolt in his neck?'

Sky Noonan had noticed the tiny steel bolt before Rudy had been fully covered. Cooke had spotted it earlier but didn't want to have to deal with the questions it triggered, not in front of the whole town. But it was too late now. Others spoke up, grief quickly turning to anger.

'Hunters, Sheriff? D'yer think hunters could have done this?'

Mayor Adam's voice shook as he tried to rationalise what he saw. The group gathered around them had gone silent as they waited for an answer from Cooke. He ignored the question at first, just focussed on carefully wrapping up the boy, thinking of the loss of someone so young, thinking of his own boy. He had helped them pull up the pale, bloated body out of the freezing water, helped wrap him, just like he was doing now, had held him that way, grief and the sickening bobbing motion of the lake bringing up burning bile, an arm around his shoulder, a voice coaxing him to let go, let the medics take him, and the finality had hit him as he'd handed the white bundle up to a pair of waiting arms, then he had dropped back heavily, back into the boat, and welcomed the numbing darkness that had engulfed him.

He looked up at the people he had come to care for, not just serve, as they waited for him to make sense of what they had witnessed.
Finally he spoke.
'Could be,' he murmured. 'Most likely an accident.'
The boy's mother had come round now, still held by her husband. They stood on the edge of the group, looking down, at Cooke, at the body of their son.
Mrs Miller spoke, her voice broken.
'Wrong place, wrong time, is that what you're saying Gene? Please don't tell me that. Not that.'
Questions seemed to come from everyone in the group.
'But why would they leave the boy to find his own way back here Sheriff? Wouldn't they have brought him in?'
'Maybe they don't even know they hit him, maybe they were after game, and hit him by accident and don't know it.'
'But don't you go see what you aimed at?'
Then Sky spoke across all of them, voice spiked with anger.
'We need to get a search team out there and find these assholes.'
Lou Tennent cut in then.
'Where's his dog? Where's Rhya? He never went anywhere without her?'
Cooke tried to close down the speculations that were running like wildfire around the room but it was a losing battle. He left them venting their growing anger, took Ed and Jordan to one side.

LAKE FEAR

They began discussing their next move.

Byrd stood over Seth writhing on the floor, gun trained on Seth's head.

'Jeez, man-up a little will you? Don't groan so much. It's not life threatening, just a nice neat low calibre shot. A little painful I know, but you'll live; I missed the bone and arteries. Now put your hands around your back and I'll take a look at the damage.'

Seth reached both hands behind him as Byrd slipped a nylon tie over his wrists and hitched it tight, then tied his ankles.

'Afraid you're likely to limp for a while. I just needed to emphasize to you early on in proceedings that I am not dicking around here. The plan I spoke of is *my* plan. Not *your* plan or *our* plan, just *mine*, OK?'

He frisked Seth but found nothing. He missed the short length of thin wire tucked into Seth's waistband.

'OK, now let's take a look at that leg.'

The bullet had passed through Seth's left leg, clean shot. Blood was seeping from the wound and pooling underneath, but Seth's focus was on the wire and how he might use it to free himself.

'Don't go anywhere, Seth, OK? I'm just gonna find something to fix that. You see your tax dollars working here? I clean up my own mess. I can't have you bleeding to death until we discuss my plan.'

Seth let out a low groan for effect, but he had already zoned out the pain and was planning a route out of this. Byrd manhandled him and propped him against an armchair before going in search of material to plug Seth's wound. As soon as Seth heard Byrd opening cupboards and drawers in the kitchen he reached for the lining of his combats. He found the thin sliver of wire and looped a finger around one of the small wooden end pieces, pulling it, drawing it loose. He held one end of the wire and then looped it over the plastic tie binding his hands, catching the other end. Then he began to work on the tie.

Byrd called out to Seth from the kitchen.

'Say, these Maine folk are very neat and tidy round here; I can't find a friggin' ... ah, this ought to do the trick.'

Byrd came into the room, and knelt beside Seth. He had a length of rope and a towel in one hand and a small med kit in the other. Out of reach of Seth, he pulled his gun from the shoulder holster and placed it on a nearby table.

'Like they say in the commercials, man, I hope you're worth it. Here, open up. Advil. It's all I could find.'

He dropped the two painkillers into Seth's open mouth. He continued talking as he straightened Seth's damaged leg and ripped away a piece of the combats to reveal the wound. He wiped at it with the towel then balled it up and rammed it against the entrance wound, then began looping a length of washing line around Seth's thigh, holding the towel in place, attention momentarily focused on the task.

'Y'know, they exploit our madness, Seth, don't you think? They trade on our desensitised, inhuman madness. They train us to point guns at people and not really think, not really care about pulling the trigger. We sleep-walk to the edge for them and, sometimes, step over the line. They train us to ignore that deadly momentary silence before the impact, when you look them in the eyes just before they cry out, just before they drop ...'

Seth struck as Byrd philosophised. He brought his freed hands around front fast, clapping his huge palms together against each side of Byrd's head. The impact was immediate as the pressure ruptured Byrd's right eardrum.

Byrd fell forward toward Seth's lap but Seth was already on the move, using brute force to pull the tie from his ankles and getting up on his one good leg, all the while holding in his head the position of the gun. It was perched on the end of a coffee table just a few feet away at ten o'clock. He kicked Byrd sideways as he reached forward to grasp it.

His fingers were about to curl around the handle when a shaft of pain doubled him up. Byrd had got in a blow, shockingly hard, almost square on Seth's leg injury. Seth fell on Byrd but Byrd was quick and scrambled sideways, slipping on the pool of blood but keeping going. The gun fell, slid under the table. Byrd dived for the gun but Seth grabbed at his legs and hauled him back. He slammed a fist against Byrd's temple as he pitched backward toward Seth. Byrd howled with the pain; Seth had got his damaged ear again. Byrd kicked out, sending Seth face forward onto the wooden floor, the tiny sliver of wire coming loose from the back of Seth's pants as he did. Byrd grabbed for it, pulled it taught between his hands. Seth turned to face Byrd but Byrd was kneeling, balanced and ready; he thrust forward, wire held firm between his hands, the sharp deadly thread biting into his own knuckles as he caught Seth's throat.

Byrd screamed out, 'No Seth, it doesn't have to be like this.'

But Seth ignored the words, just fought on. The wire sliced into Seth's skin as he lunged forward, made a grab for Byrd's hands to stop the pressure before it tore through into his windpipe. The momentum carried them both over, crashing into the table. Byrd hung on, forcing his hands closer together, cutting deeper, until Seth could taste his own blood at the back of his throat.

His vision began to cloud, a thousand tiny stars swimming in front of him. He leaned back to ease the pressure, and then he caught sight of the gun. He gathered his leg underneath him and drove forward, reaching out and grasping at the handle, pushing Byrd along with him, the wire cutting deeper. Still Byrd clung on. Seth had the gun but his vision was greying out. Almost blind he felt for Byrd's body, flipped the safety, and with strength draining from him he pulled the trigger.

He felt Byrd's body jerk hard as the bullet entered his body, felt its energy, sensed the damage. Byrd finally loosened his grip on the wire, his arms dropping away from Seth, his body sliding to the floor through Seth's hands.

Nate found what he was looking for in the middle of a row of neatly-maintained shops: a glass-fronted premises that had *Lake Fear Sheriff's Office* stencilled on the picture window in large gold lettering. It was in darkness. The street was empty. Nate went down a small alleyway that ran along the length of the row of buildings. At the back of the office was a window. He slid the blade of his knife into the window frame and carefully flipped the catch, raised the sash slowly, climbed in, stepped down onto sodden carpet. There was no noisy alarm to contend with.

He found himself in a small kitchen just off the main office. A single empty cell occupied the corner of the room, the door swung open. Nate quickly scanned the room and saw a tiny red light blinking on the land-phone sat on the reception desk. Nate went over and lifted the handset, listened in to the handful of messages. Most were trivial local matters. He deleted each of them quickly until he reached the boy's garbled voice. There was no description of him after all, nothing much of anything really, just a choked out attempt at his name: *Rudy*. Then another, maybe his dog's name, Nate couldn't make that out. Then the line went dead. He nodded to himself, allowing some slight relief as he deleted the message. He examined the handset more closely. It had a *Verizon* tag embedded in it, with the number of the phone and the telephone number of their tech support. He made a call.

He looked around the office then, a little jealousy creeping in. A large notice board with various codes and instructions was covered over with dozens of photographs. A tall, handsome-featured man wearing Sheriff's badge seemed to be in most of them, often with at least one Deputy at his side. A few had a pretty woman and a small boy in them. The boy looked familiar.

The place was a little untidy, lived in, homely. Nate hadn't known too much of that. The unyielding rules of the barracks, and before that the chaos and confusion of home life, but nothing that remotely passed for *homely*. He noticed a small wooden name tag on a desk: *Sheriff Gene Cooke*. The name struck a chord for Nate. That dead kid out on the lake, his name had been *Cooke*. Nate walked closer to the notice board and shone his flashlight at the photo of the small boy. It was him, the boy that'd drowned, he was the Sheriff's son. So the Sheriff knew what deep loss was like. Well so did he..

He walked to the desk and opened a drawer. He wasn't even sure why. He knew he had little time, but he was drawn to it, drawn to Cooke's little universe, drawn to the need to learn more, share in it somehow. He casually flicked through the bits of detritus there: a penknife with all the tools, a cheap flashlight, a bunch of coloured highlight markers, a keychain with a half dozen keys, maybe to the cell door, who knew? Nate suddenly got a strange compulsion to go and sit in the cell. And he did just that.

In his mind he was a local now, had been involved in a little altercation in the local bar, nothing too serious, something about a card game maybe, bit of under the table action that had escalated to a little pushing and shoving, just a drunken play-fight, drawn a little blood. The Sheriff had picked him up and carried him in there to sleep it off, hadn't even locked the bars.

Nate switched off his flashlight and sat there for a few seconds in complete darkness, part of the strange scenario he was building for himself.

After a while he shook his head and walked back into the main office, the strange thoughts that had been swirling now dissipating.

He went back to the open drawer to close it and noticed a small padded envelope with Cooke's name and home address on it wedged in a letter rack on the desk. He picked it up and examined it. Empty. He tucked it inside his jacket and closed the drawer, unsure of why he had kept it.

He retraced his steps and climbed back out of the window, lowered it back into position.

Next he had to track down the location of the telephone substation.

He wasn't aware that he'd already triggered a silent alert on Sheriff Cooke's pager.

32

Seth gathered up the med kit and headed for the bathroom.

He tore off the rope holding the towel in place and inspected his leg more closely. The bullet has passed straight through, blood from the wound already clotting. He dabbed at the entrance and exit with clean water and a towel, then pushed hard at both. He used his other hand to rummage through the med box, finally grabbing and uncapping a small bottle of peroxide and spilling it freely over both ends of the wound. He bound the towel around his leg and retied the rope. He looked up into the mirror. His face and neck were swollen and bruised, his throat had several weeping, blood-soaked welts that he bathed, revealing shallow cuts. He tore another strip of towelling, doused it in peroxide, wrapped it round his throat. He tied it in front and pulled up and fastened the collar of his sweats to hold it secure. He ran out of the bathroom, grabbed the walkie-talkie, hit the transmit button, spoke, listened, but Nate still had his handset switched off. Seth ran to a wooden cabinet, pulling out each drawer, searching for a pen and some paper. He found a pencil and a child's empty school notebook. He tore out a page, quickly scribbling a few lines and then left it on the table top. He pulled on his parka and ran awkwardly to the storeroom. Ten minutes later he tore out of the cabin grounds at full throttle, swerving the snomo into the freezing headwind. He charged toward town.

Nate found the substation easily enough; the phone company's tech support had been very helpful to what they'd thought had been an enquiry from Lake Fear's Sheriff's office. The building was a small single storey brick construction, partially concealed by bushes and a timber fence. An electrical hazard sign was fixed to the front of the building. Nate walked up to the front door and kicked at the deadlock, his weight behind his boot, shattering the wooden frame with one blow. He'd taken out a similar installation once before, that time using a few short bursts of automatic fire. Here he had his hunting knife and a crossbow. The wiring was behind a metal cage secured with a small padlock. He kicked at this with his heel until it gave, then swung the gate open and entered the cramped space. He was faced with a thousand coloured wires in looped bundles. He went to work with his knife.

Five minutes later he backed up out of the confines of the substation and stood back, looking up and beyond the structure. Then he brought his glasses up and traced the power supply cable from the station to the junction box fastened to a timber pole twenty metres away. From there he tracked its journey across town. It ran north to south following the route of the main road in and out of Lake Fear. He put away the glasses and headed back to the dirt path.

Cooke stood in the centre of the group looking into their still-shocked faces. He had a piece of paper in his hand with a list of names grouped into three teams that he and Ed had put together.

Nancy, Jordan, and Rudy's Mother had taken the boy's body to the clinic. Rudy's father had stayed. Cooke's own wife had already left for home.

Cooke's pager vibrated just as he was about to speak and he quickly read the automated message. It was an alert; the security alarm had tripped at the station. Probably the flood messing up the electrics. He switched the pager off and refocused his attention on the group. They were still buzzing with anger and adrenaline, and too much alcohol and caffeine.

'OK friends, can I have your attention now please. I'm gonna call out the names of some of you to assist with a local search.

The rest of you need to pack up and go to your homes while we respond to this emergency. The snowfall is getting heavier and storm-winds are already hitting the coast at Jonesport, from what Eddie learned from his call to Rumford earlier.

He glanced at Jess.

'You might want to get an update from 'em.'

Jessie went into the back office as Cooke continued.

'Remember the drill spelled out in Kate's newsletter. Let us deal with matters arising tonight. Be assured that we will find the culprits who did this.'

Cooke read out a handful of names who moved to form a small circle on the edge of the bar area. The rest of the townsfolk collected their belongings and filed out of the centre in near silence. Cooke reached out to many of them as they passed, shaking hands and reaching around shoulders. He shared their shock and grief.

Ed appeared beside Cooke with a large map of the town and surrounding area and a couple of spare waterproofs and laid them on the table. Cooke smoothed out the map and spoke up.

'I want three teams of two. I'll lead one with Clem and Tom, Eddie will lead the second team with Sky, and Jordan and Lou you'll make the third. The community centre here'll be our home base for now.'

He took out a pen and drew three circles covering the East of the town, the West all the way down to the lake, and the town centre itself. Rudy's father stood, arms folded across his chest, rocking a bit as if to soothe himself, listening to Cooke outline the arrangements. He shuffled forward. His face was ashen but there was a firmness in his voice.

'I'm going too Gene. I want to help find the assholes that did this to my boy.'

'Prefer you to stay here, Tom.'

'I'm going Sheriff.'

Cooke capitulated. He knew he'd have wanted to do the same thing if it had been his son.

'Good enough Tom. You can join my team.'

He now swung his gaze across all of them.

'Just a quick preliminary search. If you find them, radio in. I want them arrested and brought back here. Call in every thirty minutes; Jess here will cover the calls and relay messages to each team. I want you all back here, no matter what, by ten pm.'

'Using the winter kit Gene?'

That was Lou.

'Some of us. The latest weather report has us down for maybe a couple of feet by the early hours. So I don't want anyone wandering too far. Ed, Jordan, you take the snomos parked up in Denis's yard, ride two up, but be careful. Me, Clem and Tom will be in Town on foot. Waterproofs are here for those that need 'em. OK, let's go. And remember to call in every half hour.'

They filed out of the centre, collecting kit on their way out. Jess came back into the room.

'Landlines are down Gene, I can't get a tone.'

The wind buffeted Seth as he sped along an open stretch of countryside, each jolt causing a sharp spike of pain in his leg. The rope had loosened and the wound had begun to bleed again. He was travelling at speed, steering by the glow of a single headlight, unable to see the rocks and gullies that lay beneath the covering of snow. He could see faint lights now, shifting in and out of view through the falling snow, about a mile ahead: the beginning of the town's boundary. The sight spurred him on and he pulled on the throttle sending the snomo screaming across the packed surface. If he could find Nate and get back to the cabin, they could clear out and head north, find a new location. He had already half-formed their next moves. He was running through them in his mind as he raced ahead, when a rock appeared in his path, then another, part of a low escarpment, just its top visible above the deepening level of snow. He hit the rock full on, sending him head first over the handlebars of the snomo. The snow partially softened the impact but his shoulder and legs hit the stony summit of the ridge causing fresh stabs of pain from his damaged knee. He tried to right himself but a sickening nausea gripped him. He reached inside his jacket and pulled out his walkie-talkie.

'Nate, you hear me? Come in Nate, over.'

He felt light-headed now, a blackness descending on him until he slowly slid sideways into the snow. He lay there, unconscious, on his side, snow already beginning to cover his body, the hiss of his handset still in his hand, unheard and unanswered.

Nate was back on the path jogging down to the lake. That would take maybe fifteen more minutes and then he'd have another twenty minute hike across country back to the cabin. He had plenty of time to prepare for Seth's extreme verbals.

The noise of a motor engine broke into his thoughts. He dropped low looking for the source. A tiny single light flashed across the sky in the distance. It sounded like a motorcycle or a snomo, maybe a mile away. He increased his pace. He needed to get off this path as soon as he could and into the wooded stretch. If someone was after him, he would be safer amongst the trees. He finally reached the end of the path, and the lake shore.

The boy's dog lay where he had left it, on its side, partially covered in snow. He thought about lifting it and dragging it into the lake but that would take time. Besides, he would leave an obvious trail, and that animal had to be sixty or seventy pounds. Then he thought of covering it up completely, making it look like a snow drift, but the noise of the engine was getting louder, he wouldn't have time. He had no choice but to leave it there and reach the cabin as fast as he could. He darted into the woods just as the beam of the snomo's headlamp lit up the final stretch of path leading down to the water's edge.

He stopped and hid behind the nearest tree, watching as the two men got off the snomo and shone their flashlights down at the dead dog. One knelt down examining it while the other played his flashlight along the path and beyond. The one kneeling pulled out a walkie-talkie. Nate slipped away into the darkness, leaving the two men. He quietly put fifty metres between himself and them before he risked picking up the pace again. He had about two miles left, through thick bush and deep snow, before he reached the cabin.

Ed Lister spoke into the walkie-talkie as he and Sky nervously scanned the area.

'Sheriff, it's Ed, copy?'

Cooke responded immediately.

'Copy Eddie over.'

'We found the dog Sheriff. She's dead, has a crossbow bolt in her and slash wounds to her neck like someone took a butcher's knife to her. Jesus she's a mess. There's a lot of footprints here too Sheriff. One set look fresh, they go off into the woods. Do you want us to follow them, over?'

'Negative Ed, do not follow, repeat, do not follow. Take some pictures on your cell and go back to base. I think we need to go over things in light of your discovery, it doesn't look like an accident anymore, over.'

'Copy Sheriff. We'll take the East route back, it's a little quicker. Getting' pretty bad out here.'

'Copy that. Be careful of the ridge, Ed. Out.'

Sky gripped Ed's jacket and pressed his face into his back as the snomo cut across a flat open field. Then they headed south, the open ground gradually becoming enclosed on one side as a sharp ridge emerged and reared up almost vertically for over two hundred metres. The path narrowed here and Ed slowed the snomo to a walking pace. Then he stopped completely as he tried to make out what lay in front of them.

Nate finally reached the grounds of the cabin, breathless and sweating despite the cold. The floods had been tripped. He crouched down and glassed the cabin looking for trouble. A single light was on in the main living area, the rest in darkness. The snomo was gone, a fresh set of tracks leading off past the edge of the forest and into the open fields heading across country towards town.

He circled the cabin listening for voices, looking for movement. There was none. He kept low, crossbow armed and ready as he walked towards the front of the cabin. He could see the churned up snow and footprints now as he neared the door. He crept the last few steps and stood silently, holding his heavy breathing as he peered into the cabin through a tiny gap in the window shutters. Furniture was strewn around the room. A body lay motionless at the side of the table. Pools of blood seemed everywhere on the wooden floor.

The sight of the body shocked Nate into action. He dropped the bow, pulled out his knife and turned, hitting the door with his full weight, shattering the frame and sending him full tilt into the room. He hit the floor and rolled, his mind taking in the room like flash photography, his voice screaming out the name of his brother. He went towards the body, skidding in pools of blood, already concluding that the scale and shape was wrong. This wasn't Seth. He grabbed the still body and turned it over, shining his flashlight at the bloodied features of a stranger's face.

'What the hell?'

He dropped the body and shouted out for his brother, running into each of the rooms. Finally he noticed the scribbled note on the table top;

Nate, switch on your walkie-talkie! Security breached. On my way to town to pick you up. Contact me ASAP. Injured but NOT life-threatening.
Seth.

Hell, he had switched off his handset after he'd contacted Seth earlier and had forgotten to switch it back on. He did so now and slammed his finger on the transmit button.

'Seth it's Nate over, Seth come in, over … Seth it's me bro, copy?'

The message went unanswered. He continued calling Seth as he ran back out of the cabin and into the storage room, throwing the door wide and scanning the equipment on the wooden trestle shelves before him. He took off his coat and shrugged into a protective vest and then put it back on. He reached for the rifle and began loading it. He threw more ammunition and kit into a rucksack along with arrows, plastic, a med kit. He grabbed his bow. He hadn't yet retuned it but it would have to do; he might need it as backup in this temperature. He tried the walkie-talkie again.

'Seth, respond, over … I'm on my way and following your tracks. I'm at your back, man.'

He ran to the back of the cabin and ripped off the tarp covering the old snomo. It was a battered Yamaha Phazer that seemed to be held together with rust. Two ignition keys were tied together with a piece of wire and looped around the handlebars. He grabbed them, straddled the machine, kick-started the engine. It turned over but failed to start. Nate lowered his head close to the fuel tank and swung the machine from side to side listening for the slosh of gas. Nothing. He jumped off and ran to the rear of the storeroom, returning seconds later with a small container of fuel. He emptied it into the tank, gas washing over the machine as he raced against time. He threw the empty tank to the ground and tried kick-starting again. The engine fired up briefly then died. He was about to try again when a voice sounded from his walkie-talkie, flooding Nate with palpable relief that quickly turned to horror.

'This is Deputy Edward Lister please confirm your name and location over.'

Nate was stupefied.

Had they captured Seth? Or had they just stumbled upon their frequency?

'What the fuck is your game friend and why are you on this frequency? Where is my brother?'

'I say again, this is Deputy Sheriff Lister. We've come across an injured male on east shore track and we are taking him into town to get medical treatment. Please confirm your name and position, over.'

Nate recognised the location that the Deputy had mentioned. He could reach it in around fifteen minutes on the snomo.

'Not important. Is my brother secure, over?'

'If by secure you mean his condition, that I can't confirm. He's breathing steadily, has a strong enough pulse, but beyond that, it's for the medics to handle. Give me your location and we will pick you up, you can see your brother for yourself, over.'

Nate pondered this information. If Seth had a regular pulse, he was pretty sure he could get to him in time and treat him himself, maybe get him to a medic out of the area.

'That doesn't work for me, friend. I want you to put him back where you found him, leave him secure and leave the area. I'll take care of my brother myself.'

'Negative. I am instructing you to –'

Nate switched off the handset and sat perched on the snowmobile. He had to think. He was having that falling sensation again. The note had said the injuries were *not life threatening*. But what were the circumstances now? Had Seth come off the snomo and caused more harm to himself? Would it be for the better if he let them treat Seth and only then rescue him? But once all of the evening's trouble fully emerged, wouldn't they put him under arrest? Jesus. Nate pounded his fingers into his forehead. No, he had to act now before they got a fix on things. If he could get Seth away from his captors, get him away from here, he could get him medical help. Jesus, this was all *his* fault? He pulled the map of Lake Fear from his pocket, frantically looking for a hospital building or a clinic. There was no such facility marked on this map. *The man had said he was taking Seth into town. Did he mean the town of Lake Fear or further afield? Seth had been following Nate, had to be part way into Lake Fear, they had to be going that way now, especially in these conditions, but where?*

He tried kick-starting the engine again and it finally spluttered into life. He ran back to the bench and threw the rucksack, rifle and bow across his back. He ran back to the cabin, looking frantically for the final thing he needed. The ready-bag lay on a cabinet. He grabbed it and threw a strap over one shoulder, then returned to the snomo and sped off following Seth's tracks. He had to make this right. He had to recover his brother and make it all right.

33

'Sheriff, it's Ed, copy.'

'Copy Eddie, Cooke here, over.'

'Sheriff, we've come across an injured male close to east shore. Seems he trashed his snomo on Howard Ridge, think he was heading towards town. He has wounds to his leg and neck, needs urgent medical help. I found dog-tags on him Sheriff, and he was armed. He's army, over.'

'Copy all that, Ed. Get him to the clinic for now, over.'

'Can you get Scarlett down to us, at level two of the ride? It'd be a lot easier than trying to get this guy all the way back on the snomo, over.'

'Affirmative Ed. I'll call Jordan, get him to send her down. Can you reach the station, over?'

'Think so Gene, I can just about see it from our position. Sky's tying the guy to me right now. He'll walk alongside us, then ride the snomo to the top station. We'll be able to bring the guy in by sky-ride, over.'

'Copy that Ed. Me, Clem and Tom are just leaving Bethel Road. I'll call ahead to Nancy and meet you at the clinic, over.'

'Sheriff, that's not all. There's another unidentified male out here, says he's the brother of the injured male. I intercepted a walkie-talkie message. He ain't friendly, Gene. Think they could be responsible for the trouble, over?'

'I'd say they're prime candidates. Get the injured one back here and we'll worry about the brother later.'

Cooke, Clem and Tom Miller had just made it back to the clinic. They were helping Jordan and Lou clear a narrow path through the snow on the access road when Lister's snomo appeared out of the frozen gloom, Sky walking a little way behind, slip-sliding on the snow. All five men ran to the vehicle, shocked by what they saw.

'He's a big 'un Gene. Damned near dragged me off a couple of times.'

Ed had Seth tied to his body and had ridden the short journey from the sky-ride station, pitching and swaying on every bend he hit. Sky had tried to keep up, initially holding Seth in place, but the snow had made his footing awkward and unsteady.

Cooke untied the injured man while the others held him upright on the seat. Seth was shaking and slipping in and out of consciousness, his skin cool to the touch, pale and clammy and showing signs of hypothermia. It took four of them to lift Seth and carry him to the front door of the clinic. Nancy was waiting there with a gurney and fully-loaded saline drip. She covered Seth with an insulating blanket and wheeled him into the consulting rooms. She'd already changed into her white uniform and was totally focused on her task. She inserted a cannula into a vein and released the valve, then checked his pulse. It was running fast. She carefully located a thermometer under his tongue and strapped a blood pressure cuff over his right arm, took his temperature. The thermometer read thirty two degrees.

She had heard about all the trouble, but to her this stranger was a patient first and foremost, and he needed urgent care. The four men had followed Nancy into the small med room, jostling for space to stand. Cooke spoke up first as they all stared down at the stranger.

'You heard from his brother?'

Cooke was deeply troubled about all of the recent developments: the death of Rudy and his dog, the comms down, the appearance of an unidentified and injured male here, another one out there somewhere. And the storm was getting wilder by the hour.

The community would look to him for leadership. His thoughts were to question the injured man and try to capture the other male. Then at least he'd feel like he had his hand on the tiller.

'Not since that first contact.'

Cooke nodded, thoughts swirling in his mind. He reached out.

'I'll take his walkie-talkie in case the brother calls again.'

The man was out cold now and Cooke took each of Seth's arms and secured them tightly to the frame of the gurney with Velcro straps that hung there. He then secured Seth's good leg. He leaned in closer to inspect Seth's damaged leg, lifting it a little. Nancy looked at Cooke and frowned.

'It's necessary Nance, just as a precaution, until we find out what the hell is going on in our town. That look like a bullet wound to you? Looks like entry and exit to me.'

She never answered him directly.

'I'll take it from here. He needs fluids, quickly. I just hope the saline doesn't screw up the clotting process. I need to get his core temperature up, and his blood pressure is ninety over sixty. Not a good combination.'

Nancy leant over Seth and eased the dog-tag chain from under his bloodied chin, then looked across at Cooke.

'Yeah, I spotted it. He looks the type, but what the hell is he doing here?'

'I don't have blood here Gene, this clinic is more used to dispensing flu shots and handling dog bites. Let's hope I can stabilise him and do a temporary wound closure, else it's a journey to Rumford somehow if we're to save him.'

Cooke left the room and headed to a small training facility at the rear of the clinic. In truth it had been a storeroom until Nancy had cleared it out the previous year, set it up to train some of the townspeople in basic first aid and use of the defibrillator.

He returned a few minutes later carrying an old white board and a box of magic markers.

'Need these Nance. I'll bring 'em back when we're done. I'm leaving Ed and Sky here to keep watch for the time being. Jordan, could you, Clem and Lou head for the community centre? I'll join you there in about twenty minutes.'

'I'll stay here too Gene.'

Tom was stood at the bottom of the bed where Seth lay. The man seemed mesmerised by Seth, didn't take his eyes off him as he spoke to Cooke.

'OK Tom, for a little while at least. But I'd say your priority was being home with your wife.'

Cooke took Sky to one side and quickly whispered an instruction to him. Sky uttered an oath in return. Cooke looked across to his Deputy and mouthed a few words, then left the room and took off, leaving Nancy checking Seth's vitals once again.

Cook took one of the snomos and headed to his office. He needed to collect a few things and check out the security alert he'd gotten on his pager earlier. It was a short distance but the snow had already begun to form unstable drifts along the main streets, making his journey slow and hazardous. He let himself in; the front door was still locked and undamaged.

He checked in each of the rooms, paced to the front window, looked out onto the street. He figured that it had been a false alarm. Nothing appeared out of order. It was then he noticed the footprints and remnants of snow leading to and from the cell.

Nate came upon the upturned snomo without warning, almost ploughed straight into it. The wind was driving intermittent ice particles almost vertically now, cutting vision down to just a few metres at times. He pulled back on the throttle, slid to a halt, jumped off, quickly surveying the scene under the illumination of his headlight. The wrecked snomo was half buried in snow and lay scuttled across a ridge of jagged rock.

There were a lot of footprints trampled into the fresh snow and the tracks of a snomo heading south. A single pair of footprints ran parallel to the vehicles tracks.

Seth walked around the snomo, kicking and scraping at the snow with one boot. The snow turned a dark red as he scraped deeper. It seemed to spread in a wide arc around the vehicle, then trail off into the darkness.

He climbed back onto his own machine and followed the tracks. He pondered what he saw as he slowly inched forward. *Were the footprints Seth's? Were the bastards making him walk while injured?* His anger rose with each new scattering of blood.

The small sky-lift station appeared out of the frozen mist, just a small timber-slatted structure that was positioned to the side of a steel support. Twin steel cables ran the length of the route from the side of the lake below to the highest level that was the town of Lake Fear. Nate dismounted and swung his rifle into position, shined his flashlight at the building. A hand-painted sign came into view: *Lake Fear Sky-Ride $5 return*. Under that, an arrow pointed downward annotated *Lake Fear (Lakeside)* and another pointing upwards saying *Lake Fear (Town)*. Nate walked toward the open structure and played the flashlight over a wooden bench that sat this side of a counter top. The ground here was trampled and bloody, a lot of blood, heavy and clotted. It had to be Seth's. Something else caught his eye, half-buried in the snow. He bent down to scoop it up. It looked familiar. The fingers and cuff were stained with dried, frozen blood. He looked inside at the tiny label, matched it with his own. Identical make, gloves that Manny had gotten for them both. He grabbed the bench, dragged it beneath the cable and reached up. It was still warm from the friction, but he didn't detect movement. They'd been here with Seth maybe ten minutes before. He replaced his own glove and rammed Seth's into a pocket. He walked back outside and scanned the ground more carefully beyond the station. Just snomo tracks now, headed for the town of Lake Fear. He spun his own snomo that way, then pressed the transmit button on his walkie-talkie.

Cooke puzzled over the footprints. *Had he himself made them?* He didn't recall going into the cell as he'd moved around the office looking for signs of entry, but he couldn't now be certain that he *hadn't*. God knows he had a lot on his mind. He leant down and compared boot size. Those in the cell were bigger than his own. *But maybe the snowmelt had just distorted the size? Jeez he needed to slow down a little, organise his thoughts, chill, as Ed often told him.*

He grabbed the cell bars and was about to close them when the walkie-talkie he'd taken from Ed earlier shocked him to attention. A deep booming voice, distorted by the background noise of the storm, echoed round the confines of the cell. Cooke stood and listened with growing alarm.

'You still out there Deputy Dick?'

Cooke pressed transmit, hands shaking with the suddenness, the dread.

'This is Sheriff Cooke. Who is this, over?'

'Seems I've traded up. I just hope you can solve my problem before I become yours. I want my brother, Sheriff, I want him back before this goes any further. You bring him back to where you found him. Do it now. Do it alone. Then me and my brother, we leave your town. You got that?'

The man sought an answer but Cooke wasn't ready to give one. He sat on the bunk in the cell and wiped his mouth. The handset crackled to life again.

'You hearing me Chief?'

Cooke gave his head a shake, tried to clear it.

'You need to come in, talk this over, see if we can clear a few things up first, over.'

'You're making it difficult for me to be reasonable Sheriff. Now I'm telling you. You give him to me or I'll take him from you. Anyone gets hurt, that'll be your responsibility not mine.'

The guy's voice was rising, almost shouting now above the noise of the wind.

'Doesn't work that way. We talk first, investigate a death. You have nothing to do with it, you and your brother go free.'

'Oh but it *does* work that way. You'd better make it that way. Now I'm gonna wait here for ten more minutes for your call, telling me you're on your way with him. I don't get that call, I'm coming to take him. You hear Sheriff Asshole? You hear me?'

Cooke was left with the screech of static in his ear. *Jesus, who the hell were these people?* He pulled the cell bars shut and returned to the main office to collect the equipment he'd come for.

34

Cooke walked into the community centre, a large cardboard box under one arm and a whiteboard in his other hand. Jordan, Clem and Lou had already arrived and were stood huddled around a small electric radiator drinking coffee and talking to Mayor Adams and Good Jay. Two of Rudy's friends had showed up, Ricky Jacks and Tully Machin, and they stood leaning against the bar, shocked, angry at the news, keen to assist the efforts to catch whoever had done this.

They all came across and made a single group around Cooke as he lowered the box and whiteboard to the floor and began making two piles: protective vests, and rifles.

'Jordan, go get the walkie-talkies from the backroom there. Harvey has already set the frequencies.'

Good Jay took Cooke by the arm as he was setting up the whiteboard.

'I'm heading to the church Gene – I need to say a few words for Rudy.'

'OK Jay, but don't stay too long. And take one of these.' Cooke picked up a walkie-talkie from the table and switched it on, handed it to Jay.

'Contact me when you get to the church and when you leave and once more when you reach home, OK?'

Cooke gave Jay's shoulder a squeeze and walked him to the door. The snow was a foot deep now, swirling in wild eddies.

'Later Jay, and don't stay too long.'

Jay waved and walked out into the frozen mist.

Cooke turned and walked back to the centre of the room.

He stood and relayed the call he had taken earlier, then grabbed a vacant chair and leaned the whiteboard against it.

'Bring your chairs in closer, we've got some planning to do.'

Cooke bit off the cap of a felt marker and began writing on the board, a handful of one-liners, as he spoke.

'First up I'd like us to get a few things straight. Some things you know about, some things you don't.'

Rudy shot in neck with cross bow
Dog shot/knifed – found down by the lakeside track
Stranger shot – found east shore track
Landline and cells are all down – weather?
Contact from second stranger (brother?) – very threatening
We're ON OUR OWN – for now!

Cooke stood back and ran through the points in his head, nodding at each one, then verbalised them to the group. He lingered over the last point.

Jordan glanced round and nodded.

'That's about the size of it.'

Cooke turned and faced the group.

'OK, here's my take: either we've got two maniacs in our town, one of which is still on the loose, or else it's a hunting accident that got out of control. Whichever it is, our priority is to find that second individual.'

Jordan spoke up again.

'Think there might be more of 'em Gene?'

'Good point Jordy. Could be, who knows?'

Cook grabbed the map they had used earlier, turned it over to reveal a detailed street map of the town and draped it over the whiteboard.

'Think we need to concentrate our attentions on the town. I figure this second individual will come here looking for his brother. Also, we need to consider moving the brother to a more secure location once Nancy gets him stable.'

Cooke stood throughout the session, pacing on the wooden

floor as he organised the search teams.

'Jordan, I'd like you and Lou to cover everything west of Addis street.'

He pointed out the area to cover although they knew it well.

'Clem, you and me will cover everywhere else east of Jordan's position. I'm gonna leave Ed and Sky at the clinic for now.'

He pointed to Lou and Clem.

'I'm also gonna deputise you two for the duration. I've already deputised Sky.'

Earl Adams spoke up then. Adams defined the town of Lake Fear, his family having moved to the town in nineteen seventy from Boston. He and his wife ran a small law firm dealing in conveyancing and estate matters.

They had a daughter called Chloe who had moved to Portsmouth in the nineties. She had hit the skids. Her son Ricky, had been practically brought up by Earl and his wife. Earl had taught the boy to fish and hunt and had bought him a Remington 260 for his sixteenth birthday and paid for shooting lessons at Rumford hunting lodge. On his eighteenth birthday, he traded up to a Mauser and Earl bought him his first hunting license.

They often camped out during the summer, fishing and hunting for rabbit. Sometimes Ricky would take his friend Tully along and both boys became accomplished marksmen, which was why Earl spoke up for them as they stood taking in all of Cooke's plans.

'Sheriff, we need all the hands we can get. I'd like you to consider deputising Ricky and Tully here. They know how to hunt and shoot, and we'd cover the ground quicker.'

The two boys smiled and nodded enthusiastically. They had a score to settle for Rudy.

Cooke looked shocked.

'Now just a minute Earl, they're just boys.'

'Gene, they're grownups and they've been hunting since so high.'

Cooke dismissed the idea flat out, stared Adams down angrily for even suggesting it.

'Can't do it Earl, I want them safely at home. You too for that matter.'

He wrapped up the final details of the search plan, and began handing out the rifles and vests to each of the men. It was Lou who voiced all of their concerns.

'Who are these people, Gene? And of all places, why did they pick on our town?'

'You still up for it Tull?'

The two boys had quietly left the community centre as the Sheriff was in a huddle with his deputies and a handful of other townsfolk. They were picking their way through the snow in the direction of their homes. Ricky was pissed that Cooke had blocked them both from being deputised.

'You kidding?'

'No I'm not kidding. You plan to just head home and read your Hulk comics while all this is happening in our shitty little town?'

The two boys had stopped under a street lamp as they talked, Tully dancing from one foot to the other trying to keep warm and keep his nerves in check.

Ricky nudged him.

'Come on man. Listen, I overheard Cooke telling the teams about the radio channel and frequency that they're gonna use, so we can call in if we see anyone. We're totally safe man.'

Tully was hesitant. He was up for the hunt but his father and the Sheriff were close. He could get into serious trouble if he ignored Cooke's instructions to go home and stay home, but he also knew that Ricky would ride him forever. Besides, if they happened to get lucky they could be town heroes. He danced some more and rubbed his hands together for warmth.

'OK Rick, I'm in.'

Ricky punched at his friend's arm again.

'OK man, I'll go back to my place and get my rifle. You go collect yours and pick up your walkie-talkie. Meet me at Turner's place in one hour. I'll leave the side door open for you.'

Turner's was a furniture store, with storage at the back, just off the High street. Ricky worked there most Saturdays. Old man Turner trusted him with a set of keys, trusted him to open up the store first thing Saturday mornings. Ricky exploited this to the full when he and Tully went back some Saturday nights with a little bag of weed, a few bottles of bud and sometimes, when their luck was in, a couple of the local girls. Turner had figured young Ricky hosted weekend smoking dens at the back of his store; he lived with it on account of the fact that he was friendly with Ricky's father. That and he wasn't averse to a little pot himself.

'Here.'

Ricky handed Tully his hunting knife and laughed.

'Just in case you meet the boogey-man on the way.'

Seth lay still on the bed, a dull pain engulfing his entire body. The sedative was wearing off. He opened his eyes a fraction, taking in his surroundings. He flexed his limbs. Both his arms and one leg had been tied down. A drip was attached to his left arm. A nurse had her back to him checking some readings. He could hear the drone of voices nearby, occasionally punctuated by a raised voice, but couldn't make sense of the conversation. His leg and neck had fresh dressings on them. The wounds underneath felt bloated and raw.

He raised his head a little to get a better view. Nancy must have caught the movement because she turned to him now.

'Glad to see you are back with us Mr Stone.'

Seth eased himself back down and stared up at the ceiling. He quietly tested the strengths of the straps; they were firmly looped around the metal frame of the bed. Spikes of pain ran across his shoulder blades and down his spine with the effort. He relaxed again and let the pain subside. When he spoke, his voice was hoarse, barely a whisper.

'How's the boy?'

'You mean Rudy? The boy who was shot with a crossbow bolt?'

Seth just nodded, slowly, the bandage pulling taut against his neck. Nancy's features seemed to drop, any semblance of generosity to her patient vanishing.

'The boy died from his wounds.'

Seth closed his eyes at the news, genuinely shocked, saddened, that they had visited such dread on this community. Five more minutes passed before he spoke again, in the same raspy voice.

'You found my brother yet?'

'You are my concern right now but there are a lot of people here who want to talk to you. I'm your only line of defence right now so I would appreciate some cooperation.'

Seth liked her directness, and the fact that she had probably saved his life.

'The name's Seth Stone.'

Nancy nodded.

'That much I know.'

She pointed to the dog-tag attached to its chain that she had removed earlier from Seth's neck and placed on a nearby table.

'Shouldn't have removed those, Ma'am. I'd appreciate them back.'

'How was I to dress your wounds Mr Stone?'

'Seth.'

She reached over for the tag and carefully placed the chain over Seth's neck.

'Where's the other one?'

Nancy appeared puzzled.

'The other chain, a smaller one, hangs off the main one here.'

'That I don't know, that was all I found on you when you came in here.'

Seth thought back to the fight with Byrd.

'Well Seth, you seemed to have brought a lot of misery to our little town.'

He felt himself answer a question then that she hadn't asked.

'Sometimes life is stacked against you, sometimes, you make bad choices.'

'But why us. Why here?'

Seth ignored her, just one thing on his mind now.

'Do you know anything about my brother Ma'am?'

'Only that they have sent search parties looking for him.'

The hum of voices could still be heard. He listened in more intently, caught a few sentences, a few names, cast them to memory. Then he pointed his chin in their direction.

'I need to talk to your friends next door. Warn them about my brother.'

'Mr Stone, your vitals are off the chart and you have a bullet hole in your left leg that I haven't managed to fully stop bleeding yet. I can't let you speak to anyone right now.'

Seth had to warn them, had to get them to let him talk to Nate before this escalated out of control. He filled his lungs and shouted out as best his damaged body would allow.

The tiny room was filled within seconds, everyone jostling for position round Seth's bed. Nancy tried to shoo them back out but Ed put a flat hand up and strode to the bed.

He checked the straps, then spoke first. Sky and Tom were

watching over the prostrate figure.

'Let's start with who you are and what the hell you're doing in Lake Fear.'

Seth noticed the Deputy badge on the man's shirt but afforded him greater office for the effect it often got.

'My name's Seth Stone, Sheriff, and you need to listen to me. If you have sent out search parties for my brother, you need to recall them. Negotiating with violence will only end badly. You have to stop this before it goes any further. You send search parties out there after him he'll see them as the enemy. Please Sheriff, let me talk to him, let us walk out of here. I promise you, you'll never see us again.'

'Are you serious son? We are not letting you and your brother walk out of here. You're both suspects in a killing and God knows what else. No, we will catch him and bring him in and let the law deal with you both.'

'With respect Sheriff, you can't stop him. Trust me when I say –'

Clem weighed in then, anger building.

'Trust you? You and your brother bring murder and mayhem to our town and you want us to *trust* you?'

Seth tried to raise himself off the bed, the restraints digging into his flesh, face flushing with the exertion as Nancy gently tried to ease him back down. He only managed to speak one more warning before he passed out on the bed.

'Please Sheriff. He knows death. My brother only knows death.'

35

Nate arrived on the outskirts of town, pulled over, and parked the snomo against a long bank of thick hawthorn bushes that ran parallel to the road into town. He was angry that he hadn't got the call back from Cooke. He pulled out the town map again and shone his flashlight along the route into the centre, picking out the main buildings. His map gave no clue. He needed intelligence.

He dismounted, slung his rucksack and weapons over his shoulder, and began the walk toward the centre of Lake Fear.

He heard faint voices as he crunched along the sidewalk, and he slowed, zoning in to the source. He peered through a stretch of bushes and watched as two men stood on the snow-encrusted steps of the old church. One of the men had a cop's uniform. He watched them until they split up, the officer walking west, into town, the other going into the church. He waited another few minutes before he crossed the street.

He let himself in by the back door of the church. It was a simple spring latch and he picked it in less than a minute. He followed a flickering light down a narrow corridor, his bulk almost filling the space as he slowly eased forward. The old church smelled of candle grease and polish. It transported him back to his Sunday School days when he and Seth attended together in Rumford. It was there that he and Seth had made up their special prayer after their Sunday school teacher had set them all a project. Nate had read it out to the class that day, feeling foolish but sincere, the words all about him and Seth.

The corridor opened onto a small nave and Nate scanned the dim candlelit room, looking for movement. He saw a dark solitary figure knelt in prayer in front of the altar, illuminated by four tall candles. The man was dressed in a black tunic, dog collar slightly askew. Nate stayed in the shadows until the man had concluded his prayers and slowly, awkwardly, got to his feet. Nate was beside him in an instant.

'Let me help you up Padre. I'm hoping you can help me out, help me find someone.'

Good Jay looked up in shock and swayed a little until Nate grasped him more firmly. He was like a bag of bones to Nate, fragile, worn down. Good Jay stared up at Nate all the time he spoke, mesmerised by Nate's calmness and control. Then his attention switched to the two distorted black scorpion tattoos on the back of each of Nate's hands.

'You like my tats Padre? I designed 'em myself. They signify the Praetorian Guard, y'know, protecting the roman emperor? I do a lot of protection work. Me and my brother have protected all kinds of assholes. We've also killed a few too.'

Jay seemed hypnotised by Nate's gentle cadence, but he sensed that beneath that serenity, he was just as calm cleaving flesh from bone. Seth slowly unsheathed his knife and held it up, catching the dancing candle flames. Jay finally found his voice.

'What do you want with me?'

He reached inside the pocket of his smock and felt for the walkie-talkie that Cooke had given him. His fingers tried to find the operating buttons but he couldn't tell which he was pressing. He had to hope that someone could hear the conversation.

'I have no interest in you. I just want you to tell me where your friends might be keeping my brother. Could you tell me that Padre?'

'I can't help you son. I don't know anything about your brother. All I know is what the Sheriff told me when –'

A voice, tinny and slight, seemed to emanate then from somewhere within Jay's clothing. Jay stiffened as Nate cocked his ear and leaned towards Jay.

'You holding out on me Padre? You got a squawk box on you there?'

Nate reached for Jay's hands and pulled them out of his pockets, one still holding the handset. He dragged it from Jay's grip and listened in, but the message had already ended with a man's voice telling Jay to call in. He left it on and tucked it in his own pocket.

'You were saying, Padre? About my brother?'

Jay had clasped his hands together, he seemed distant, seemed to be mouthing something, slowly, part of some sermon maybe. Nate focussed on his words, recognised them.

'*...man is born to trouble...*'

Nate interrupted, finished the piece from the book of Job.

'*...as the sparks fly upwards.*'

The reference seemed to anger Nate and he squeezed Jay's shoulders together until his bones cracked.

'You got that right, trouble finds me wherever I go, but God isn't ever home when I need him.'

Jay cried out, his pained voice echoing around the cold stone walls of the church.

'I know that's gonna hurt, big man like me, but I'm not really trying yet.'

'I only know a little of what's going on, only what they tell me from the radio that you took from me. They found someone out on the ridge just out of town, brought him in. That's all I know. Maybe they took him to the Sheriff's office, put him in the lockup.'

Nate felt his spirits rise then. He was here. Seth was right here in town. He hadn't been taken to Rumford or even further afield.

'Well Padre, let's get down to business. Now, FYI; I don't think my brother has been taken to the Sheriff's office. I was there earlier. It's closed up, blacked out. No med facility. Also, I saw you talking to the uniform earlier, so, any new information for me?'

'I don't know son, I honestly don't know. I thought that was where they may be headed.'

Nate pursed his lips and nodded, like he was making mental notes in an amicable meeting of minds.

'When I was in Afghanistan a few years back I was captured by some very unfriendly people. They had me for ten hours before my brother and four other soldiers rescued me. I owe my brother a lot for that. And all of the other times of course.

'They did a lot to me in those few hours. I ain't got that long with you friend. I figure maybe ten minutes and I'll have to go. Know what I remember most about those long hours?'

Jay slowly shook his head.

'Not the death threats – we're all gonna die right? Death is sometimes a blessing. It was the *pain*, the *gut-wrenching pain*. I can still feel them working on me in my nightmares. They started with my feet. The soles are very sensitive, all the nerves end up right there. Fuckers took my good boots too.'

Nate placed one of his huge booted heels over the toes of Jay's left foot and leaned heavily, then stepped off just as quickly. Jay let out a tiny yelp of pain.

'Then they worked on my joints, just here.'

Nate cupped Jay's bony knee in his massive hands and began applying sideways pressure to the ball joint. Jay cried out. But Nate had already stopped.

'Then they took some teeth. See here?'

Nate opened his mouth and shone his flashlight towards it to show several gaps, his face looking ghastly and distorted in the fixed beam and the flickering light from the candles.

'I still feel the pain on a cold day, like now for instance. Makes me irritable as all hell y'know? So please understand Padre, once I start on you, I won't be able to stop. Now, tell me, where are they keeping my brother!'

Nate laid the flat of the knife blade on Jay's cheek as he spoke this final warning, his voice arcing upward in anger.

Good Jay knew real fear then, for the first time in his sixty eight years, a bone-deep wash of sickening fear that loosened his bladder a little, here before the altar, before the flaking plaster image of The Lord.

It hadn't taken Nate the full ten minutes to realise that the man genuinely didn't know where they had taken Seth, but the man could still be useful.

He wiped the tip of the knife blade clean on his combats and returned it to its sheath. Then Nate forced Jay to make a call on the walkie-talkie before leaving him the way he'd found him, in his crouched position, in front of the altar.

If they got here like they said they would, he would live. He'd live long enough to give them a message and for them to patch the old timer up.

But Nate's estimates were out. He didn't know about the alcohol in Jay's bloodstream that was helping to quicken the pace of blood flow through his veins.

He walked out of the church and stood under the stone arch of the narthex. He opened his ruck, withdrew a few items, and pushed across the street towards the nearest roadside lamp, barely visible through the driving snow. The storm was raging now. When he was done he lifted his face to the sky, collecting huge fat flakes that melted on impact, leaving a sheen on his tanned skin. His face began to freeze, but Nate didn't mind one bit, he enjoyed its anesthetising effect. He wiped at it with a sleeve and turned towards town. He'd find someone in Lake Fear sooner or later that knew where his brother was being kept. But until then, time to raise the stakes.

36

Ricky looked up and down the street as he took the keys out of his pocket. He had his rifle in a slim leather pouch slung over one shoulder. A box of shells and the walkie-talkie were in his jacket pocket. The street looked deserted. Heavy snowflakes swirled in the currents as the wind snaked around the town's streets and buildings. He let himself into Turner's furniture store, using a flashlight as he entered instead of flicking on the light switches. He wasn't keen to attract unwanted attention. The store was like a museum. It was stuffed with new and second hand furniture and light fittings, rugs pegged from lengths of rope that had been looped over timber rafters. His flashlight reflected off a collection of dull brass lanterns stacked together on a makeshift display stage, the distorted reflections stopping him in his tracks. A musty smell permeated the air, together with the faint but unmistakeable smell of pot. He negotiated around the furniture to the back of the store and unlocked the side door that led out onto the street, then went back into the main room.

He unpacked the gun and placed it on a nearby table, pulled out the shells, began loading them.

Nate was crouched under the awning of what looked like a warehouse. The snow was relentless and Nate slipped round the side of the building out of the worst of the wind to study the map. The scrape of feet dragging through the fresh snow drew his attention and he pulled into a narrow alcove and peered back out onto the street. A young slightly-built kid of maybe seventeen was stood at the front door of one of the stores opposite, huddled against the biting wind as he fiddled with the lock. Nate watched unseen as the kid looked up and down the street, then let himself into the store. The kid had a rifle slung across his back. Nate needed intel and he figured some had just come his way. He waited a few minutes before coming out of hiding and crossing the street. He peered into the building. It was in darkness save for a thin beam of light flitting about the store as the boy used his flashlight to navigate around. Nate tried the door but the boy had locked it behind him.

Nate went round to the side of the building.

He was faced with a small door let into the side of the timber-lagged wall. He tried the door. Not locked. He turned the handle and let himself in to a darkened musty space. He was closing the door when the single shot missed him by fractions as he was turned closing the door and he dropped instantly and rolled away toward a wall of packing cases and pile of old furniture.

Muffled footsteps then and a voice, a young voice, screaming hysterically.

'Tull, you on line yet man? I got him Tull, I think I got him, he's in the store, I saw him go down. I'm coming out.'

The boy was still screaming excitedly into his handset as he ran toward the front door. Nate had no time to ready his own weapons so he reached out and grabbed a small wooden stool just as the boy passed his line of sight running full tilt. Nate was ready and he flung the stool at the legs of the runner hitting him in the knee and sending him face down onto the floor. Nate ran to the boy, kicking away the rifle and grabbing the walkie-talkie from his hand.

The boy was groaning and clutching his leg.

'Hey pretty boy, what'd you do that for? That could have injured me man. I can't believe that's what you intended you know? Shouldn't ever aim a gun at a man, not unless you intend to kill him. And then you'd better make sure you do, 'cause guys I know would come after you with plans of their own if you left them alive.'

As Nate dragged the boy nearer to the front door, a voice screeched from the walkie-talkie in Nate's hand. He'd got Tully within a few yards, so let him drop heavily back onto the floor while Nate reached across and unlocked the front door.

There were a couple of small stools positioned at the side of a large chest of drawers. Nate retrieved one, picked the boy up and sat him down hard. He reached inside his own jacket and withdrew the wire he'd made at the boathouse. Delicately he placed it round the boy's neck like it was a valuable necklace.

'You see this wire? It can slice through flesh in the blink of an eye. I know it can 'cause one just like it became my close friend in Iraq. What's your name son?'

The boy managed to croak out his first name.

'Ricky.'

'And your numbnuts friend out there?'

'Tully.'

'OK, now, I want you to call to Tully to drop any weapons he might be carrying and come in here, through the front door. Tell him he needs to do this right away.'

Nate had tightened his grip slightly. To him it was nothing, but he knew the wire was now beginning to cut into the boy's neck. The boy slowly nodded to Nate, his eyes wide and panicky. Nate held the walkie-talkie in front of the boy's face as the boy shouted out to his friend.

'Tully, drop your gun and get in here, slowly. He got the drop on me man. He's gonna kill me if you don't.'

Nate nodded and smiled down at the boy confirming his good work. Tully immediately shouted back over the noise of the storm.

'No way man, I'm going for my dad. He'll call the Sheriff, we'll catch that asshole, and we'll be local heroes like you said.'

Nate whispered in Ricky's ear.

'Nooo, that's no good at all. Tell him he has exactly one chance or I'll kill you now and him within thirty seconds. That's no idle threat. I'm just telling you what's gonna happen. Your deaths would be no hardship for me. Tell the little shit that.'

'Tully, no, don't go. He means it man you've got to get in here or he'll kill us both. Don't leave me with him, he's....'

The wire tightened around Ricky's neck choking off the final few words.

Nate spoke into the walkie-talkie then, his voice calm, like it was a conversation between the best of buddies.

'Hey Tully, I'm gonna do the counting thing now y'know? Like in a movie or something? You seen that happen? Five, four...'

Ricky managed to shout out too, over Nate's metronomic counting.

'Tully, he ain't kidding, get in here before he slices my frickin' head off.'

'... three, two...'

The front door pushed open, just a crack. Nate dropped Ricky, reached through the gap, grabbed the barrel of the rifle and pulled the other boy gripping it through the doorway in one violent jerk, leaving the terrified kid on his knees in front of him. Nate flicked on one of the light switches illuminating a single row of dull yellow bulbs.

Tully was on all fours like a scared puppy, gasping and hiccoughing in fear, staring up at Nate. Ricky eased the wire from his throat and threw it on the ground. Nate nodded and retrieved it, then smiled at them both.

'Listen, I'm not gonna harm you OK? No more than I have to at least. I just need some intel and a small favour from you both. Think you could do that for me?'

Tully nodded enthusiastically but Ricky just stared, still rubbing the weal around his neck.

'Appreciate it. Now. You know about my brother?'

Tully nodded again.

'Know where they're keeping him?'

Tully was about to answer when Ricky stood and blocked Nate's view of the boy.

'We ain't telling you shit.'

Nate laughed at that, genuinely laughed. He reached out and slapped Ricky across the mouth, sending him sprawling hard onto the floor by Tully.

Nate was still looking at Tully.

'Forget your buddy, have *you* got anything for me, kid?'

'He's at the clinic. I think they took him there to patch him up.'

Nate took out his map and flashed it in front of Tully's face.

'Show me.'

Tully pointed with a trembling hand to the building. It wasn't far from where they were. 'They got firepower there?'

Ricky spoke then, a look of disgust as he looked across at Tully.

'Enough to take you on.'

Nate smiled at Ricky.

'Yep, well, they're gonna need it son. A lot of it.'

Tully spoke again, his voice without any real strength, shocked and now shamed by his friend.

'Still won't do you any good to go there.'

'Oh, why's that?'

'Cause they're moving him, somewhere safer.'

Nate dropped the map in front of Tully a second time.

'We don't know, we honestly don't know.'

'Can't be far though can it, jerkwater town like this? Let me just make your friend more comfortable. Then you and me can find out. '

Ricky lay on his side, bound with his own shirt, as Nate and Tully spoke quietly together.

Fear had done its job on Tully so Nate went through the words one final time and then handed the walkie-talkie to him. Tully tuned it to the channel that Cooke and his team were using, then the hit the transmit button and spoke the script that he thought would save their lives.

'Hey Sheriff, dyer copy me, over? It's Tully, Sheriff. We have him. Me and Ricky have him. We've tied him up in here but you need to get here quick 'cause he's trying to get loose. We're in Turner's Store. But be careful when you…'

Nate snatched the handset out of Tully's hand, ending the call and gave him a polite applause.

'That was one shit-kicking performance kid. That should send the cavalry here pronto. Just enough time for our next little trick.'

Nate re-arranged the stools, reached into his ruck and pulled out a length of bandage from the med-box. He grabbed Tully and bound his hands and feet. He scanned the room, ran to one end, reached up, grabbed at the length of rope holding up a display of rugs, and tore it all down in one pull. He ran back to where the boys were huddled together and began making a couple of slip-knots at one end of the rope. He kicked out at Ricky, still lying on the floor.

'You. Stand.'

He pulled Ricky to his feet and looped one end around his midriff. He threw the other end over the double rafter above his head and pulled.

'Step up there.'

Nate pointed to one of the stools with his chin.

'Fuck you.'

Ricky dropped to the floor.

'You'll pay for that, son.'

Nate heaved on the rope and Ricky was pulled upward violently, his whole body momentarily airborne.

'Up.'

Nate cut a piece of bandage and tied a gag around Ricky's mouth then pointed to the stool.

Ricky stepped up and stood balanced there as Nate turned to Tully.

'Think you know what to do.'

Tully stood as Nate gagged him then he climbed up onto the second stool, positioned ten feet or so from the first. Nate tied the rope around Tully's wrists, then he sliced off the spare rope left dangling at Tully's side.

He bent down and tied one end of the second piece to the spindles of Tully's stool, the other to the handle of the front door.

When he was done, he reached inside a nearby packing case and pulled out a handful of paper and began twisting it into small bundles, then pulled out his cigarette lighter, lit the paper, and dropped it back into the case. He dragged the burning packing case into the centre of a collection of wooden tables that were positioned against a wall, building a makeshift bonfire there. The fire took hold fast, giving off toxic clouds of thick black smoke that rose and impacted with the low tiled ceiling, then curled back down and began to fill the room with choking fumes.

He returned to the two boys. They were already coughing, spitting out bits of floating ash from around their gags, awkwardly trying to turn away from the source of the smoke.

'Hey asshole, got one more job for you while you're hanging around up there.'

Nate stripped off his own jacket and placed it round Ricky's shoulders, then placed his own rifle in the crook of the kid's bound right arm.

He switched off all of the lights and retreated into the shadows.

Jordan Washington heard the message at the same time that the

Sheriff did but he was nearer. He and Lou had parked the snomo at the end of the street and were walking the lower east side of town, when the message from Tully came in. Jordan was younger and fitter than Lou and soon outpaced him as they ran stiffly through deepening snow for the store.

'I'm just a few minutes away Sheriff. I'm going in there, over.'

He turned the corner and saw flames beginning to lick the side of the store.

Cooke sensed there was more to this but couldn't stop him in time.

'No Jordan, don't go in the front, fall back, wait until I get there, over.'

But Jordan had already reached the store's half-open front door through which the wind was howling, whipping the blaze into fury. He raced in, pushing the door all the way open with his full weight, the door resisting at first. He had his gun cocked and ready in his hands.

A scraping sound came from his left as the door reached its limit, followed by a dull thump and pained squeal.

He dropped low and pointed his gun at the jerking swaying movement that had suddenly appeared in front of him. At first he couldn't make it out in the smoke filled room. Then it began to sink in. He saw a rope pulled taut that ran from the handle of the door and hooked around an upturned stool.

Dear God, he had done this. He'd walked into the trap. The Sheriff had warned him and ...

He looked up and across and recognised Tully's wild-eyed face as he swung by his wrists. He dashed to his side, taking his weight and looking around frantically for something to cut the boy free. The boy was screaming something but Jordan couldn't make it out over the roar of the fire.

As he scanned the room his eyes went to something else out

of place. Through the smoke he made out a figure looming there, tall, dressed in a camouflage combat jacket, the sort that army personnel wear. The man had a rifle raised. He too seemed to be screaming something, angry, threatening.

Jordan had to let Tully go. The kid screamed. Jordan took aim at the armed man and pulled the trigger, letting loose a full chamber of bullets. The figure dropped, its dead weight pulling on the rope jerking Tully further up.

Jordan turned back to Tully, choking smoke everywhere now, and went to lift his body by its legs as the kid continued to spiral. He sensed rapid movement then, behind him, but he was too late to respond as a huge hand curled around his neck, then another, cutting off his air. The last thing he saw before darkness took him was a pair of scorpions.

Jordan dropped at Nate's feet and he pushed him aside. He cut down the boys with two quick slashes at the rope, retrieved his rifle and stripped his bullet riddled jacket from Ricky's bloodied body.

Nate went back to Jordan, stood over his prostrate body. 'Fuck you man, you ate up my jacket.'

He picked him up and swung him over his shoulder, reached down and grabbed at Tully's collar, dragging him to the side door. He pulled him through and dropped him semi-conscious in the snow as a window exploded behind him. He spotted the snomo parked up at the end of the street. He took a quick look back as he kept to the shadows and watched. A figure peered into the flames from the front entrance. Nate put his ruined jacket back on, turned and headed for the ride.

He reached the end of the street and began to search the Deputy's pockets for the ignition key. He seized it from Jordan's jacket, then manhandled the limp body till it was perched in front of his own. He took fresh cold air deep into his lungs, forced himself to calm his breathing, then fired up the snomo and fishtailed away. The fire lit up the town's skyline behind him.

Cooke and Clem finally reached the corner of Amos Street to see the store fully ablaze, flames pouring through shattered windows. The next building, where *The Mariner* was produced, had also begun to smoulder. They ran to the front door where Lou had uncoiled a heavy roll of canvas hose he'd retrieved moments earlier from the emergency fire hydrant across the street. Cooke grabbed at the brass end piece and raced to the hydrant. Clem reached for the coil, helping Lou unravel it. Clem screamed to Cooke over the din of the fire and the soaring wind.

'Called Kenny and the boys out?'

Kenny Sheehy headed up the volunteer fire protection team for Lake Fear. Cooke shook his head.

'Comms still down. We're on our own for now.'

'We could hit the button Gene?'

Yes, he could run to his office, press the Town's emergency siren button, but did he really want townsfolk turning up on the streets? With a maniac on the loose?

'I'm hoping one of them has seen the fire, without us bringing out the whole town.'

Cooke grappled with the heavy metal ring, trying to find the thread, screaming out at himself in frustration. Finally it caught and he quickly spun it until it tightened home. Then he turned the wheel, releasing the pressured water.

He ran back to Lou who was already aiming the jet at the front of the building.

'Douse me Lou.'

Lou looked puzzled and Cooke grabbed at his arm and aimed the jet up and down his body.

'Now keep it aimed through those broken windows.'

Cooke sprinted past Lou and Clem, almost losing his footing, his back taking a blast of water as he raced through the open doorway.

He screamed the names of his Deputy and the two boys as he entered the building. His voice was lost against the roar of the blaze.

The flames were everywhere now. He dropped low to avoid the worst of the smoke. The shape of a town flier hung from a display stand; it was the one announcing the double centenary dance, the town square sketched in the background drawn by one of the Town's school children. He had helped judge the entries. This one had won out because it was a simple line drawing, no fuss, not even coloured in, just a black on white crayon drawing, but it worked, it typified the town and its people. The flyer caught fire, the background image turning to a crisp. He pressed on deeper inside the building, making his way on hands and knees, his wet clothes steaming from the heat and the bare skin of his face already cracking . The acrid smoke began to burn his lungs, every breath scorching, searing his throat. He could feel the heat through his thick parka now, his hair beginning to singe and curl, but he carried on.

His hands found the body. It was bloodied, tied, lying motionless on the floor, a trail of rope coiled behind. He grabbed at the legs and pulled, dragging it backward, back toward the front door, shuffling along low on his haunches, knowing that he was probably just retrieving a corpse from the flames but doing it anyway. His hand slipped and he fell sideways against a burning carpet display, upsetting the base so that the stand toppled towards him. He turned and shouldered it out of the way, flames searing into his parka, his zip-through. He slapped at his jacket with gloved hands, fumbled for the body again, grasped at it, pulling again, trying to see through the deadly smoke for his way out.

Finally, he reached the door and first one pair of hands, then another, grabbed at him, pulling him through the doorway and into the street, showers of freezing water from the hose soaking him again as he gulped for air and stared up with desperate bloodshot eyes at Lou and Clem.

Nate had only travelled a few hundred metres before he'd been forced to pull over. The Deputy's weight had dragged Nate slewing across the snowbound street a couple of times and he'd grappled with the snomo to keep it upright. The man was still out cold. Nate checked the Deputy's pulse. Nothing. *Jesus. He hadn't used such force had he? Maybe it had been the smoke. Maybe the guy'd had a heart-attack. Who the hell knew?* Nate no longer had his leverage. No matter.

He knew where he could get all the leverage he would need.

He grabbed Jordan Washington's shoulders angrily and heaved him sideways off the vehicle onto the snow. The body almost disappeared in a drift. He looked around but the street was empty. He pulled out his walkie-talkie and pressed transmit.

'I have to go back in, I have to find Jordan and Tully. They're still in there.'

Cooke struggled to raise himself off the freezing ground but Clem held him firm as Lou continued hosing the building.

'We found Tully. he was at the side entrance. Burned up a little but he's OK.'

'Jordan?'

Sky shook his head.

'Then we have to go back, I –'

'No point Gene. Not now.'

Again Cooke tried to stand, but a coughing fit wracked his body and he fell back down on the ground. The soft snow was soothing and he lay there letting its numbing effect work on his burned, cracked face.

'Here, drink.'

Clem held a flask to Cooke's mouth. Coffee with a hit of rum. It scoured his throat and he heaved most of it back up onto the ground.

'We've lost 'em Clem, we've lost 'em.'

Cooke stood, staggered away from the burning building, left them to tackle the flames that had already ruined the store and threatened the full row.

He stood now in the middle of the street, arched over heaving more bile, scooping handfuls of snow into his parched bitter mouth.

His walkie-talkie sounded and he fumbled with his gloves, dropping them to the ground, grabbing at the handset from an inner pocket, pressed the receive button.

'Sheriff, you listening to me? You know who this is. You know you really ought to clean up your streets around here, 'cause from where I'm sat, it looks to me like a stiff in a Deputy suit messing up the place. Oh and your two lost boys of course, you found them yet? You might want to check the ballistics by the way cause the bullets didn't come from my gun. Your Deputy here did all the good work. You listening Sheriff, you getting this? I want just one thing.'

He screamed the remainder of the message before he clicked the handset off and sped away.

'Remember Sheriff, it's me out there in the dark. Let my brother go or I will tear your little town apart. D'you copy me Sheriff Asshole? GIVE ME BACK MY BROTHER!'

Cooke clicked off his handset and rubbed at his swollen eyes. He tried to think but his thoughts ran in ten different directions. He spat out the remains of the snow, reached inside his jacket, switched handsets, clicked on.

'Ed, it's Cooke. I need Sky here pronto, Turner's Furniture store, or what's left of it. We got dead and injured. I need you to keep the clinic secured, watch for the brother showing up until I can get there, out.'

Cooke ran back to the burning building, stood in its glow and grabbed Tennent's arm as he and Clem grappled with the fire. He had to shout to be heard.

'I'm going looking for Jordan, you two stay here and do what you can.'

Both men looked puzzled. They hadn't heard Nate's call to Cooke, but they just nodded and played the hose into the flames as Cooke ran to the end of the street following the fresh tracks of the snowmobile.

He found Jordan's body face down in the gully. As he neared him, the whine of a snomo dully surfaced amongst the background noise. He pulled his gun from its holster and aimed it in the direction of the sound.

He could just make out the outline of the snomo ploughing down the street toward him. He braced to fire, cursing the snow driving into his eyes.

The driver waved.

Cooke eased his trigger finger, sleeved away the residue on his face, raised his aim. . Sky slid into view. Cooke clicked the safety on and shoved the gun away, pushed through the snow toward Jordan. Sky slewed to a halt a few feet away and jumped clear of the vehicle. Cooke felt Jordan for a pulse but there was none.

'Help me get him onto his back.'

They man-handled Jordan over and out of the gully. Cooke began pounding at Jordan's chest and breathing air into his lungs.

'My God Gene, who did this?'

Cooke just kept up the CPR as the snow continued to fall, covering Cooke, covering Sky, covering their dead friend.

Finally Cooke gave up.

The two of them lifted the body and placed it under shelter on the sidewalk. Cooke took off his hat and reached down, placed it over Jordan's face, turned to Sky.

'Ricky's gone too. Found him shot full of holes in the burning building.'

Sky crossed himself, muttered a few indistinct words.

'I need you to take Tully to the clinic, have Nancy look him over. You go on to the Church, make sure Jay is OK. I want him safely back home if he's still there. Call me when you're done. Once the fire is out I'll make my way to the clinic, want to keep a close eye on the suspect myself, watch for his brother showing up. We'll bring in Jordan and Ricky later.'

Sky nodded and slung a leg over the machine. He fired the engine and slowly pulled away.

Cooke let the noise of the engine die in the storm before he pressed the button on his handset. Nate answered almost instantly.

'I've called the state troopers you stinking son of a bitch.'

'Oh I doubt that, Sheriff. I don't see how you could do that without any comms.'

'Why, why are you doing this to us?'

'You know what I want. Release my brother to me and it ends here.'

Cooke clicked off the handset and trotted back to the smouldering building. Lou and Clem were still hosing it down. The flames were almost out now, black filthy smoke and ash mixed with the falling snow leaving dirty smears and run-off cascading down the walls and sidewalk.

Cooke shouted out to them, shaking with fury, grief, disbelief.

'Found Jordan back there.'

He looked at them both, shook his head. He grabbed at Lou's shoulder.

'Need to ask you something Lou.'

Clem waved them both away and took up the strain of the hose as they walked a few steps from the smoke and the roar of the fire hose.

'I need to ask you to try reach Mechanicsville, get some help. Think you could do that? Take one of the snomos, go the back way.'

'Sure I can Gene, but not the snomo. I'm not good on those contraptions. Prefer to go get my girls, take my sled to the lake, get my boat, plus it'll be a darn sight quicker than going all the way round.'

'Good enough Lou. Tell 'em everything, but tell 'em quick, we need firepower here, troopers. And change your radio channel, change it to channel twenty four.'

They both walked back to Clem.

'I need you to get Lou home, then come back here. Take my snomo. I'll take over for now.'

He reached over and grabbed Lou's hand, shook it, pulled him close.

'Good luck Lou.'

The men hugged briefly. Then Lou and Clem ran to the snomo. Cooke looked at the blurred shape of the retreating vehicle carrying the town's hopes, looked up into the smoke- and snow-filled sky, saw one the town's ancient buildings in ruin, saw the bloody images of Rudy with his neck torn open, the lifeless forms of Jordan and Ricky.

His town was at war with a deadly stranger.

All he had to do to stop it was let a man go.

37

Sky had taken a short route across open fields. He stamped off the loose snow and entered the church. Jay was kneeling in front of the altar. Sky hit the transmit button on his walkie-talkie then let it hang across his chest on its wire. He shouted out to Cooke as he switched his attention back to Jay.

'He's here Sheriff, Good Jay's right here, just prayin', you copy over?'

Sky ran up the aisle and put his arms around Jay's shoulders.

'Jay, Gene's been trying to reach you. You got your box switched on there?'

Good Jay slowly turned and looked up with milky eyes. He seemed to be mumbling something, over and over.

Sky didn't see the blood at first in the flickering light, but he *smelt* it. He smelt *something* anyway, something metallic and a little ... *pissy* mixed in with it.

He leaned across Jay and went to help him up. Then he saw the tiny wound, on the right side of his neck just below the jawline where a slow but steady stream of blood flowed out and down the front of Jay's cassock. Cooke finally answered but Sky grasped the handset, cut him off.

'Jeez, he's bleeding Sheriff, the asshole cut Jay's throat.'

Sky realised his use of profanity in a church. crossed himself. Cooke came back on the line.

'Sky, ball up a piece of rag or something and keep it pressed against the wound, try get him back here, over.'

'Why'd he do this Gene, hurt him but let him live?'

'He's causing diversions, making us feel threatened, giving us no time to think. The son of a bitch knows his brother is in town somewhere. I need to get back to the clinic and move the brother someplace else before he works out where he is.'

Good Jay lay on his side looking up at the model of Jesus. *He'd been a good man hadn't he? Good enough for heaven he'd say.* He wasn't really listening to the soothing words from Sky, who had a cloth he'd taken from the altar balled up and pressed against his neck.

But the blood still oozed between the folds all the same and Good Jay was dying a little more each time his withered heart pumped another beat.

Sky took off his belt and fastened it carefully around Jay's neck, holding the cloth in place.

'Just hang in there Good Jay, we'll get you to the clinic in no time, get you fixed right up and home before the ball game comes on.'

Jay gave a slight nod which let loose a gout of blood that soaked his collar.

'Come on, I'll help you to the door. You have to get on the back of my snowmobile. You have to try stay on until we reach the clinic. I'll stick to the road, make it a little less bumpy for you.'

The two men clung to each other as they made their way to the snomo. Sky helped Jay onboard.

'Hold onto me, Jay, tight as you can.'

Sky set off down the road heading for Town, slow but steady. They hadn't travelled far, just about left the church grounds, when Sky saw it. But he was too late by then. He slammed on the brakes but his momentum carried him forward on the snow. Jay slid off the side of the snomo as it hit a thin stretch of wire pulled taught between two huge oak trees on either side of the road.

A flash of yellow and amber lit up the darkness and a deafening noise like thunder echoed across the landscape. Both trees were blown from their roots, came crashing to the ground burying the two riders under tons of burning timber.

Jay was pinned by one leg. He began scraping away the snow holding him in place, driven by the cries and screams of Sky who was lying under the main trunk of one of the trees, his . hair and clothes alight. Jay finally freed himself, crawled towards the burning figure.

Sky tried to roll in the snow to extinguish the flames engulfing him. He frantically tried to push the weight off himself but it wouldn't shift. Jay scooped handfuls of snow and heaved them over Sky's charred, distorted features, oblivious of his own blood loss, somehow finding the strength, but it wasn't enough. Sky whimpered one last time before his head slowly slid sideways into the snow.

The stench overwhelmed Jay. He turned his head and heaved where he knelt.

He turned back to his old friend. Sky just stared back, lifeless, the whites of his eyes a shocking contrast against the incinerated mess that had been his face.

Good Jay leaned across Sky's dead body and dug away some of the snow. He stretched a hand inside Sky's pocket and withdrew the walkie-talkie. His hands and feet were numb now, his body weak, trembling. He tried to work some circulation back into his fingers. It didn't help, but the movement drained him. He dropped onto the snow, lay on his side, then managed to fumble with the handset in the light of the burning branches.

'Gene, Gene, it's Jay over ... can you hear me Gene?'

He prayed that Cooke would hear over the noise of the wind.

He waited an eternity, a few short painful breaths, and Cooke came on line.

'I hear you Jay, over.'

'I have a message Gene. He said to give it to you.'

'You OK, Jay? Is Sky with you, over?'

'Sky's gone Gene, Sky's dead. There was an explosion.'

'Did you say explosion, Jay?'

'I need you to listen to me, I haven't got much time. The man who was here? He said to give you a message. He said to tell you he won't stop. Not until you let his brother go. He said to tell you that. You do it Gene, you let him go. Promise me that you'll do it?'

'I hear you Jay, I'm coming out there.'

'No Gene, you stay there, protect the Town from him. And you let his brother go.'

Jay's heart had almost pumped the last of his blood onto the ash-smeared snow. The handset slid from his frozen fingers. He tried to move his head back toward the mouthpiece, tried to say something else but just rambled.

Cooke held the handset tighter against his ear, tried to decipher the words. They sounded like paper rustling, almost drowned out by the roar of wind and fire. He turned. Sheehy and a couple of his fire volunteers had finally showed up, two of them steering a tractor down Amos Street, pulling a flatbed packed full of equipment. Another followed on a snomo. All three were kitted up with hazmat suits, masks hanging round their necks. Cooke put a finger in one ear, jammed the earpiece tighter against the other.

'What is that Jay, what did you say, over?'

But there was just static coming from the handset. He heard nothing more from his friend.

Seth was alone in the room. He had come round and was straining against the straps on his wrists again. There was now some play in his right, enough to work on. He lifted his head and scanned the room, fully this time. Two doors. One led into the corridor that he'd been wheeled down on the way in, the other led to the next room. He needed a weapon. The people here were no match for him, even in his condition, but they had guns.

A pair of surgical scissors lay alongside fresh dressings on his bedside table.

Miller was the weak link. He'd caught the name as the group out in the corridor had talked together earlier. He thought he'd heard mention of a fire in town, wondered what Nate was doing now, whether he was mixed up with it.

Miller was angry, fraught about the death of his son, that much was clear from the conversation. Anger led to mistakes. If he could get him in the room alone, work on him, on his raw emotions.

He called out through the open doorway to Nancy who was moving around in the adjoining room.

She immediately came to Seth's side.

'One of those men out there, he the dead boy's father?'

'Tom Miller? Yes, he's here.'

'Think I might talk to him? Apologise, seek his forgiveness for my brother?'

'That I don't know. He might just as soon shoot you dead as listen to what you have to say.'

'But I could try, right?'

Nancy pondered the request. Maybe it *would* help, help dispel some of the fear that had grown since Rudy's death.

Ed had told her and Tom of the call from Cooke about the fire but that was all.

'I could talk to Deputy Lister for you, see what he says about it.'

'You would do that?'

'I could try.'

Nancy walked out of the room.

Seth was rehearsing his lines as Ed and Tom Miller came in. They were both armed. Miller spoke up, voice angry but broken.

'You wanted to talk to me, Stone?'

'I was hoping we could talk about your boy. Just you and me. Think we could do that?'

Ed cut in.

'You want that, Tom? I could wait right outside the door, leave it open a little in case you need me?'

Miller nodded and Ed walked out into the corridor, pulled the door to.

'OK, we're alone. So talk.'

Seth waited, stared at Miller, then lowered his head.

'Mr Miller, I lost my Momma and baby brother, I know that kind of pain.'

'Your Momma and brother shot like some kind've animals, then left to die? Did they die like that?'

'No, they –'

'Then you don't know shit. That all you got to say?'

Miller fidgeted with the rifle's trigger guard.

Seth lowered his voice, enticing Miller to come closer, out of earshot of the Deputy stood the other side of the door.

'I just wanted you to know what happened.'

Miller edged nearer.

'You were there?'

'My brother spoke to me, about how it happened. It's not what you think. My brother needs help.'

Miller hefted his rifle higher and thrust it forward.

'I got some of what that son of a bitch brother of yours needs.'

Seth spoke again, close to a whisper.

'Your son's death was an accident, that's all.'

'What did you say? That's *all*?'

Miller leaned in, spittle spraying in Seth's face.

'My boy's dead and you say *that's all*?'

Seth lunged forward, pulling hard on the right wrist-strap, splitting the Velcro fastening His hand came free. He grabbed at Miller and pulled him down across his chest, the rifle dropping to the floor as he did, then his hand travelled up to Miller's throat, fingers digging into each side of his windpipe, silencing him. Seth whispered to him.

'Lean over and loosen the other strap.'

Miller did as instructed. Seth held Miller firm as he reached with his free hand for the scissors on the cabinet, then he twisted Miller around and placed the sharp point into the side of Miller's neck. He loosened his grip on Miller's throat and Miller screamed, a choking high pitched sound that brought Ed rushing into the room. Ed already had his handgun drawn and aimed at Seth's head.

'Let him go Stone.'

'Can't do that. What've I got to lose? You on the other hand could lose your friend here, so drop the gun. Do it man, your friend isn't in any kind of shape to take this.'

Ed lowered his gun as he took in Seth's expression.

'Drop your weapon onto the floor.'

Ed bent down and placed it at his feet, then stood.

'Good. Now you need to get over here and free me up. I don't want trouble. I just want to find my brother and leave your town before there are any more needless deaths.'

There was a clatter of dropped equipment in the next room. Seth shouted out.

'Ma'am, you'd better get in here.'

Nancy came into the room and walked to the side of Seth's bed.

'Please let him go Seth, hasn't he suffered enough? Haven't we all suffered enough?'

'Just trying to end the suffering is all.'

Nancy stretched a leg under the bed and felt for the pedal. She had to move a little to her left but she kept her eyes on Seth, kept him talking.

'They let you go, you would just leave? No more trouble?' Seth was about to answer her but Ed shouted across the room.

'That's not gonna happen Nancy. We can't do that.'

Nancy waved a hand at Ed, cutting him off, trying to talk him down.

'Let's all just be prepared for what's best in the long run, OK?'

She stared at him unblinking.

'OK Ed? Just be prepared is all I'm saying.'

She shifted her balance, felt again for the pedal. And pressed down, hard, against the spring's resistance, all the way, and the bed dropped, throwing Seth and Miller sideways. Ed ran forward and dragged Miller clear, then bent and picked up Miller's rifle. He slammed the butt down hard against Seth's shoulder, sending him towards the floor, his body twisting violently as one of his legs pulled taut against the retaining strap.

Ed pointed the gun at Seth as he hung there awkwardly.

'Give me one more reason, Stone.'

Seth held a hand up in supplication and dropped the scissors, but he was angry, his face contorted with fury and frustration. He screamed at them as he grabbed the back of the bed, easing himself upright back onto it. He looked at each of them slowly, in turn, finally resting his eyes on Nancy.

'You want more deaths? You all want that? Well I tried to help you. You remember that. Remember that when you run out of body bags.'

38

Nate shone the flashlight down at the envelope he'd taken from Cooke's desk, then found the address on the town map. He figured just a ten minute journey by snomo, then he would have his prize. He was about to set off when the walkie-talkie sounded. He listened in to the brief conversation between two men.

Damn. A detour. Not what he had planned. But it had to be done.

Cooke had watched as Sheehy placed sheets over the bodies of Jordan and Ricky. Then all three fire-fighters had switched on their head lamps and entered the building, playing the hose out in front of them. He had left them with instructions. *Don't lose the building.*

He headed for the church, his borrowed snomo rearing and dipping on the fresh drifts of snow, twisting fresh knots of cramp in the pit of his stomach. He thought he had left all of this behind when they'd fled the City. The murder, robbery, assaults, all just a terrible nightmare that had left scars on him, scars he thought had healed. But they hadn't, not fully, and they had been violently ripped back open. Now he realised that nowhere was truly safe. There could be one, maybe two, more deaths. Good people, folks that didn't deserve a violent end. He slowed and pulled in, leaned over and wretched again until he was empty, then sat wiping at the mess left on his jacket. He was shivering from the cold made worse by the buffeting winds. His mind was a chaotic mix of hatred and sadness and confusion.

Jay's last words reverberated around his head. *Let him go Gene, promise me you'll let him go.* But he couldn't do that. Not now. Because all he had now was justice. Justice for those that had given their lives for Lake Fear. He engaged gear and set off again, thinking of the loss, the terrible, unnecessary loss and his burning need for justice. Then he thought of Lou and hoped to God he was close to getting the help his town needed.

Lou Tennent was still anxious about his error.

Cooke had told him to change radio frequency. But he'd forgotten when he'd called in with an update.

He could see the lake shore now in the beams of the flashlights lashed underneath each grab handle, but he had his main attention on the unseen horizon as he skipped over the fresh snow on his sled, thinking ahead to the boat journey across to Mechanicsville and hoping he had enough fuel. He didn't see the man hidden behind the gorse bush touch his lighter to the gas-soaked bandage that ran neatly across the track in front of him. It flared instantly, brilliantly, shocking the two harnessed dogs. They reared up, barking and squealing, pulling away from the flames, sending Lou crashing to the ground, twisting his knee violently on impact.

'Here Jenny, Lola, come here girls, come here now.'

The dogs tried to run back to Lou, yapping and squealing, but the sled had been upended and dug into the snow as they pulled against their harnesses. He scrambled to a sitting position and reached across to the sled, pulled his rifle from its leather sheath, then stretched for the dogs' straps and untied them. They both ran to him, still fearful. The flames retreated, smothered by the falling snow.

'What have we got here girls?'

Lou pulled one of the flashlights free and played it across the path, picking out the still glowing dressing.

'Son of a bitch. The bastard laid a trap for us.'

Lou looked around wildly then, feeling vulnerable even with his rifle cocked. But he was mad. The pain from his knee had riled him.

He shouted into the darkness, above the noise of the wind and the increasing barks of his dogs.

'You got me you son of a bitch. Come on out. Show yourself you murderin' chickenshit lowlife.'

The arrow came from his left, whistling as it accelerated through the bone-chilling air. It hit one of the dogs in the side of the head sending her spinning off her feet. She gave out a single whimper and lay dead at Lou's feet. Lou stared down at her, shocked by the suddenness of it all, and then another arrow flew, found its target, and the barking stopped altogether.

'Next one's for you old man, unless you drop your weapon.'

Lou levelled the gun and loosed off a couple of shots in the direction of the voice, but Nate was fully concealed now behind a row of cedar. He shook his head.

'Wrong choice friend.'

Another volley of shots came and then a clicking sound penetrated dully through the shifting night air. Nate walked out into the open then and shouted out to Lou from twenty metres away.

'Gun jam? Weather can do that. That's why I hate guns so much, honest to God. It's why I hunt with this. Happened to me once, when me and my brother were in Afghanistan.'

He spoke to Tennent conversationally as he closed the distance on the hunter, and then he steadied his bow and took aim again, almost casually, firing an arrow at Tennent's arm, shattering the bone and sending the rifle spinning across the snow to fall out of sight in a drift. Tennent screamed out.

'Just in case, y'know? Sometimes they can free themselves up all on their own.'

Nate slung the bow across one shoulder and continued the chatter.

'We were in a place called Kandahar on a hush-hush security job, and we got the drop on a group of unfriendlies. They were sat in the dirt playing cards in the remains of a bombed out building. It was hotter than a snake-pit in there. My brother had gone round back and I came in front, preferred it that way. I watched them for five or six minutes all told, watched them laughing and smoking and talking in that speeded up high-pitch way that they do. Their guns were laying in the dirt beside them. That's a court martial on its own right there, abusing your weapons y'know? I watched the remaining few minutes of their lives, and I tried to imagine what that would be like, the countdown to the end. Then my brother gave me the signal from a low wall behind the group and I made my move to arrest them.'

Nate had closed the distance with Tennent now and stood looming over him. A pool of his blood was seeping into the snow, mixing with that of his dead dogs. He groaned as Nate carried on his story.

'Well I'll tell you right here, our motto used to be *believe in God and your M16*, but never after that, 'cause I levelled the gun, released the safety, and joined the game. They were smart enough not to reach for their weapons at first, which probably saved my life though I didn't know it at the time.'

Tennent had collapsed now, convulsing from the pain and blood loss.

'You still listening to me, man? I waved my gun at them and pointed to a wall behind them in full view of my brother. They were very compliant. They stood and walked backward together like a troupe of dancing girls. Dancing girls wearing flip-flops. I kid you not. I kicked away their rifles. But what my brother didn't know was that I was whispering to them all the time in their own language, goading them, or trying to. They ignored me, just kept backing up, their eye balls on stalks. All apart from one.

He wore a strange smile on him, mouthful of dirty crooked teeth, big creased-up face. The others, they looked at each other, looked behind, looked all around but this one never took his eyes off me, and me still whispering and staring back at him. It was going textbook and I was pissed about it. Until I got my wish. Mister Smiley reached for a handgun inside his shirt. Who knows why, y'know, I mean why risk it? Maybe I'd got to him.

I lifted my rifle and pulled the trigger but nothing happened. Can you imagine that? The man pulled out his gun and aimed it at me. They say your life flashes in front of you when you're about to die don't they? Well mine was just a long dark tunnel of shit as I stared down the barrel of his gun. The others in the group broke rank and went for their guns on the floor beside me. Jesus, people running everywhere, dust flying, ya gotta keep cool at times like that. Now big fish eat little fish over there, but sometimes the little fish bite back. I had to admire them for that y'know? Although not for long, because they came across my brother. He's the shark, he eats everything. I used to say that you need more than Kryptonite to take him down. Just the one bullet hit me. Here.'

Nate pointed at a spot on his left shoulder.

'The guy only got a single shot off 'cause Seth took him out, took them all out. Rat-tat-tat, fast like that.'

Nate mimicked the actions, the sounds, as he continued with his strange monologue.

'Lit those mothers up in one pull. Back in the days, man, back in the days.'

Nate nodded absently.

'Gun jams, happens. Usually a death sentence, but I beat the dice that day. My brother always says that bad things happen quickly around me. Guess he's right. Jeez would you listen to me? You'd think I had all the time in the world, but you ain't going anywhere are you fella?'

He knelt beside Tennent and looked into his contorted face.

'Listen, I can't have you running for the cavalry. We've got to keep all this trouble between us OK? I have some questions for you friend, won't take long and then you can finally be on your way. You must be getting cold down there.'

Nate folded up his collar and hunkered down with Tennent right there in the bloody snow like friends pitching up for the night.

They stayed that way for a full ten minutes.

Nate stood then and stretched his legs, arched his back, looking around the wondrous scenery and then back down at Tennent.

'Just one more question for you friend. Do you want burying with your dogs?'

39

Burning embers still glowed despite the driving snow as Cooke rounded a bend and came across the wrecked trees and ruined snomo. He jumped off his vehicle and switched on his flashlight, frantically searching for the two men. He spotted Sky first, in amongst the burning debris, scorched, lifeless. He wheeled around, the beam bouncing off snow drifts and broken branches that littered the ground. A dark figure lay motionless, ten metres from the burning site, half buried in fresh snowfall. Cooke ran to Jay and dropped down on his knees, turned him over. Jay's mouth was moving as if speaking but nothing came out. Cooke reached for his hand, checked his pulse but he found none. He leaned in, pressed his face close to Jay's, close to his still moving lips, strained to catch his words. He unzipped his jacket and pulled the sides around Jay's head, trying to lessen the noise of the wind. He could hear a little of it now. It seemed to be a bible verse, the Psalms maybe. He closed his eyes and concentrated on every word so that he received the last offering from his dear friend, so that he could cast the words to memory:

'The words of his mouth were smoother than butter, but war was in his heart: his words were softer than oil, yet were they drawn swords.'

The modest, white clapboard was set back off the road. A child's swing took centre stage on the front lawn, swaying wildly in the wind. The smoking chimney and several lights on the ground floor confirmed that someone was home. Snow on the driveway was churned up and a Subaru Forester was parked up next to a side door.

Nate was back on plan after the diversion. He put away his

binoculars and followed the tree-line, heading for the rear of the house, snow drifts halfway up his thighs making movement difficult even for him. He caught snatches of music between the worst gusts of wind. He was close now, close enough to see movement at the rear window. From this distance, in the well-lit room beyond, she looked about right, maybe in her forties. A serious looker, or had been, would still turn heads. Someone who wouldn't give Nate a second glance; unless she was being paid. He looked on from his hiding place; what would it be like to live in such a community, have a wife to love, a life like this. *Oh man, what was wrong with him thinking this crap? Must be part of the cold turkey from his meds.* But still, the strange homely thoughts lingered.

The back door opened suddenly and he ducked low, keeping the figure in his sights. She was small, trim, in a jumper and jeans. She seemed to be standing at the back door and staring straight at him. *Had she spotted him?* He didn't think so but he stayed motionless and reflexively calmed his breathing.

And then she was gone and the back door closed. It had happened so quickly he scanned the rear of the property in case she had gone outside, but she reappeared at the window. He kept low and moved out of the arc of the light coming from the window. Quickly he closed on the back door. Scraps of food lay atop the fresh snow. That's what she had been doing as she stood at the back door, feeding the wildlife, not watching him. Doing the dishes, taking care of the animals, having a life. Nice.

And not locking the door.

Her life's biggest mistake.

He reached for the door handle that she had held moments earlier. He almost expected it to still be warm from her touch. He had an amazing vision of him just turning the knob and walking in, saying 'Honey, I'm home'. *Oh man, but life was so screwed up,*

LAKE FEAR

he was so screwed up.

His hand was still on the handle and it turned as though by someone else, door pushed open by someone else, nice pretty lady looking up from the dishes, wiping her forearm across her face, long strands of shiny dark hair dropping alluringly across her dark eyes, smiling across at him, gently nodding, mouthing *hello* sweetly to him (screaming), *asking if she could fix him a drink* (still screaming). Then Nate heard reality. He was shocked that she had screamed that way. *Jesus, what the hell was he expecting?* He reached and grabbed her shoulder with one hand, covering her mouth with the other. He forced her to the floor, one hand pushing down on top of her head, and she crumpled in on herself like an empty cardboard box. Nate was fully back in reality now as he whipped a plastic tie from his jacket pocket and bound her hands. He shushed her, speaking quietly, gently, as a friend might do about a delicate private matter, the news just for her.

'I have to ask you to be quiet Mrs Cooke. Could you do that for me?'

She looked up, eyes black behind narrow, slitted lids and nodded. She was even prettier close up; Nate drifted again momentarily.

'I see you keep your child's swing in good order out front.'

Mary Cooke looked baffled, said nothing.

'That's what I would have done if I'd have lost him, tried to keep it as it was. What else could you do? Take it down? Dispose of it? Let it rust? No, I'd oil the springs, paint it. Bet that's the first thing that you do each spring, am I right Mrs Cooke?'

Mary nodded, without really understanding the nature of the conversation, yet it *was* true. That's what she and Gene did the first decent weekend every spring since...

They'd rub off any rust that had collected with a wire brush, then clean every inch of the swing and apply primer and a fresh coat of red paint, always red. Like his little fire engine. They did it because they couldn't give him up. *Oh my God, who was this man and how did he know her name, know their deepest, secret, unspoken things?* And they *were* unspoken because she and Gene had just picked up the wire wool and brushes that first spring and begun the job. Nothing really planned, nothing discussed even. They had just sat there in the milky, spring sunshine and looked across at the swing, swaying in the cool breeze. Gene had gone into the garden shed and come back out with a boxful of materials and they both set to work wordlessly, both crying and working furiously until their fingers had bled.

'Please don't hurt my baby.'

The words shocked them both, her because she hadn't told anyone yet, not even Gene. She was waiting for the results of her twelve week scan and bloods done secretly at Rumford General the previous week. Too many false promises left her fearful that the act of telling him would somehow curse their luck. And now she had told a stranger; a huge terrifying stranger that had tied her up and forced her to the floor. Nate stood shocked too. *Did this woman think he was going to harm her?* Not his game. He shook his head awkwardly as he loomed over her and then looked away. There were photographs everywhere here too. Lots of them. Hung on the walls, attached to the refrigerator, stood leaning on a cabinet. Pictures of her and her Sheriff husband, and the boy.

He answered her in almost a whisper as he stared at a blow-up of all three of them smiling widely at the camera as they sat in a canoe, boy at the centre of the craft with the oar, holding it in both his hands above his head like it was a trophy.

'No Ma'am. I won't do that. You have a coat?'

Mary pointed with her bound hands to a door leading off from the kitchen. She couldn't find her voice. Nate opened the door to a small cloakroom and plucked a woollen jacket from a hook. He leaned down and placed the jacket around her shoulders. Then he noticed her bare feet. He pointed to them, almost shyly.

'You'll need shoes.'

He went back into the cloakroom and found a pair of walking shoes. They were tiny in his hands, doll's shoes. He went down on his knees and carefully placed them on her feet. He did this without looking into her face, he couldn't look there. Then he stood, reached down and picked her up like she was made of delicate paper, walked out the back door into the frigid night air, headed for a location Nate had spotted earlier on the town map.

The journey took less than fifteen minutes on the snowmobile. Mary Cooke had done her best to sit as far back on the passenger seat as possible to avoid contact with Nate, but occasionally turns and speed changes had thrown her against his huge back. It had felt like he was made of steel; he was wearing some sort of protective vest. She had thought of sliding off the onto the soft snow and making a run for it but she worried that she would harm her baby. Besides, he would just turn around and chase her down. She recognised the building as they rode up the slight incline toward the dark hulking mass. It was Hancock's timber mill. She had been here once before a year or so back to collect some fence posts for a repair project to their garden. It was in complete darkness, now, save for two low-grade spotlights fixed to the top of wooden stakes and aimed at the large, rusting entrance gates. Nate rode up to the gates and shined his flashlight at the latch. There was no padlock, just the slider in its groove holding the gates in place. Nate figured that little got secured in Lake Fear. He eased the slider across and pushed one of the gates open just enough to allow the snowmobile through, closing it again when they had entered the yard. He drove up to the main entrance, killed the engine and climbed off, leaving Mary sat perched shaking from the bitter wind.

'Just be a second Mrs Cooke.'

He untied his weapons and backpack from the rear pannier, slung them across his shoulder and walked up to the two huge wooden doors aiming his flashlight towards the handles. This time they *were* padlocked but one swift downward kick from Nate and the hasp containing the padlock shattered and came loose from the timber frame. Mary was still huddled on the seat shivering and watching trancelike as Nate worked in a tiny circle of light as he man-handled one of the doors open. Again she had images of herself dropping silently from the seat and running into the darkness, but he turned then and came towards her. A fresh wave of fear spasmed across her stomach and she suffered an aching terror for the life inside her. Nate reached around, picked her up with one arm and lifted her off the seat. He carried her inside the building, just illuminated now by the thin beam of light from his flashlight. The vast open space smelled acrid, of burnt wood and engine oil. He spun round, quickly surveying the building, and then headed for a flight of stairs in the distance.

'Thank you for cooperating Mrs Cooke.'

There was that voice of concern again. It unnerved her more than anything else. Being the wife of a Sheriff had taught her a few things about the criminal mind but who the hell was this man, this gentle savage?

Nate followed a narrow concrete path, heavy machinery and huge band saws either side, until he reached a metal stairway. He followed it up and on through a door into a large office that overlooked the shop floor. Gently he lowered Mary onto a chair and shined his flashlight around the space. Mary had kept quiet throughout the journey but she spoke now, voice wavering.

'Why have you brought me here?'

'Leverage.'

That was it, just one word. He said it with his back to her, busy now pulling equipment and small electronic devices from his backpack and laying them out on a nearby desk. A flash of fear raced through her nerve endings as she recognised the timer in his hands. He was making some sort of bomb.

'Please don't do that.'

Nate turned and looked across at her.

'I'm praying I won't have to use it Mrs Cooke. If your husband does as I ask and lets my brother go, we all walk away happy.'

So that's what this is all about. Gene had arrested this man's brother. She hadn't been party to all of the discussions at the centre but she knew a little. She spoke then, though she wasn't even sure why she should risk antagonising the man. She knew it would be best to keep quiet but she asked anyway.

'Did your brother have anything to do with shooting Rudy?'

She didn't yet know of all the other deaths.

'Boy with the dog? Nope, not a damn thing.'

She hesitated now, wondering how he knew about Rudy and his dog. Had *he* done it himself? She didn't dare ask. Nate spoke again, almost detached, absently, as he worked on his device.

'All anyone needs to know is that it was an honest to God accident. If they'd given me back my brother, the others wouldn't have happened.'

Others? There were other *deaths?* Mary was shocked at this news. Her hands began to shake, her knees. She pulled herself into a foetal position in reflex and ran through the names, the faces of her friends. *Were they still alive, injured?*

Nate checked his watch, fiddled with the timer. It began ticking. It brought Mary back from her thoughts of loss.

'Do you plan to leave me with that thing ticking away next to me?'

'No Mrs Cooke. I ain't Mr Right but I'm not crazy either. I need you to stay here, right here in that chair until… until they let my brother go and this is over. I don't think the wait will be long but you have to remain in *this room*, that clear? Do not attempt to escape. This device has a movement trip that will detonate if disturbed by vibration. I'll leave you comfortable but you have to stay put until someone comes for you.'

'Won't they set it off?'

'Things will be resolved one way or another before that happens, ma'am.'

But he hadn't wired it with a trip, he'd just used the threat to keep her from straying too far. The fact was he had no intention of leaving the device in the building at all, had just been testing the timers, making sure they worked.

He walked in turn then to each light bulb in the ceiling fittings and desk lamps, tapping them with the head of his flashlight until they smashed. He walked to her and reached inside his jacket and pulled out a knife, then he cut the plastic tie around her wrists.

He strode from the room then leaving her in total darkness.

She heard his boots clank down the metal stairway. Then nothing more for ten minutes. Maybe more. Her mind was racing, unable to think clearly enough to judge. She was about to ease herself out of the chair when the noise of Nate's boots on the floor below stopped her and she sat back down again in reflex. *Had he planted a bomb somewhere in the mill workshop, maybe directly below where she now sat? A bomb that could be triggered by vibrations.* She sat in the pitch blackness absently rubbing her stomach, willing herself to stay calm. She had no cell phone and, even if she had, the network had been down for most of the evening. She thought of the landlines but couldn't risk walking around in the darkness. No, she had no choice but to sit it out until someone came for her.

Nate sat in the darkness too, thinking through his next move, next conversation. He knew he was running out of options. They would find him sooner or later; he had to make this one last play count.

40

Cooke was back at the clinic now. He couldn't remember much about the journey from the church grounds, practically nothing. He skidded up to the front door on his snomo, surprised to find himself here, face, hands numb with cold, his mind slowed, running on empty. He had gone to find Tully, to be with a survivor for the hope it brought him. He sat on the end of his bed and absently stroked the boy's back, spoke to him, even though he lay asleep on the bed, swollen, covered in bandages, barely a hint of life. Nancy had given the boy a painkiller and slathered him in antibiotic cream.

Finally Cooke assembled Ed, Tom and Nancy, told them about the deaths, told them how they had all died, about the fire at Turner's and the explosion, the carnage, the bodies, their friends' bloodied bodies.

'Had to leave them all where they lie for now.'

Cooke raked his fingers down his face as he was explaining what he'd witnessed these past few hours. He told them with no power in his voice, as if he didn't really believe it himself.

'Clem?'

'He's still at the fire in town with Sheehy and his boys.'

'Heard from Lou?'

Cooke shook his head.

'He hasn't called for a couple hours and I can't raise him. Could just be that he's out of range is all.'

Cooke turned to face Tom Miller.

'Need for you to go home now Tom. Go home to your wife. You take him there Ed, make sure he gets home safely. Call in when you're done. I'll stay here with Nancy; I want to talk to Stone again.'

Ed spoke up, wary, anxious for Gene.

'You watch out Gene, the guy's already had a go at Tom here. Nance will explain while we're gone.'

Cooke stood and they all followed. Tom and Ed collected their outdoor gear, shook Cooke's hand, hugged Nancy, then left.

'You'd better sit back down again Gene.'

Nancy steered Cooke back to his seat and put a fresh mug of coffee in his hand.

'We've had some trouble of our own.'

She told him about Seth's attempted escape, his warnings.

'Does the brother know where we are, Gene?'

'I guess if he did he'd have been here by now. You go look in on your patients Nance and I'll check security, make us as safe as I can for now until Ed gets back.'

Cooke went to the back of the building and was there making sure the windows were locked when the walkie-talkie sounded. It was the one belonging to Seth. Cooke stood rigid as the handset buzzed in his shaking hand, images of his dead friends flooding back, ones that he had blotted out just for now so he could survive the night, but they came anyway.

'Sheriff Asshole? You know who this is. I want you to listen and share what I have to say with no one. I have something of yours now and you have something of mine. I want to trade, Sheriff: my brother for your wife.'

Cooke pulled the handset away from his ear like it was poisonous and stared at it. The voice continued and he quickly brought it back, concentrating on every word, every nuance of the man's speech.

'I'm speaking just to you now, no one else need know if we do it right. I'm giving you one hour to prepare my brother for travel. Now I'm gonna give you a reason to be afraid. Your wife is in a secure location, but the bad news is she's in the kill radius of a device I've set up.'

The handset slipped from Cooke's grip then, his hands slick with sweat. He quickly picked it up, focussed back onto the voice that carried a hellish message for him.

'... has a timer set for... oh I'll tell you that in my next call. Please don't try searching for her, you'll never find her in time and even if you do I've rigged anti-tamper so anyone so much as coughs or farts within twenty metres of its position, it'll blow. I have no interest in your wife, Sheriff, just my brother. Now, this isn't a threat, just something that will happen unless you act on my instructions and stop dicking around playing cops and robbers. I want you to meet me in a four by four that'll get me and my brother away from here. You got all that? I must say by the way, I prefer Mary with her hair done dark, like in the photo down by the lake, don't you?

Oh and Sheriff? Let me be the first one to congratulate you on your new kid – I hope mother and child don't come to any harm. You seem to be a little careless with them.'

The handset clicked off before Cooke could unscramble his thoughts and respond. His head fogged with the shock of it all. *Mary taken? Holed up in God knows where and tied to some kind of a bomb? And what was that about the child? Was Mary pregnant? Had Nate got the wrong woman? But he had used her name and he had known about the loss of his son.*

He had no way of checking if this was a bluff. The phones were down and the journey home would take too long in this weather, time he didn't have. He had to believe that Nate had Mary. He was stunned by his own train of thought. Had he already decided to release Seth, with no ifs or buts, so he would to get Mary back?

He checked his watch.

He had already used up almost ten minutes pondering the call.

Fifty minutes to get Seth ready and out of the clinic. He would move Seth on the pretext that it wasn't safe here. They needed to be in a more secure location where they could guard him. Yes, that was it, move him and then encounter Nate by chance, let Seth go at gunpoint, but how would he explain Mary? That Nate had taken her and roamed the streets of Lake Fear looking for his brother? Didn't make sense, didn't fit. Cooke's mind swirled with chaotic thinking. He checked his watch again. Forty two minutes to the next call. Perhaps he should share the conversation with others, get a search party on it? But that might get her killed. No, he had to cooperate, had to let Seth go, but how would he explain it? He would negotiate for Nate to return Mary to their home before Seth's release. Mary would call him to confirm this, then he would take Seth to his brother, make it look like… He knew all of this looked bullshit, but it was the only story his frazzled mind could construct. But would Nate go for it? He would have to insist that he did. Insist? Yeah, take it or leave it, your brother rots in jail and I spend the rest of my life hunting you down you evil asshole. Cooke rubbed at his forehead trying to massage some sensible thinking into his brain, remove the hate-filled vitriol that kept clouding his thoughts. He looked at his watch again; the second hand seemed to have sped up like in a cartoon. *Oh God, just thirty eight minutes left, what had he been doing?*

He raced down the corridor, slowing as he saw Nancy about to enter the room where Stone was being treated.

'Need alone time with Stone, Nancy.'

She had no chance to answer before Cooke was past her, opened the door and slammed it shut.

He sat down on the chair at Seth's side and leaned across, whispering with his heavy coffee breath into Seth's face.

'I need you to listen Stone; I'm getting you out of here. Your brother has taken my wife and has her wired up to God knows what. He says there's a timer.'

He outlined the call he'd taken from Nate and the makeshift plan to exchange them, all the time watching Nancy's figure through the frosted glass of the door. Seth kept silent, watching the fear grow in the Sheriff's eyes as he explained.

'Can I trust your brother to stick to the plan?'

Seth just nodded and stared into those eyes.

'You good for travelling?'

'I'm good. Pocketful of tramadol wouldn't hurt though.'

Cooke leaned in again.

'I'm gonna get Nancy in here to get you dressed for the journey. Say nothing OK?'

Seth nodded again.

Cooke stood, opened the door, and faced Nancy. He checked his watch again, twenty four minutes before the call.

'Nancy, I need you to prepare Stone to be moved, I don't like the security here.'

'That would be unwise Gene, he's too weak to travel and he needs the medical facilities I have here.'

'Understood, but I can't take the risk that his brother shows up and puts you and Tully in harms way. I can't lose any more of you, Nance. I need to move him to my office, put him in the cell. We can set up the equipment there if we have to.'

Nancy looked pensive but finally relented.

'OK, give me a couple of hours to –'

'No, I need him ready in fifteen minutes.'

'That's impossible, Gene.'

'Sorry. I have a duty for the safety around here and –'

'Yes and I have a duty to my patient.'

'Nancy please, you'll have to trust me on this. Now hurry or I'll have to haul him out on my back.'

Cooke ran outside to the car park. Ed and Tom had already left on a snomo leaving deep ruts in the snow. His foot hit the edge of one, sending him skittering onto the ground. He rolled, righted himself, calculating the seconds wasted. He hoped to God that Jordan had left the keys in the old Tucker Sno-Cat, that he could get it started.

Nancy was baffled by Cooke's sudden urgency but she set to work.

Fourteen minutes later, she almost walked into Cooke in the corridor outside Seth's room. He was shaking snow off his jacket. He seemed flustered, face reddened. He looked across at Nancy but looked away again, making a big deal out of cleaning himself up. He just gave a few words of disjointed explanation.

'Been fixing the Sno-Cat. Left her running.'

'OK, he's as fit as I can make him so long as it's a short journey. I'll give him minimal sedation before we go, make him as comfortable as I can.'

She placed a syringe of midazolam on the bedside table next to Seth.

'Now, give me ten more minutes to get my med bag ready and I'll give you a hand.'

She hurried down the corridor towards her office. Cooke moved into the room and helped Seth from the bed. He was dressed with a saline drip still attached to his hand. Cooke looked haggard, frightened. He spoke with a tremor in his voice.

'Good to go?'

'I'm good.'

Cooke pulled out his handgun and pointed it at Seth, then reached down and untied the straps, snatched the syringe and pocketed it. He helped Seth to his feet, shocked all over again by the size, the sheer weight of him. They hurried down the corridor, out the front door and into the freezing cab of the waiting Snow-Cat. Cooke reached across and locked a handcuff on Seth's right wrist, pulled him upright and fixed the other cuff round a steel support pole behind the passenger seat.

Cooke checked his watch. Five minutes to go.

'What's your brother called?'

'Nate. His name is Nate.'

Cooke jammed the gear stick forward and spun the Cat in the snow, catching a glimpse of Nancy as she stood frantically waving at the front door of the clinic.

He drove a few hundred metres down the road out of sight, pulled over, sat idling in the Snow-Cat, eyes shifting from his watch to the walkie-talkie and back again.

Nate listened to Mary Cooke scraping her feet back and forth on the floor above but she had stayed put. He checked his watch. Time to call.

'Sheriff, you made the arrangements?'

'Yeah, I have your brother right here with me.'

'Put him on.'

'No Nate, not before –'

'Don't fuck with me Cooke or I'll press the little red button I have in my hand right now and make a real mess of your life.'

Cooke held the handset in front of Seth and nodded for him to acknowledge his brother.

'I'm here Nate, I'm fine, they've treated me good. You have to let her go man.'

Cooke took back the handset.

'Listen to me Nate, I want you to take my wife back home before we do the exchange.'

'Nope, not gonna happen. I already explained how this is gonna work.'

'Just hear me out. I have to have a reason for all of this. I've worked it out. It means my wife can't be any part of this.'

'Sorry cowboy, I've dealt with people like you before. It's the fear. Makes people do strange things. Sorry man. You give me my brother, I give you the whereabouts of your wife. I also give you my little box of tricks here to neutralise the explosive remotely. You go save your wife, be a big hero, and me and my brother leave town. That's it, that's the deal. Tick tock cowboy.'

Cooke looked across at Seth but he was looking out of the window into the dirty night.

'Where?'

'There's a boathouse on the north east shore of the lake, has a big *Castrol* sign on the side of it. D'yer know it?'

'I know it.'

'OK, the car park in twenty minutes.'

'Longer. I need longer, got to find a safe route, and have to drive real slow in this white-out. Can't guarantee to be there in under forty minutes, might take longer.'

'OK, one hour. Just you and my brother. You know the consequences if you bring someone else along. Don't screw up, Sheriff.'

Cooke opened the door of the Cat and dropped down onto the snow. Seth watched him as he walked a few metres from the vehicle and turned his back to him, thought he heard a conversation, but the wind was drowning out everything. Cooke returned a couple of minutes later, slammed the door and kicked the Cat into gear. Timing was everything now.

The wind was howling. Heavy flakes of snow were being driven horizontally by gale-force winds now gusting stronger than ever. Visibility was down to a few yards. The Sno-Cat rocked in the gusts as they headed for the rendezvous point.

41

Nate arrived first.

The wind blasted skeins of snow across the landscape, buffeting Nate as he crouched beside the snowmobile he'd hidden behind a hedge of privet.

If they did the exchange swiftly, Nate and Seth could be on their way out of Lake Fear in a few minutes, find a new safe location, start all over again.

His night-vision goggles were useless in these conditions as he watched the snow-covered road and he dragged them from his face, left them to hang around his neck.

Two high-intensity lights and two more forward spots sliced through the curtain of snow whiting out the landscape. He peered at the vehicle and then beyond for anything following. It seemed alone. The noise from the engine sounded dull and laboured as the Snow-Cat came to rest ten metres from where Nate was crouched. It flashed its lights twice, then switched off its engine and lights.

Nate held up his flashlight and signalled back, then switched it off and changed his position.

The driver's door opened and a tall figure dropped down into the thick snow. It was Cooke and he lit up his own flashlight and waved the beam of light across his body and then began walking forward towards Nate's position with his hands raised.

Nate scanned the vehicle. He could see movement in the back seat. He stood and aimed his rifle at Cooke.

'Keep walking, Sheriff. They call this advancing into ambush.'

Cooke turned back and pointed his chin toward the vehicle.

'He's in there, Nate, connected up to a drip and ready to travel, but he needs medical help so I wouldn't travel too far with him.'

'I bet you wouldn't, but I'm all the help he needs for now.'

The two men closed on each other and Nate patted him down for weapons.

'Unarmed, Nate, as I promised.'

'On the ground, face down.'

Cooke got down on one knee. As he was lowering himself onto the snow, he slipped a hand into one pocket and gripped the barrel of the syringe. Still far enough off the ground to reverse direction, he twisted and launched himself at Nate, thrusting the needle at him and pressing the plunger, emptying half its contents into Nate's right thigh.

Nate slammed the stock of the gun down onto Cooke arm, knocking him onto the snow. The syringe was driven from Cooke grip, shattered, leaving the needle hanging from Nate's leg. Nate gripped it and tore it out but the drug was already taking effect. He stumbled. Cooke raised himself and stepped back away from the swaying Nate, then raised his arms and screamed out into the darkness.

'Hold your fire, hold your fire!'

But a shot whistled through the air hitting Nate in the arm sending him spinning to the ground.

Cooke screamed out again, telling the shooters to hold off. He ran to him but Nate was already recovering, fighting the drug, using the pain of his arm wound to focus his actions.

He lashed out with his foot at Cooke, knocking him down onto the snow.

He sensed movement to his left.

Ed and Clem were closing on him.

He dropped low and twisted, facing them, then took aim. His shots were wide, the drug distorting his senses.

They pulled back and dropped below a ridge.

Nate stood, swayed, began running towards the Snow-Cat. More shots set him zigzagging away towards the cover of the trees.

Cooke ran back to the vehicle and climbed in. Seth looked pale, waxy, his eyes were wide with anxiety, his bandages beginning to bloom with blood from exertion; he'd been pulling at the cuffs, trying to dislodge them from the roof support. He turned on Cooke, his voice shrill with menace.

'Hell is going on out there Sheriff, you set my brother up using me as bait?'

Cooke didn't answer. He fired up the Snow-Cat.

The two men could hear more shots being fired as Cooke headed back to Town.

Nate was still bleeding but the flow was already slowing. The drug had all but expired but it had left him nauseous and he leant over and puked at his feet. He reached inside his ruck, ripped out a piece of bandage, wrapped it round his arm. He knelt down, shoved his goggles back over his eyes, switched to night vision and rapidly scanned the immediate area for the shooters.

Between the bursts of snowfall he could just make out glimpses of movement below a decline. There were two of them, thirty or so metres from Nate's position. He did a second sweep to be sure, then centred his vision on the two men. They began wading through the snow, heading back to their snomos fast as they could, one leading, the other moving in the tracks being made.

Nate quickly turned to trace the direction of the Snow-Cat, then turned back to the shooters. They were slowing now with exhaustion, not quite fully concealed by the trees and bushes. Nate lifted his rifle and steadied his aim, calculating for wind shear. The cross hairs of the night scope filled with the bobbing, wavering hood of a winter parka. He took out the runner in front, a single head shot, the fizz-zap from the bullet lost in the fury of the storm.

Nate watched as the first man dropped, the second almost

falling over him before recovering, lifting his rifle, swinging round frantically looking for movement, looking for the source of the shot. Nate stood motionless, concealed behind the thick trunk of a fir tree, pulled the trigger once more.

Nate screamed obscenities into the night as the second man dropped softly onto the snow. He slung his rifle over one shoulder and ran to the snomo, the pain of his own wound forgotten. The Snow-Cat was a half mile distant now, its running lights strobing as the storm blasted across his vision.

He fired up his snomo and headed after his brother, screaming again as he opened up the throttle.

'You're dead, you're dead. You're all dead!'

Cooke's handset bleeped as the Snow-Cat thundered along on its four massive tracks. He punched the button and held it to his ear, trying with his other hand to keep the Cat from slipping sideways off the narrow, snow-packed road.

'Sheriff, you double-crossing asshole, I'm gonna destroy you and everything you ever cared about, you hear me Cooke? I'll kill what you love.'

Nate sounded wild, breathless. His voice rasping from the radio, the noise from the Cat, howling wind all adding to the cacophony in the cabin. Cooke tried to reason with him but he knew he'd screwed up, taken a chance, a big chance, and blown it. More of his men dead and now Nate was coming again, coming for them. And it was *Cooke's* fault.

'No, listen to me Nate; we can still do the deal.'

'Then stop your vehicle, Sheriff, and walk away. I'll call you when we are out of the area. That's the deal now.'

But Cooke sped on, the community centre within view now, illuminated through the blizzard by a string of coloured lights along its roofline.

He couldn't just walk away now, he would have no bargaining chips left. He had to keep hold of Seth if he was to get Mary back safely. He had no time to think up a response before Nate's voice filled the cabin again.

'Cooke, you ain't slowing. I'm serious, you go any further and there are no deals left, just more dead people.'

Nate was screaming now, almost hoarse with the effort.

Cooke could see a single headlight in his mirror.

Nate was gaining on them.

He quickly snatched a look at Seth. He'd gone quiet now, lids half closed, leaning heavily against his own raised arm, the handcuffs digging deeper into his flesh as the Snow-Cat shuddered and shimmied on the freezing snow covering the road.

He ended the call and pushed the throttle all the way to the floor. He reached down onto a shelf slung under the Cat's dash and pulled out his gun, resting it in his lap.

Cooke tore into the car park of the community centre and brought the Cat to rest. He threw open the door, jumped down and peered behind, gun raised.

Nate's snowmobile was nowhere to be seen.

Nate watched the Cat pull into the car park of a building set on a mound overlooking the Lake. He watched through his night scopes as the Sheriff jumped from the Cat and looked back down the track, but when Nate had seen the Cat pulling off the road into the grounds he'd slewed to the edge of the road and hidden behind a drift. He sat in darkness scanning the site.

A large signpost read, *LAKE FEAR COMMUNITY CENTRE.*

He could see movement through the curtains.

He focused back on the Cat, watched as the Sheriff went back and helped Seth out of the vehicle, held him up as they trudged through the snow and entered the building. Hands grabbed at the two men as they crossed the threshold, helped them indoors. The door slammed shut. Curtains and shutters closed.

So now he knew, knew where his brother was being held, and he would make them regret ever taking him.

42

Mayor Adams helped Cooke steer Seth to a bench at the back of the centre and sat them both down. He was shocked by what he saw. He ran to the back of the centre and pulled out the med box and immediately began wiping at the wound on Cooke's face.

'No, leave me Earl, he needs you more.'

Cooke pointed his chin at Seth who had come round but lay slumped on the bench, his head angled back against the wall. Seth was trying to speak but couldn't, just shook his head from side to side.

Cooke jumped up and headed for the front door. He stumbled, fell forward. Adams caught him and lowered him back down, felt for a pulse.

'You need to rest up Gene. I mean it.'

'Later, Earl, later. When this is over, that's when I'll rest.'

Nate headed further along the road and stopped, stopped next to a powerline pole. He'd been following the route of the power lines for several minutes now. He checked all round and then turned and grabbed his ruck, reaching inside and withdrawing his flashlight and a small plastic box. He removed his gloves then prised off the lid and broke into the block of waxy substance. He molded a small square, selected one of the detonators, set the small electronic timer.

The wind rocked the snomo, peppered him with needles of frozen particles of snow. He blew on his hands to warm them.

He collected up the C4, dismounted, walked over to the timber pole. He wiped away the build-up of snow that had collected there, pressed the plastic around the base of the pole, inserted the det.

As he rode away, he heard a small whump, then a rending noise.

He slowed and looked back, as the shattered pole collapsed onto the road, dragging wires loose and causing the junction box to crackle and spit out a short burst of blue-white sparks that left momentary dancing images on his retinas.

The street lights winked out all across Lake Fear plunging it into complete darkness.

He turned and headed back to the community centre.

43

Byrd slowly came to.

He could smell the heavy, cloying stench of blood. He reeked of it.

And he felt wet, slippery.

He ached everywhere. His left side felt as though it had been roasted over a fire pit. A stabbing pain emanated from deep within his right ear and it hummed like a shorted amp.

But he was still alive.

He strained beyond the muffled whistling in his ear but heard nothing else; he sensed no movement in his vicinity. He thought he had heard the high pitched whine of a snomo start up earlier, or had he imagined that? Was it just his damaged ear? He couldn't be sure; his thoughts were scrambled, indistinct.

Had he heard someone else arrive soon after the snomo leaving? Images returned in uneven form. Someone shouting and rummaging around in the cabin, pulling him off the floor, his body roughly turned over, a light shone in his face, then being dropped heavily to the floor again. He couldn't yet think straight. He made a mental map of his recollection of events starting with his most coherent thoughts.

The fight with Seth came rushing back. He had shot Seth, not fatally, just to focus the big man's mind and to disable his fighting powers. He thought it would make his plan to help the brothers escape more realistic. But the whole idea had crashed and burned.

Seth had somehow gotten hold of the gun and shot him. Just grooved his side, not penetrated. But it still hurt like hell. That was why his side felt like it was on fire.

The sequence unravelled fully then as he lay awkwardly on the floor. He was sure now about being manhandled, the light in the face, that had been Nate looking for his brother. Great, so he was shot and bruised and in the middle of a game of hide and seek between the brothers. Seth had taken off to find Nate and Nate had somehow circled back looking for Seth. And found blood, lots of it, and a wounded stranger, but no brother. Jesus, Byrd had to contain this, somehow, because if any locals were dragged into this and Slater found out, he'd be dropped from a very great height, like out of a plane.

How long had he been laying on the floor? It was dark now. Was he in any fit state to go after the brothers? Byrd voiced his own thoughts to the empty room as he lay on the floor.

'Well there's only one way to find out isn't there, dumb ass?'

Five minutes later Byrd was sat on the sofa wrapping bandage around his midriff. He winced every time he passed the material across his body. He he'd found a med kit in the bathroom, alongside splashes of blood, in the sink and pooled on the drainer. He had cleaned himself up and taken three Advil, then inspected the damage. Nice war wound. Survivable. He would need hospital treatment once all of this was over, but for now he had to stay in the game. His cell was positioned in front of him on the table, its signal indicator flat. Damn, this must be the only place in America where he couldn't get a signal. He had checked the landline in the cabin but this too was dead. He needed to know if Slater had called. *How the hell do these hicks live out here for Chrissake?*

He finally ran out of bandage and tucked the loose end inside the wrapping. His attention turned to the cabin. It was a chaotic jumble of broken furniture and splashes of blood. His gun was missing. He saw the note then on the table. He quickly read it, balled it up and dropped it to the floor. He would need to arrange a clean-up crew when this was over.

The painkillers were kicking in and his strength and alertness were returning – he had to get after the brothers before they fled the town or caused any trouble; this was about as good as he was going to feel. But what chance did he have with no weapon, no backup, no comms? He quickly searched the cabin on the half-chance that the owner had left hunting gear, maybe a rifle, a knife, anything that might give him an edge. The brothers would be armed to the teeth. Jeez, what a mess. But maybe his plan could still work. If he could just get to them.

He spotted the dog-tag then, still threaded on its broken chain. He reached down for it and read the engraving. *Seth Stone.* Other numbers and codes: *Social Security, Blood Type, Religious Designation, Service Branch.* And one other set of numbers. He puzzled over this last. He turned it over. A small key was fixed to the back, a single spot weld, enough to hold it securely in place but easily removable without damaging the key or the tag. He pocketed the tag and then tried the cabin's telephone handset again, but it was still dead. He remembered then that Seth had been coming from the outside store when he'd shown up. Maybe there was something he could use in there. He grabbed his cell, ran to the cabin door, flung it wide, and stood frozen in place for a moment, shocked at the scene before him. Just how long *had* he been out. The floods had been tripped by the wind, illuminating the grounds like a Christmas greeting card, snow was piled nearly two feet thick, far deeper in places where it had been whipped by the wind. It was still snowing but lightly now, and the wind had dropped. But the sky was still black with storm cloud.

Tracks left by two snomos were barely visible in isolated spots. Both headed towards town.. His four wheel drive, left out of sight, would be useless in these conditions. Unless he found another snomo somewhere on site he would have no choice but to call for support – if he could get a signal. He went back indoors and returned to the kitchen. He found what he was looking for, tested the flashlight for power. He ran back out and headed for the store room.

Just walking those few paces took minutes instead of seconds. He could feel blood soaking the bandages on his damaged side. He'd live.

The door was wedged partly open by drifted snow, a sliver of bright light seeping from inside illuminating the blood-spotted mush around the doorway.

He kept out of the light and put his good ear against the door. He could hear nothing but the storm.

He pushed at the door and ducked low as he entered.

A fluorescent strip light was on, maybe left that way by one of the brothers in a hurry. Byrd eased further in, still cautious, watching for movement. His eyes were drawn to a black box with a row of tiny green-coloured lights sat on a nearby bench. He recognised it immediately. A cell jammer. *What the hell were they doing with one of these?* Byrd reached across and switched it off. His cell bleeped and a small but steady signal appeared on the screen. Just two bars, but enough. He quickly scanned the room. No vehicles. He walked over to a tattered armchair stashed in the corner of the storeroom, carefully lowered himself into it and made a call to his office. He'd realised he could no longer contain this. He needed a new plan.

He'd get Donna to scramble Portland SWAT. He would just have to handle the consequences. His call got through. He summarised the situation and his location in a handful of crisp sentences.

As he ended the call the lights went out.

44

Ice particles blew past Nate's vision, but it was calmer now. He viewed the community centre through night goggles from the safety of a row of pine twenty metres away.

He'd spotted two figures earlier as they peered out through the window slats. The beam of a torch had been visible somewhere inside. Then they'd closed the slats again.

It had been enough.

One of them was the cop.

He heard the low rumble of a generator starting up, casting a dirty yellow glow within the building.

The car park remained in complete darkness.

He reached inside his rucksack and pulled out a roll of bandage. He tore it into thin strips then wrapped them around the tip and shaft of some of his arrows.

One by one, he dipped them into the fuel tank of the snomo and carefully laid them against his rucksack.

He checked his watch: seventeen minutes to go.

Seventeen minutes before the cable car blew.

His brief detour hadn't taken long. He'd fixed and primed the plastic and then hand-cranked the cabin a few metres so that it hung out over a small ledge.

He checked his guns and waited.

The Pave Hawk heli dropped from the sky, carefully navigating between the bare trees and bushes, two powerful spotlights criss-crossing the site and burning holes in the strange silver luminescence of the cabin grounds.

It had almost stopped snowing now; just a few large flakes whirling on the wind, but the sky remained heavy, ominous.

The craft hovered a few feet above the layer of snow in the front yard, its rotors retaining their high speed, the whine deafening. Byrd had been waiting at the cabin door and made his way toward the craft, hunched over against the wind and the rotor wash. A door slid open as he neared and a man in black combats dropped a rope ladder down and helped him aboard. There were two of them alongside the pilot: shooter and spotter. Byrd shouted instructions over the din, about shot placement. The shooter nodded without looking at Byrd, continued testing his laser guide.

Byrd touched his shoulder, rougher than he'd intended.

'Are you serious?'

He nodded at the device as the red beam flashed round the cabin.

'In these conditions? Plus: the targets see that they'll blow us out of the sky. Suggest you use your normal sights, friend, keep us a lot safer.'

The wind buffeted the craft and the pilot fought to keep it stable. The chopper rose unsteadily creating torrents and eddies of swirling, fluorescing snowflakes. They turned and roared forward, lights tracing the smear of tracks in the snow.

Byrd spotted an upended snomo through stinging, raw eyes as he hung out the side of the heli for the short journey.

They flew low heading south, toward the town of Lake Fear.

An explosion somewhere on the outskirts of the town lit up the sky, illuminating the heli's cockpit with a dazzling burst of light. Byrd watched as sheets of steel and cable were hurled thirty feet into the air below them. He watched as the sky-lift was torn from its housing, rolling end over end down the hill, crashing through the under growth until it hit a row of trailers, knocking two of them from their bases, embedding itself in their shattered remains, a molten tangled mess.

As the chopper curved away from the rising heat he saw trailer doors being flung open, couples and children running out into the night, their homes igniting one by one until the whole site became a firestorm.

Nate never took his eyes off the building. A man ran out, smaller, slighter than the cop, and peered in the direction of the blast for several seconds before going back inside. A minute later he re-emerged and jumped into the Snow-Cat, fired it up and began turning it around. Nate watched him pull out of the car-park, heading for the source of the explosion.

He pulled his lighter from his pocket and touched the tip of each arrow until he had nine alight in front of him. He reached for the first, loaded it, aimed, sent the arrow spiralling through the bitter air as snow began to fall once more.

It hit the front door, immediately spreading fire down its length.

The second and third hit the east side of the building.

The fourth and fifth hit the eaves.

The rest went through the windows into the room beyond.

He heard Seth scream at Cooke from somewhere inside.

'He's here Sheriff, it's started.'

The building was ablaze in several places now, flames and thick black smoke billowing into the raging, snow-filled night.

Nate picked up the final arrow and bound a grenade to the shaft with a piece of bandage. He pulled the pin, took aim and released. He'd calculated for the weight and drag. It hit the front door, rested there, just momentarily, grenade hanging loose, then it blew, sending shards and splinters of timber in all directions and leaving a gaping hole in the structure.

Nate looped more bandage around his hand and grabbed a handful of snow, packing it inside and fashioned a makeshift mask. He tied it around his face to protect himself against the worst of the smoke. He tapped a fresh magazine against his chest and loaded up. Then he set off, racing toward the front door spraying a stream of bullets in front of him.

He reached the front door and charged through it, flames and black smoke everywhere now. He shot out the lights and screamed his brother's name as he ducked around the fires spilling from the ceiling and walls.

The smell of melting plastic grew as he reached the far side of the room.

Nate screamed out his brother's name a second time. A blast of fresh air hit him then as he reached deeper inside the building. He could see a side door hung open, but his path was blocked by a molten curtain of flames from the ignited partition wall. He turned and headed back towards the front door, charging across the room, vaulting and ducking the flames, on out through the front door. He ran around the side, gun reloaded and cocked. Flames leapt from the open doorway illuminating the path.

A trail of footsteps led around the rear of the building and Nate sprinted forward, chasing them down. He reached the corner of the building and turned, dropping low, ready for gunfire but he only saw the broad back of his brother, half stumbling in the snow, held up by someone else, two indistinct figures against the black landscape.

'Seth!'

Cooke half-turned, still holding Seth in his grip, the wind whipping at their clothing, Larger flakes of snow were drifting down in a cloud now, creating a kaleidoscope of slow motion action.

Nate ran on, closing the gap between them, shouting at the pair, gun trained on the Sheriff's head. He was within a few metres now and Seth spoke, but his voice couldn't be heard over the din.

Nate was on them now.

He was the bear of his nightmares, teeth bared, roaring like an animal.

'Let my brother go Sheriff and I'll let you live.'

Cooke still gripped Seth, holding him upright with one arm but swaying now with the weight. He swung his other hand into view, holding his gun, pointed at Nate.

'Where is my wife you asshole?'

But he was too weak. The weight of Seth and the cold wind battering at his back were forcing him forward.

He lost his balance.

Nate instantly aimed and fired, hitting Cooke in the shoulder sending him and Seth spinning to the frozen ground. Nate ran forward kicking the gun from Cooke's grasp and then turned to his brother and laid him flat. He covered Seth with his own jacket.

He turned then and reloaded his gun, walking the short distance to the stricken body of the Sheriff. He took aim at the Sheriff's head as Cooke looked up into Nate's black hate-filled eyes.

Seth screamed from behind.

'No Nate, leave him man, no more killing.'

Nate spoke back with a strange tone to his voice, pitchless, almost inhuman.

'It's unfinished business Seth. My life is one long list of unfinished business.'

He stared down at Cooke as he said it, trance-like, distant.

'No! Let's just get out of here. The place will be swarming with guns any minute. We need to move.'

Nate still had his back to Seth, staring down at the Sheriff, gun unwavering.

Cooke lay hunched and defeated.

He winced with the pain from his wounded shoulder.

But he could only think of his missing wife, the loss of his friends, of the damage to his town. Anger and frustration filled his mind with rage. He threw himself headlong to reach the gun but Nate easily stepped ahead of him and put a heavy boot on his bloody wound. He cried out and dropped back down onto the snow. Nate leant down, shouted into Cooke's contorted face.

'You think that's pain Sheriff? That ain't pain...'

Seth had crawled nearer to the two men. He shouted as loud as his smoke-damaged lungs would allow.

'Nate. Please. Listen to me. Look at me man and listen. Haven't I always got us out of harm's way? Just leave him and let's go.'

Nate seemed to come back a little. He wiped a gloved hand across his mouth, looked up at the sky. He seemed to be trying to make sense of a new sound, something distant, like a metallic heartbeat, drifting in on the wind and then lost.

Nate turned and nodded at his brother as though seeing him clearly for the first time that night.

'You're right Seth. You're always right.'

He lowered his rifle, stepped closer to Seth, reached down to lift him to his feet, intensity diminishing, thinking of his brother, thinking about getting away from Lake Fear.

And then a roar broke through the noise of the storm as a helicopter rose from behind a row of tall trees, search lights flashing in the darkness, finding Cooke's prostrate body on the ground and then washing over the brothers, half stood, holding each other up, one armed.

The shooter in a harness was leaning out of the chopper door, invisible to the men below blinded by the spotlight. He steadied his rifle for a clean shot.

Seth twisted in Nate's arms, caught a glimpse of the shooter, knew what he was working through, rhythmic breathing, seeking a supported rest position, and he knew they only had another second, maybe two. He raised himself high enough to cover the shot, screamed at Nate.

'Eyes on, eyes on!'

And Nate saw the shooter now too. He threw himself forward, pushing Seth to the ground, rolling, removing his Kevlar vest, placing it over Seth's body, continuing to roll, shielding his eyes from the searing lights, the deep pulse of the heli's blades coursing through him, reaching, prepping his own gun, and the shots finally came, but wide of the mark, missing both brothers.

The heli pitched in the air, snow momentarily blinding the pilot's vision, clearing, then back again as the wind shifted direction violently.

Byrd screamed at the shooter, reminded him to shoot to maim, femur shot. The shooter aimed lower, seeking Nate's legs.

Nate moved fast, reactions instinctive, years of training taking over, switching to automatic fire, spraying the cockpit and engine compartment, a stream of bullets punching through the plexiglass, sending a thousand shards of glass flying inside the cabin.

Byrd ducked behind the heli's thick steel door and looked across at the pilot. Blood seeped from the man's arm and shoulder as he grappled with controls that bucked in his hands.

The wind was raging again, storm returned in force.

Byrd screamed through his mic and pointed to a clearing beyond the trees. The heli hovered a few more seconds, spiralled, lost stability and height before the marksman could get any more shots off.

Nate watched it roar away into the darkness, smoke belching from its engine.

He turned and headed toward Cooke, gun aimed at his head, hatred returned for the man who had caused all of this.

Seth, screamed from behind him, voice hoarse and pained and full of battle-weary sorrow.

He stood over Cooke now, gun barrel just inches from his temple.

Seth got to his knees, reached, seeking something half-buried in the snow, then steadied himself, screamed out again, bracing for the recoil.

'No Nate, no!'

The shout broke a link in Nate's brain. He hesitated, just for a few milliseconds but it was enough, enough for the squeeze of a trigger, the red hot bullet hitting home.

45

Nate took the shot in the side of his chest, the bullet blasting flesh and bone. He dropped heavily to the ground in shock and pain, panting and hiccoughing frantically in an effort to fill his ruined lungs. Seth threw Cooke's gun into the snow and crawled the short distance to his brother, shouting out at Cooke to get help. But he knew his shot had been fatal

He rolled himself into a sitting position, lifted Nate's head and rested it gently on his own lap. He began rocking Nate gently then, tears spilling down onto his brother's face. Nate stared up at him with a look of confusion. He moaned softly in between each short tortured breath and then seemed to gather himself for the effort of speaking.

'Jesus it hurts so much y'know? Hey, what're you crying for bro'? We've been in worse scrapes than this. I just need to sleep a little is all, I'm so Goddamned tired. Then we'll make our move. Go to Canada like you said. OK? OK Seth? You and me? Become oilmen. Stop shooting people for a living. What d'yer say bro'? Momma would've liked that.'

'Yep to that little brother. You and me. Same as always.'

Nate began to shake then, his eyes slowly starting to roll back in their sockets. His demeanour changed, like he knew he had just moments, like he couldn't fool himself any longer. He looked haunted.

'Fuck the dice. Fuck the dice, Seth, 'cause they've won this time.'

Seth held him tighter.

'But how else would it end y'know? I'm the kitten in the tub now aren't I Seth?'

Seth was baffled but didn't seek an answer from his brother. He figured Nate was hallucinating from the pain and the blood loss.

'I'm the piles of bodies at the bullet parties, I'm the bleached bones at the side of the road, I'm the Iraqi family riding in their rags, I'm the dog, I'm the boy just out walking, I'm the cop, the priest, the trackers, I'm the young guns, I'm Leon, I'm everyone and everything I have ever killed. I'm all the monsters locked away inside of me. I met them on the way up and I think I'll meet them again on the way down. But not Momma, Seth. I didn't kill Momma. She did that herself. She loved us. She loved me, didn't she, Seth? She didn't kill herself because of me, I wasn't to blame for that was I?'

Seth just stared into Nate's pained, dying eyes. He saw blood beginning to bubble through his brother's open mouth as he struggled to find more words.

'What say we do our special prayer together now, Nate, just until the medics get here and fix us both up?'

'I'd like that Seth. I'd like that a lot.'

They started their private prayer together then, whispered it, until Nate's head slumped back.

Seth mouthed the remaining few words for the both of them just as the snow finally stopped falling.

EPILOGUES

I

Byrd's heels clicked sharply as he walked the corridors of Chase Bank. He could have been mistaken for a business man, maybe a banker himself; suit, shirt, tie, smart briefcase swinging at his side. The guard walked a few steps ahead, armed and wired. He waved at the camera as he reached the inner vault door, and then placed his eye next to the iris scanner. He hadn't spoken to Byrd the entire journey through the outer door, just did his job. That suited Byrd. The bolts slid away and the door released. The guard flicked the light and air-con switches and the room began to hum with a slow rhythmic heartbeat. He closed the door behind him then, led Byrd through into a second room laid out with dozens of safety deposit boxes on all four walls. A small table sat in the centre of the room, single leather chair pulled up to it. There were cameras in here too. Byrd was relying on that. He looked up at one of them and smiled. He resisted the temptation to wave.

The guard unfurled a roll of green baize at the edge of the table and laid it flat. He turned to Byrd.

'Press the buzzer when you're done, Sir. I'll come get you.'

Byrd nodded pleasantly.

The guard turned and unlocked the door, walked out. Byrd watched the barrels roll back into place. He dropped his briefcase onto the table and pulled out his wallet, withdrew the dog-tag and key. He quickly scanned the numbers on the boxes for the first three digits on the dog-tag. He located it and stood in front of it.

He held up the tiny key, hands slick with sweat, a slight tremor there, as he hovered over the keyhole. The air con seemed to suck out all of the air from the room at that moment and he reached up and pulled at his collar, loosening it. He need this to work, he needed it badly. He slipped the key into the slot, tapped the remaining numbers from the dog-tag into the keypad and turned the key. The tumblers turned effortlessly and the door sprang open. He closed his eyes, thanked his God, thanked Seth.

He reached inside, withdrew a black tray, walked over to the table, sat down. The tray contained just a single item, a small black bag. He pulled at the drawstrings, reached in, took out a battered Motorola cell phone. He stared at it a few seconds. Just a cell, just a damned cell, but so much more.

He unstrapped his brief case and pulled out a notebook, fired it up, unspooled a cable with attachments fixed to it. He found the one he was looking for, connected the cell, fixed ear buds in place. This time there was no hesitation; he loaded the software and hit *Play*.

The images were grainy, the sound distorted with background noise, but they were good enough, good enough for the leverage he needed. Relief flooded him and he looked up at the camera again and formed a circle with a finger and thumb. He inserted four data sticks into the notebook, one after the other, and downloaded the footage onto each before pocketing them. He returned the cell to the bag and put it back on its tray, stood and placed it back in the deposit box. He powered down the notebook and returned it to the briefcase.

The air in the room was fresh and cool now.

He fastened his collar, straightened his tie, reached for the buzzer.

He turned left out of Chase and walked a few yards along East

Tropicana, found Sammy's Sports Bar and ordered a chilled beer. He settled in a booth in back and sat nursing the beer, gathering his thoughts, absently scratching the scar tissue above his right eye. The heli pilot hadn't been so lucky. Then he made a call.

Donna answered on the third ring.

He let her know that his hunch and her research on Seth's R and R, stateside visits had indeed led him to the security box. The numbers had sprung the code and the key had worked like a charm once he had removed it from Seth's cleaned-up dog-tag.
    Then he'd given her the other news, asked her to clear his desk, send his stuff on, made her a promise to come good on the dinner he owed her.
    He closed the call and pulled three envelopes from his brief case. They were already addressed, one to Slater, the others to friends in Tampa and Newark. He dropped a data stick into each, and sealed them. The fourth he kept.

He checked his watch.
    The crystal of his Tag was cracked, courtesy of Seth, but it still worked well enough. He figured he'd leave it that way.
    It was just a couple hours before his flight. He hated the usual heat and noise of Vegas but his work was done here now. He drained his glass and called over to the bartender.
'You got a UPS store near here?'
The man pointed through the window.
'North, on Flamingo.'
    Byrd dropped a ten on the counter and walked out into the brassy Vegas sunshine.

II

Cooke stared at the tiny image as it twitched and stirred on the scanner.

Tears fell freely down his face.

He looked up and held out a hand to Mary.

The nurse came back into the room with a still of one of the images. She handed it to Cooke.

'Well, now you know to paint the bedroom blue.'

'Oh, he's already done that Connie, along with a poster of the Patriots.'

'How's that shoulder now Mr Cooke?'

He smiled and nodded in answer, gently lifting his right arm which was still in a sling.

The nurse handed a card to Cooke and took on a more serious tone. News of the events in Lake Fear had hit the nationals and Cooke had become high profile, something he didn't particularly relish, the media interviews hindering his efforts to help rebuild the town.

'Congratulations on your re-election *Sheriff.*'

III

Seth stood hunched, like an old man. From here he could look out over Hanover Falls, one of Nate's favourite spots, deep inside Ellis River State Park. A biting wind was pushing at his back, seeming to urge him forward into the narrow rocky chasm. The smell of pine wafted around him and then was gone. The sky was clear and uninterrupted all the way to the horizon and he closed his eyes and filled his raw lungs with cold clean air.

It had taken him weeks to negotiate this with the authorities. He'd freely offered them the location, code and key for the locker containing the cell phone. He wouldn't need it anymore.

Then it had all gone quiet.

Until he'd received an anonymous call asking him if he needed anything. The voice had sounded familiar.

Within twenty four hours the suits had appeared in his cell, anxious to deal.

He eased the lid off the urn and shuffled the few awkward steps that his chains would allow towards the chasm's edge. One of the guards fed the chain through gloved hands as the other looked on. They both stood back allowing Seth some privacy.

Seth went down on his knees then, in the patchy remains of the snow, the grinding pain from his injuries ignored. He held the container out in front of him, head bent, tears streaking down his weathered face.

He felt empty now, in this place. A hole had opened up within him, deep and dark. He knew it would never heal.

He turned the container over in his hands and held it high, letting the wind carry its contents over the trees and streams and ditches and rock pools beyond.

He placed the urn on the ground and stood then, his balance barely holding on his ruined knee. He reached down and grasped the chain to steady himself, all the time looking across at the guards and smiling. Then he pulled it violently from the guard's grasp and stepped back, into the void.

The author

Michael Willetts has spent most of his professional life in computing but harboured a passion to write since he was very young.

Lake Fear is his first published novel. He is currently working on his follow up novel which is provisionally called *Capture + Kill*.

He is married with a daughter and lives in Bolton, England.

The publisher

Adel Publishing has been launched with the publication of this novel. They are a small enterprise aiming to find new authors with real potential and help them develop that potential.

They also wish to give the author a fair share of any profits on sales, and involve the author closely in every aspect of the book's preparation for publication.

Lightning Source UK Ltd.
Milton Keynes UK
UKOW04f0002291013

219966UK00006B/772/P

9 780992 699208